For All We Know
Angela M. Rosati

Cover Art:
Michelle Crocker

http://mlcdesigns4you.weebly.com/

Publisher's Note:

This is a work of fiction. All names, characters, places, and events are the work of the author's imagination.

Any resemblance to real persons, places, or events is coincidental.

Solstice Publishing - www.solsticepublishing.com

FOR ALL WE KNOW

Angela M. Rosati

Chapter One

There was a noisy rapping on the table. "Hey, can we get some service here? We're starving!" They were four robust young men; starvation was not one of their immediate concerns, and they were at Lorraine's table. She knew a group of wise guys when she saw them but she hurried to their table because it was lunch hour.

Serving the famished, impolite, screaming lunch crowd would make anyone absolutely nuts. There were smells of coffee, food cooking, and the clanging of utensils and the shouts of the servers to the short order cooks. Ordinarily this was a very busy diner and at this time of day, it was such a madhouse that the servers constantly cursed under their breaths. Lorraine, a pretty, young redhead, cursed in English and Italian.

She arrived at her table, ready to take orders from the four young men, who had given Lorraine the once over as she approached their table. She knew what was coming and braced herself.

"Hey, Red, where did you get all those freckles?"

"Red, do those spots wash off?"

"You know what those freckles look like, doncha?"

If only they only knew how many times she'd heard these annoying questions, these hotshots wouldn't think they were so hot… or appealing.

She made up her mind she would be her sweet self, just like the wise cracking actress everybody said she resembled, Ann Sheridan, the Oomph Girl.

"Change the record, boys. I've heard it all before. What'll you have? We're busy, in case you haven't noticed." Lorraine pushed her lips to the side to show she was used to their crap.

"Whoa, she's a tough one. Okay, you guys check

out the menu and give Red your order. And be nice; she looks like she works hard."

He seemed to be the leader of this rambunctious group. He made sure they all gave her their orders in quick succession, trying to give her a hard time. He didn't know Lorraine. Her pencil flew across her pad. She looked at the leader and said with a snide look on her face, "Anything else, Buster?"

The guys laughed. "Walter, she's got your number." They laughed again. Walter, who had the biggest smile on his handsome face thought, *now if only I could get her number*. He was determined to do so, but not with the knowledge of his buddies.

They all watched, with great appreciation, as she walked away. She was slim and they liked the way her hips swayed gracefully and her red ponytail bobbed tantalizingly. Whistles and sounds of approval came from all of them except Walter, who said, "Hey, you guys watch what you say. Yeah, she's beautiful, but you can tell she works hard. Mind your manners. Let's make our mommies proud of us!" They all laughed because Walter was full of baloney, but they also knew that Walter had eyes for the beautiful redheaded waitress. So, being full of vinegar and vim, they did behave; up to a point. It was a strain.

She brought their orders and as she distributed them to each diner, they watched her freckled, shapely, arms as she reached across the table to place the proper order in front of the proper diner; they looked at her ample breasts and tried looking down the open top of her uniform, and smelled her perfume. They were so silent, she became ill at ease. Of all of them, Walter gave her the most intense gaze. She started to feel her face redden and stole a glance at him. His blue eyes penetrated hers and she sort of moved her head. When she was done, she quickly moved away and went to her next table.

As she wrote down new orders, she stole another glance at Walter and saw him looking at her, his mouth trying to smile as he chewed on his hamburger. He gave her a quick wink and she looked away immediately. She was flustered. She'd never seen him before and wondered if he would become one of the many regulars. "Friggin' torture," she thought.

When the lunch crowd left, it was very quiet and peaceful in the diner, she and her friend, Lucy, the other waitress, sat at the counter and had their lunch. Lucy complained about her aching feet. Lorraine knew what she was talking about.

"Lucy, I told you you're wearing the wrong kind of shoes for this job."

"What should I wear, nurse's shoes?"

"Yes."

Lucy looked at Lorraine with a pained expression on her face. "Oooh, they are so ugly. Do you want me to wear white nylons, too? Ugh!"

"Lucy, you don't have to wear nurse's shoes. You can get the low heeled shoes I get. They're not expensive and they're comfortable."

"But, they're ugly."

"Well," Lorraine said, "I don't care. My feet don't hurt when I'm finished my shift. Anyway, who the hell do you think you'll meet in here, Mr. Rockefeller?"

Lucy looked pensive, "Yeah, I know. You're right. Ow." She rubbed her right foot against the back of her left leg. "I think you're right, Lorraine. I never hear you complain about your feet and you never limp at the end of the day."

"Well, I wonder why." She smiled at Lucy. "And you never can tell, I might meet Mr. Rockefeller! Or better, his son!"

They both laughed.

Lorraine and Lucy were the same age, nineteen and had been friends for many years and socialized together. They had attended many local dances hoping against hope that they could tell their mothers that they had met "the guy."

Lucy was a bit chubby, had shoulder length black, soft, wavy hair, lovely skin tones, and was starting to give up hope. "I don't know, Lorraine, my mother is driving me nuts. All I hear is, 'You don't have a boyfriend, why? All your cousins have boyfriends and the girl next door has many boyfriends. Maybe she could lend you one!' How do I know why I don't have a boyfriend? And I told my mother that the reason the girl next door has so many boyfriends is because she opens her blouse! With those heavy provolones, who wouldn't have a load of boyfriends!? I can't throw myself at these guys. And they're all looking for Hedy Lamar. The last time I looked in the mirror, I didn't see that face, I saw only my own."

Lorraine smiled at Lucy. "Lucy, you gotta have patience and you don't have to look like Hedy Lamar. You're more beautiful than she is because you don't wear all the make-up she does. And we just can't go out and find a boyfriend. It's not that easy. Don't forget, a lot of ladies our mother's age were matched up with their husbands. The girls had to marry the boys who were introduced to them, it didn't matter if they loved each other or not." She sipped her coffee and heaved a sigh.

"Your mother didn't. She married your father, the one she loved. You told me that."

"Yeah, my mother married my father; she fell so in love with him, she didn't want to marry the guy her father picked out for her. And she was in big trouble for it.

"I had a table full of guys and I heard the usual baloney about my freckles. I'm so sick of that! They left a nice tip, though. That made up for the small aggravation.

But, one of the guys gave me a look."

"Yeah," an interested Lucy said, as she popped a fry in her mouth, "what kind of look?"

"Oh, ya know, a kind of look, like he looked at me a little longer than usual."

"Did he ask for your number or anything like that?"

"No," Lorraine looked aghast, "and I wouldn't even consider giving it to him. He looked like a wise guy. I've had enough with wise guys. Remember my last date I told you about?"

"Yeah," said Lucy, as she plunged her fork into her apple pie. "He was a real piece of shit."

"I know and he thought he was such hot stuff, acting like he was Tyrone Power. Maybe I look like I'm love starved. And he's the one to feed me."

"Agh, get outta here. You're beautiful and I've seen a lot of guys looking at you." Lucy looked at her friend. "Lorraine, do you think, well, I mean, I don't want to offend you, and maybe I'm wrong, but do you think that maybe you scare the guys?"

"Geez, I never thought of that. I don't think so." She sipped her coffee and her eyes showed she was thinking back to her recent dates. "Nah, I don't scare the guys." Another thought of one of her dates, "Well, maybe, but sometimes the guys scare me and I have to let them know that I don't do some things they want to do. Sometimes a little slap and they behave."

"A little slap!" Lucy laughed at the recollection of one of Lorraine's dates. "You remember that guy who told you he was an orphan and had no brothers and sisters? Looking for sympathy. You told me you slugged him!"

"Well, I had to," she said, a small smile on her face, while she scraped her fork to try to get all the crust of her apple pie, the part she liked best, "While he kissed me, he put his hand on my chest and took my hand and pulled it toward his crotch. Hey, whaddaya think I am! And this was the first date… also the last."

Lucy was in hysterics. "Lorraine, you're hot shit!"

"And as my little, Italian immigrant grandfather used to say, 'you soft shit'". They both laughed heartily.

"Well," Lorraine said, "are we gonna go shopping for dresses tonight for tomorrow night's church dance?"

"Oh, sure," Lucy said, a smile beginning on her face. "I'll be ready."

"Of course, you'll be ready," said Lorraine, "we're going right from work."

"Okay," Lucy smiled.

They finished their lunch and began to do the little things that were included in their jobs, and they moved faster when they saw the gorilla who owned the place walking around banging pots and pans and yelling Greek words the girls didn't understand but knew he wasn't saying his rosary. Behind his back the girls called him King Kong because he was big and hairy. It was their secret because if King Kong ever found out, his ferocious temper would come into play and they would both be canned. On the other hand, Stavros was a good guy, fair and respectful of the girls.

Stavros' son, who possessed the same dark Greek good looks as his father, had come to work in the diner for the summer and he eyed Lorraine, which earned him a slap on the back of the head from his father and one from his uncle. When Lorraine saw that, it recalled the many times she'd seen her father and grandfather do the same to the males in their families. She thought, what is it about a good slap on the back of the head? It didn't get results because Thomas continued to eye her. And the slaps continued, much to the enjoyment of Thomas, the cooks and the customers.

The girls were good workers and earned good tips.

They planned to go shopping that evening to buy something really spiffy for the church dance Saturday night. Stavros had asked them if they wanted to have a bite in the kitchen of the diner. But the girls refused, thanked him for his kindness, and they went shopping.

In their little Astoria, New York, neighborhood, they went to Steinway Street to shop. It was the only street with many stores and many selections. Lorraine, with her auburn hair and freckles tried to keep to the colors that enhanced the beauty of her hair but toned down her hated freckles. In the second store they entered; you could never find something in the first store, she found a very pretty light green dress with a portrait neckline. She bought it at once and was happy she didn't have to have it shortened.

Lucy, trying to hide a chubby body, looked for a dark color, preferably black that would disguise ten pounds. She was having a hard time and feeling the ache in her feet was about to give up.

"Lorraine, all these dresses make me look like an old lady."

"Not old, Honey," said the saleslady, who raised her eyebrows, "just mature"

"Oh, there's a difference?" Lucy said, annoyance showing on her pretty face. As the saleslady walked away, Lucy told Lorraine, "Why doesn't she just come out and tell me I'm a fat slob! That bitch, I'll show her." And she started to go after the saleslady.

"Lucy, Lucy, hold it. Stop acting crazy. The saleslady was being tactful. Come on, let's get out of here." Lorraine turned to the saleslady and said, "We don't find anything here. Sorry." The girls left, Lorraine pulling Lucy by the hand and Lucy giving threatening looks to the nasty saleslady.

"Lucy, that saleslady was a bitch. She'd no right to speak to you that way." She had angry lines on her forehead.

"Then why did you stop me, for God sakes?"

"Because you're my best friend and I didn't want you to go to jail for assault and battery. Besides, she lost her commission; what better revenge for her insensitivity?" Lorraine smiled with satisfaction.

"Gee, you're a pal. I never thought of that." She smiled at Lorraine and said, "Let's go across the street to Young Maids."

Lucy found a pretty dark blue dress with a bit of rhinestone trim. It fit her perfectly and concealed any imaginary flaws; she bought it. Lucy was thrilled and thanked Lorraine for preventing her from serving a jail term. But, as they walked to the bus stop, Lucy remembered what the first saleslady said and it bothered her. "Ya know, I think I'm gonna go on a diet. Whadaya think, Lorraine?"

"That's a fine idea. My advice is to keep it a secret from one and all."

"Why?" asked Lucy, not understanding why such a little bit of business should be kept secret.

"Because, my friend, when you tell people you're on a diet, everyone and their enemies want to shove food down your throat."

"Nah, I don't think so."

"Oh, yeah? Remember Edna? She announced to one and all she was gonna go on a diet. People wouldn't stop feeding her and you know, we all have healthy appetites and she ate and ate. She gained thirty five pounds in a few months. I saw her last week and would you believe she crossed the street not to speak to me."

"Maybe she didn't see you." Lucy looked concerned because Lorraine never insulted people.

"Yes, she did. I waved to her and she looked the other way. She was ashamed to face me. I feel so sorry for her. She's such a nice girl and I really like her. Please, Lucy, do what I say. Please?" Lorraine had a pleading look on her face.

Lucy looked at Lorraine, a lot of sisterly love rising in her heart and smiled, "Yes, I'll do what you say."

"Okay, let's concentrate on tomorrow night. We bought gorgeous dresses to go to the dance. I can't wait. I hope we meet a couple of nice guys. But…" Lorraine said, with a smile on her face.

"Oh ho, I know." Lucy said, with a knowing "wise guy" smile. "You don't want to go to the dance tomorrow night. You got your eye on that guy at your table in the diner. Come on, admit it."

"No-o, I don't. He's a wise guy. I don't want to associate with guys like that. Besides, I didn't say I didn't want to go to the dance tomorrow night. I do. It's just that I—I—I don't know what I want to say. I just hope we have a nice time."

"Ah, I see you're beginning to smile. Come on, admit it. You like him."

"No, I don't. We-el, maybe a little bit. Anyway, when will I ever see him again?"

"Probably tomorrow!"

Lorraine gave Lucy a look, "Nah, I don't think so."

"Oh, yeah, you'll be hard to find. Gee, he'll have to hire Dick Tracy to get your trail. Or how about Charlie Chan who has his number one son to help him!"

They both laughed. Lorraine realized that Lucy was right and it sort of gave her a thrill and some hope. She really did find Walter, which was his name, attractive. But…

The girls had arrived in their neighborhood and parted to go to their homes. They lived close by and made plans to meet on the corner Saturday night to go to the dance. It was 1959, and that's what friends did.

***

Lorraine opened the door and called, “Ma, I’m home. Where are you?” As though she didn’t know her mother, Lena, would be anywhere but in the kitchen. She was cooking fish; they had fish every Friday night and the aroma made her head spin. She didn’t realize that she was hungry.

Lena looked at her beloved daughter; a big smile on her flour stained face. “Ciao, bella. I’m glad to see you. What have you in the package?”

Lorraine kissed her mother, wiped off the flour from her mother’s face, and smiled, “I bought a new dress for the dance Saturday night Lucy and I will go to.”

“Ah, I want to see, but get away from the stove, the oil is spitting. I don’t want a stain on your dress before you wear it.”

“Right, Ma.” And she moved to the other side of the kitchen table and opened the box; carefully she removed her dress, held it by the shoulders, and shook it out. There was a big smile on her face as she held the dress against her for Lena to see.

Lena lowered the heat under the fish, which she never really did because it wasn’t a good idea. She looked carefully at the dress, came close to judge the fabric. “Ah, yes, it’s very pretty.” She nodded her approval. Lena occasionally sewed for the members of the family and she knew fabrics and style, and she approved of the dress. Lorraine smiled.

“Ma, I’ll run upstairs to hang it up, wash up and come down to set the table. Who’s home so far?”

“Nobody,” she yelled because she had raised the heat on the stove and the oil was spitting.

In a few minutes, Lorraine was downstairs and began to set the table. She smiled remembering the table of four guys she’d served lunch to.

Lena noticed the slight curve on her daughter's lips and as she brought the serving dish with the fried fish to the table, she looked closely at her daughter. "Beh! You wanna say something to me?"

"Oh, it's nothing, Ma," Lorraine said. Her mother's eyes never left her daughter's face. "Oh, Ma, I can't hide anything from you. It's nothing, really. Just a table of four guys came in today and they made some remarks, you know, about my freckles. It was all silly fun for them."

"Okay, cut the lemons and put them on the table; Papa, Vinnie and Joe will be home any minute. The crabs are almost finished cooking and the water for the spaghetti will soon be boiling. Please get me a box of spaghetti."

"Sure, Ma. Everything smells great. I'm hungry."

"They don't let you eat in the diner? What kind of place is that to work?"

"Oh, Ma, it's a good place to work. Stavros is a good man, he allows us to eat lunch there, but he can't keep feeding us all. He'd never make money. Besides, if I ate too much, I'd get fat and I don't want to do that."

"Hmmm," said Lena. "I know, you're right. Oh, I hear the footsteps. Somebody's home."

In walked the first born; it was Vinnie, who was an unusual six footer, broad shouldered, dark and handsome. "*Buonasera, Madre*." He hugged and kissed his mother. "Hiya, Red." He pulled her hair. "How's it goin'?" And he started to make his way upstairs to wash his hands and face and comb his hair.

Before either female could respond, Joe, the youngest son, a duplicate of his brother walked in kissed his mother and said, "Hello, Ma, I smelled your cookin' from a block away. Hiya, Vin and Lorraine. What's new?" The brothers worked in the same auto mechanic shop but didn't always come home together; sometimes there were girls they talked to and thrilled with their deep, handsome eyes.

"Agh, you didn't smell anything. Hurry and wash up. Papa will be home soon."

At that moment, in walked Papa and it was no doubt who his sons took after. He had a scowl on his face. Everyone greeted him respectfully and quietly. Papa had been born in Italy and demanded the respect due to him as the head of the household. He quickly washed up and in no time, they were all sitting at the table enjoying the delicious dinner Lena had prepared.

The children had an animated conversation about sports, movies and a little politics thrown in. Lena and Papa looked curiously at their children. Lena understood their conversation. Papa, baptized Carlo, didn't understand the fascination with baseball or football and as he ate he listened carefully, always trying to learn a new word and its definition. Since he had a scant education in Italy, he listened to his children to improve and increase his vocabulary. He was well muscled and stubborn; he had found work in construction and the many years working under the sun had roughened his good looks. He was proud that Lena married him; a greenhorn.

Upon his arrival in this country, the Italian American girls would have nothing to do with the new arrivals because they spoke no English and soon learned to speak broken English. They'd grown up with parents speaking thus and were ashamed; they didn't want their future children to endure the smart aleck remarks from kids whose parents spoke English without an accent; no matter that their grammar wasn't correct.

Many years before, at a christening party, Carlo had seen Lena and immediately fell in love with the redhead. She tried to avoid him at the party, but she couldn't resist his good looks and his romantic conversation, even though it was all in Italian, which she easily understood. Her friends laughed at her for failing to free herself from the guinea; she shouldn't waste her time with him, they advised her. While at first, Lena agreed with them, she couldn't resist him. She and her friends were looking to marry somebody like Tyrone Power. While she had her eye on her Irish employer's son, once she met Carlo, she was hooked.

Carlo, for his part, couldn't resist her beautiful red hair and he thought freckles were the most beautiful "beauty marks" in the world. That first night they met, Carlo had kissed her a few times and Lena knew she would marry Carlo. In the space of two months, they were married and within a year, Vinnie was born, followed by Joe, and then Lorraine, the only redheaded child.

Carlo insisted that Lena teach him English and she did this with gladness and gusto. Carlo was a quick learner. Many times he would come home asking what a word he'd read in the newspapers meant. And working in construction, he learned all the most potent curses, which he repeated to Lena, asking the definition. Blushing, she explained them and told him he must never say them in polite society. Some expressions were new to her and she blushed more. She told him to ask his sons. He was aghast; his sons could never know those words. Little did he know, but he soon found out and excised them from his vocabulary, in polite society, anyway. He was amazed that though he didn't know the English language that well, he was learning fast. He was proud of himself and wanted his Italian American wife and American children to be proud of him. He became an American citizen as soon as possible and when it came to vote in the national elections, he did so with much pride.

Tonight at dinner, he was quiet. Lena knew something was disturbing him and asked him about it. At first, he wouldn't answer, saying nothing was wrong. But after dinner, when he and Lena were alone, he confessed that he'd heard rumors, (a word he recently learned) that there would be some firings and layoffs at work and he was worried that he may be among them.

"Carlo, honey, don't worry about it. I'm sure you won't be fired. You're one of their best workers. You just told me that last week the boss complimented you on your work." She caressed his face, looked into his eyes with great love and sympathy, and he took that hand and kissed her palm. Then he kissed her. They went upstairs.

***

Lorraine had received a call from Lucy.

"Hi, Lucy, what's up?"

"We're already finished dinner. Have you?"

"Yes, we've already cleaned up."

"Well, I've been thinking, let's go to the movies tonight; there are some good ones out. I have nothing to do and I don't want to stay home and listen to my parents start chapter seven of why they got married in the first place. My mother has a whole list of guys she could have and should have married. My father wants to know their names; he wants to punch them out. Oofa! Is that boring?"

"Okay, yeah, that's a good idea. I have nothing to do either and I don't feel like watching TV. I think my ass is getting bigger and bigger from sitting watching sitcoms. Okay, I'll go upstairs to change. I'm still in my uniform. I'll meet you on the corner. Oh, my mother liked my dress. See ya."

In a short while the girls met each other on the corner and started walking toward Steinway Street, where the Triboro Theatre was located. They walked arm in arm, gabbing and laughing. They turned the corner and saw a long line of people at the theatre, waiting to buy tickets.

"God, look at that line. We'll never get seats!" said Lucy.

"I think we will. It's still early. Once we're inside,

we go right to the seats. No candy, okay?"

"Right you are, Miss Lorraine. Say, guess what I had for dinner and I didn't mention the word 'diet' to anyone. Oh, I'll tell you, you'll never guess. I had broiled salmon."

"What! Broiled! Not fried? How come?"

"Well, my mother, who as you know, is a bit chubby and my father has been calling her *culo grande* (fat ass) for a while, and it's been bothering her, so she heard from one of her friends that if she broils the fish instead of frying it, she'll lose weight. So, that's how she made it for the whole family. Great, no?"

"Yes, great! Lucy, you keep that up, you'll be slim in no time and you'll need a baseball bat to keep the guys away. But, you never had trouble with the guys. You were always asked to dance every time we went to a dance. You weren't exactly a wall flower, ya know. I've seen guys eyeing you, maybe it was lust in their hearts and maybe it was something nice. I think nice."

Lucy looked at Lorraine and then she looked away; she was thoughtful.

Lorraine asked, "Lucy, what's the matter?"

"Well, many times the guys would say vile things to me. They were beasts at times, saying I was loved starved or, worse, sex starved." She scowled at the thought.

"Lucy, you never told me that. And don't you think I heard the same filth?"

"You did? I always thought I heard all that rotten stuff because I'm fat. Well, I'm surprised to hear this. And now, I'm more determined than ever to lose weight and I'm gonna sock the next guy who insults me."

"Let's make a pact. We'll be the Pair of Punching out girls!"

They laughed. Since they were on line waiting to buy their tickets, they hoped no one else heard their conversation and as they looked around they found that the people in front of them and behind them were engrossed in their own conversations. They were safe.

Chapter Two

The girls bought their tickets and entered the beautiful theatre, which had a thick carpet and a ceiling resembling the night sky with stars and clouds that moved. They bypassed the candy counter and began to go toward the stairs to the balcony. But as they made their way to the stairs, they heard, "Hey, Red." And they looked around. It was Walter and he was with a friend.

"Oh, God," said Lorraine, "who would have thought we'd see them here tonight." She quickly looked away.

"Yeah," said Lucy, who couldn't help showing annoyance.

The boys came near. The girls were upset; this is not the place where they wanted to have a conversation with these fresh guys.

"Hey, Red, what good luck to meet you here, right Joe?"

"Yeah," Joe said, as he leered at Lucy, who was ready with her fist!

"Really? Why?" Lorraine said coldly.

"Well, we could sit together and enjoy the show."

"No, we can't." And the girls walked away from them. The boys laughed; they got a kick out of being rejected because they thought they knew better. They followed the girls and tried to sit next to them. The girls moved; the boys followed. The theatre was filling up and they couldn't continue to play this silly game. The girls finally found two empty seats together; the boys couldn't follow but they quickly found seats directly behind the girls. Lorraine and Lucy made sure the boys heard their exasperated explosions of breaths. This didn't bother or faze the boys at all; they found it amusing and let the girls know it.

Walter sat directly behind Lorraine and frequently nudged the seat back with his knee. At first, Lorraine was quiet, hoping he would stop. They were watching a comedy and while people laughed aloud, Lorraine turned and asked him to stop.

Walter smiled and apologized. Within five minutes, he was at it again. Lorraine didn't know what else to do. In a way she was pleased that he wanted to make her acquaintance, but in another way, she didn't like wise guys and he was a wise guy.

Joe had seen Lucy's fists and didn't try the same thing, although he really wanted to get to know her. Instead, he said in a voice he wanted her to hear, "I think these girls in front of us are gorgeous, especially the brunette sitting in front of me. Woo woo."

The boys noisily tore the paper from their candy bars. Walter leaned forward and offered Lorraine some candy. Joe did the same to Lucy. Both girls coldly refused, were embarrassed, and then turned to each other and quietly made some remarks the boys couldn't hear but knew it concerned them.

Lucy turned to Lorraine and whispered softly, "What do we do? Should we move? It looks like these guys are gonna be pests."

"Yeah, you're right, Lucy, but it looks like all the seats are taken. We have to ignore them and maybe they'll stop or be quiet, at least."

The girls became quiet and settled down to watch the movie. Lucy wished she had a candy bar. Then she remembered she was on a secret diet. She wanted to be successful and she knew Lorraine would be disappointed if she was not.

The boys also became quiet because the other people would have called the management. After all they weren't little boys; they had to maintain some sort of dignity. Walter watched Lorraine more that he watched the movie.

The movie program was continuous showing and when they came to the part of the movie they came in on, the girls got up quietly and left. A few minutes later, the boys followed and trailed them to the lobby where they began a conversation.

Walter sidled toward Lorraine and said, "Hey, Red, we're gonna have coffee. How about you and your beautiful friend join us?"

Coldly, Lorraine rebuffed him. "No. What kind of girls do you guys think we are? We don't even know you."

"Well, you remember my friends and I, which includes Joe, here, came into the diner where you and your friend work; at least, I hope you remember. You do remember, don't you?"

"I don't know. We get many rowdies." Lorraine said and looked at Lucy, who nodded.

Walter smiled. He knew the girls remembered them. "Come on. You remember us. We'll just have coffee; nothing more. Maybe a few laughs. You don't have to worry; you both will be safe with us. I swear it. We have the utmost respect for you ladies."

All the while Joe, letting Walter do all the work, was smiling at the girls but his smiles lingered on Lucy. She wasn't impressed and showed it with her lips pressed against her teeth and with impatient breaths escaping her mouth.

Lorraine, meantime, trying to be very cold and reserved, trying not to listen to her heart, was unsuccessful in keeping her eyes from showing pleasure.

"Ah, I see you want to smile." Walter said raising a finger to Lorraine's eyes. "Come on, don't deny it. You want to come with us for coffee. We'll even buy apple pie a la mode. Whadaya say?"

"No, we will not go with you guys. You look like wise guys to us."

"We're nice guys but if you think we're wise guys, okay, we won't bother you anymore. Let's go, Joe, We'll go to the diner for coffee."

Joe, bewildered, said, "Sure." But as the boys walked away, Joe, looked back at Lucy, who was aware of that look. She smirked at him.

But they waited for the girls to start to walk away and they followed at a close distance. The girls were aware and they began to giggle and look back. They kept on walking and came to a diner and entered. Close behind, the boys entered, also.

The hostess, thinking they were all together, showed them to a booth and they all slipped into the seats; the girls first and opposite each other, the boys last. Each boy sat diagonally opposite the girl he liked.

"Hey, you can't sit here. This is our booth," Lorraine said.

Lucy quickly piped up, "Yeah, the hostess made a mistake. I'll call her."

Joe finally spoke up. "Ah, come on, beautiful, it's okay. Let's have coffee; we won't hurt you, right Walter?"

"Right," Walter smiled. "We just want to talk to you beautiful girls. Unless you find us really, really repulsive, we'll leave. But, remember, you're chasing away two guys…two broken hearted guys." And he took out his hankie and dabbed at his eyes.

"Oh, what malarkey," Lucy said and the girls looked at each other laughed and didn't fight too hard; they decided to let the boys stay.

"Okay, you guys can stay but the minute you get out of line, you'll get a left hook to the jaw!" Lucy looked malevolently at them.

"Wow, did you hear that, Walter?" He looked at

Lucy, obvious admiration in his eyes, and said, "I don't want a left hook from you, baby; I'll just take a kiss. NO! NO! I was only kiddin'." And he held his hands up in mock protection.

Lucy smiled and looked from Joe to Lorraine, who was smiling, too.

Walter was peering at Lorraine and she turned to see his eyes, intense; she lowered her eyes and reddened.

The waitress came and sort of broke the mood. "Yeah? What'll you have?" she chewed her gum as she spoke. Lorraine smiled because Stravros didn't allow that. He thought chewing gum had no place in his diner and he was right, as now Lorraine could attest to that.

Walter looked at her and said, "We'll have coffee all around. Does anyone want pie, Red?"

Singled out, Lorraine said, "No. Thank you, just coffee."

"Why don't you have some ice cream on it? My treat, of course." And he smiled his dazzling smile.

Joe piped up, "Yeah, why don't we all have ice cream on our pies. I want strawberry. What about you, gorgeous?" He said this to Lucy, trying to hold her hand, but he noticed it was balled into a fist and retracted his hand while it was still in good shape. He had heard about how fierce Italian girls can be and a left or even a right hook was not what he wanted tonight from gorgeous Lucy; a kiss would be more appreciated and it was softer and the jaw was left intact.

Lucy was just about to order her favorite ice cream flavor when she remembered her diet and since she didn't want to disclose this private information to the present company, she demurely declined; she settled for the pie. Joe was enraptured.

Lorraine settled for pie only; she wanted to keep Lucy company and thought it would help Lucy stay on her diet easier if she had support.

The boys decided to stuff themselves with pie a la mode, but they again urged the girls to join them. They refused. The waitress gave the girls a look that said the girls were full of baloney and who did they think they were kidding. This wasn't lost on Lorraine and Lucy, but they simply ignored the waitress.

Their conversation started with the movie comedy they had seen and went to many others things. But, all the while, Walter's blue eyes sent messages to Lorraine, who was receiving them, with a bit of fear. She knew he wasn't joking. She licked her lips frequently, a sign she was nervous.

After they finished their treat, the boys paid and they all left. Outside, the girls said thank you to the boys for a lovely treat and lively conversation. But, the boys continued to walk with them. This time, Walter walked with Lorraine and Joe walked with Lucy.

Walter said, "Listen, Red…"

"My name is Lorraine."

"Oh, okay, that's what I'll call you, Red…I mean, Lorraine. What a pretty name. Are you sure you're one hundred percent Italian? I think there may have been an Irishman way back in your family."

"Well, if there was, it was kept a secret, because of the ancestors I know of, none were said to be Irish. Do you think only the Irish have red hair?" She tilted her head up a bit, sort of a challenge to his intelligence.

"No, I don't. I know that other ethnic groups sport red hair, too, it's just that it seems the Irish have a monopoly on red hair."

"Well, it may seem…"

They were passing under a large tree that afforded a very dark shadow, and Walter was kissing her. With great strength, she pushed him away and slapped him. His hand went to his face, but he looked at her with a message she couldn't really understand but which she understood fully. How could that be?

She instantly regretted the hard slap. "Oh," she whispered. "I—I'm sorry. I hope I didn't hurt you."

Walter smiled; he was making progress with this beautiful girl. His hand still on his face, he said, "You've got a right there that could knock out Joe Louis." His arms went around her and he kissed her again, a long, uninterrupted kiss. "I want to see you again."

"I—I don't know."

"Can you meet me on the Triboro Theatre corner?"

"Forget it!" And she pushed away from him violently, turned away from him; glad she slapped him and would do it again if he didn't walk away from her.

He followed her. "Hey, wait." He took her arm to stop her from walking too fast.

"Don't you dare touch me! Get away from me!"

"Red…I mean, Lorraine, please, wait." But she was walking too fast and he knew he had insulted her and regretted it.

Lorraine caught up to Lucy and Joe and when Lucy saw Lorraine's expression, knew it was time to get rid of Joe, which she did, fast!

The girls walked swiftly and not talking at first. Lucy kept looking at Lorraine knowing something was up but keeping silent for the moment. She knew by Lorraine's fast breathing that something awful had happened. She wondered if Walter had said something really terrible and she knew she would soon find out.

Lorraine, without looking at Lucy, said, "Can you imagine the nerve of that bastard! I should have socked him!" Her breathing was fast and hard and her lips were pressed against her teeth.

"Lorraine, what happened?" Lucy made no secret of

her concern for her friend.

"He wants to see me again but asked me to meet him at the movies. What do I look like? *A puttana?* A whore? I never met a guy on the sly in my life. My father and brothers hear of this and I'm in trouble; no telling what they would do to Walter. Wise guy Walter needs a few lessons in deportment. Maybe he thinks because I'm Italian I'm worthless. If he ever comes near me again, I'll really sock him." She clenched and unclenched her fists.

Lucy agreed with her. "You're right, Lorraine, he thinks…well, he thinks, maybe because we're waitresses he thinks we're a step above a whore. Or maybe on the same level. Maybe Joe thinks the same. Well, he's in for a surprise; too, if he thinks he can pull that shit with me.

The girls walked swiftly to the bus stop and while waiting, Lorraine looked back to see if Walter was following because she had a fist ready to meet his jaw! The boys were nowhere to be seen. Lorraine was a bit disappointed; she was ready to knock a few of his teeth out!

"Tuh! He knows he overstepped the boundary and I'm dead serious. What a conceited bastard. I hope he never comes back to the diner because I won't serve him and I don't want Stavros or anyone else there to have any idea what happened. They're worse than my father."

"Oh, yeah, Lorraine, I know what you mean. Stavros came over to one of my customers and nearly knocked his head off. On the other hand, having a guy like Stavros keeping an eye on us is good. Doncha think?" She was trying to sooth Lorraine because her friend had so much patience with guys but when she got mad, well, blood ran.

Lorraine looked at Lucy and she smiled. "Lucy, I don't know what I would do without you. You're the best pal I could have." She put her arm in Lucy's arm and made her smile. The bus arrived.

They got on the bus, sat down quietly and remained that way for the short ride home; each was lost in her own thoughts.

When they arrived at their stop, they smiled at one another, said goodnight, and promised to speak on the phone to each the other the following morning about going to the dance that night.

Chapter Three

Saturday morning burst forth in a June sunshine frenzy. Even though Lorraine's blinds were closed tightly, the sun managed to wake her. She looked at the clock and as if on cue, the alarm went off. She pushed herself into a sitting position, then swung her legs over the side of the bed and held her head. *Anyone would think I have a hangover.* Then she heard the radio announcer on her clock radio say it was ten minutes past eight and played a lovely melody for sleepy heads. *Hmm, very appropriate.*

She got out of bed and pulled at her pajamas, parts of which were sticking to her slim body. She made her way to her door and opened, only to smell the wonderful coffee Lena had made. Lorraine looked down the hall; the bathroom door was open, which meant it was free for her to dash in and shower. She turned back into her room to get her robe and made a fast entry into the bathroom.

While the water was running down her body, she thought of last night and how the boys had successfully sat with Lucy and her to have coffee. Though the girls objected strenuously, secretly they were pleased and wasn't that normal? She was starting to remember how she was feeling about Walter; she liked him and the more he spoke, the more she liked him. But, when he suggested meeting him by the Triboro Theater, he sent Lorraine spinning into rejection mode. She didn't meet boys on the corner; any corner. That's for sluts! She had set him straight immediately! *Who does he think he is? Who does he think I am?* She didn't realize that she was scrubbing her body fiercely. She would make sure she never came in contact with him ever again, even if he came into the diner and sat at her table. But...she liked him! Her scrubbing stopped suddenly; she remained motionless under the drops that caressed her body. She was beginning to feel sad because he acted so repulsively. She liked him.

She thought of his kisses, so easily taken and enjoyed by both of them. She couldn't get Walter out of her mind. *Well, I will. I don't need a guy like him who thinks he's so wonderful and sensational that I'll fall in love with him immediately. That's for jerks!*

"Lorraine, you awake?"

"Yes, Ma. I'm in the shower and I'll be down in a few minutes." Her mother's voice was just what she needed to bolt her out of her dangerous thoughts. Lorraine made haste to finish her shower, get dressed and get down to breakfast.

"*Buongiorno, tutti. Come state?*" (Good morning, everybody. How are you all?) Lorraine said.

Lena and Carlo were at the table already eating their breakfast. Vinnie and Joe had already gobbled their breakfasts and were ready to leave.

Joe, pushing his empty chair back under the table, said, "See you later, Ma, Pa. I'll call you later to see if you need me to buy something. Vinnie, stop eating, get ready! Ciao, Lorraine. You look gorgeous!"

"Thanks," she said, smiling.

Vinnie, stuffing the last piece of toast in his mouth, said, "Sure, I'm ready. I just need sustenance. I'm not like you, you shrimp. I'm still growing. So long, Ma and Pa. See you later, Red. Give my love to the beautiful Lucy."

"She hates you."

"Ha, ha, that's what she says, but in her heart, she loves me."

Lorraine shook her head. She wouldn't mind if Lucy became her sister-in-law, but if Vinnie waited any longer, he'd lose her. "Yeah, turtle, she'll wait for you."

The parents smiled at their children. It's better to

have them tease and laugh with each other than fight like cats and dogs.

"Where they go?" Carlo asked.

"Where are they going?" Lena corrected and Carlo immediately repeated as Lena pronounced. And she looked at him, lovingly, and said, "They're going to see that car that Bruno Forti has for sale."

"But, that's an old junk. Why they waste their time and money on that?"

"They are going to buy it to work on it. They like mechanics, that's why they went to that vocational high school, and this way they'll learn more. And maybe they'll sell it or keep it for themselves. Who knows? You know they want to open their own shop and this will help them. They love to get all greasy and dirty. Remember when they were little boys, who could get the dirtiest! How crazy they were." She smiled at the recollection; it warmed her heart.

"So, now they are not crazy? I want them to go to college and get good jobs. This is why I work so hard."

"I know, honey, but they want to open their own business and you know they are really, really smart."

"Yes, I know. They take after me." And Carlo puffed out his chest and smiled.

Lena looked heavenward as she rose from her chair and took their cups, "Oh, sure, they did." As she turned to go to the sink, she swayed her hips into her husband's shoulders and he smiled.

Lorraine, all this while, was making a fast breakfast of cereal, not really paying attention to her parents. She was thinking of last night; which made her sad and happy.

The phone rang and Lorraine ran to it. It was Lucy and Lorraine promised to meet her on the corner and go to work. The moment she hung up, she thought *on the corner.* That's where Walter wanted to meet her. Well, it's okay to meet your girlfriend but not a potential boyfriend. She regretted her quick actions with Walter, but she was right in letting him know that she had standards. *He would never respect me if I met him on the corner. I like him. But, there's no reason he shouldn't come to the house to pick me up. I guess he doesn't think Italian girls are worth the energy and effort. Well, he'll learn. But, gee, I like him.*

She was on the corner waiting for Lucy and she was glad she didn't have to wait too long because the occupants of almost every car that passed by whistled or said, "Hey, hey." Though it was annoying, her heart was lifted to hear all the positive remarks.

"Hi, Lorraine, how are you?"

"Fine, Lucy, how are you?"

"Tired. But, I want to tell you that I'm still on my secret diet. Thanks, Lorraine."

"Oh, you're welcome. I'm on your side, Lucy." She smiled at Lucy.

"I know and I'm glad."

They walked in silence for a block or two. Lucy looked at Lorraine and she thought it was a good time to talk about last night. "Lorraine, I feel bad for you about last night."

"You don't have to. It happened. I don't care if I never see him again. It was a rotten thing to say to me. But, Lucy," she looked at her friend with a shy smile on her face, "I like him and I've been thinking about him so much."

"Oh, gee, Lorraine, you better be careful. I know you. You don't fall in love so quickly. He looks like a great guy, but you always gotta be careful of their actions."

"I know." Lorraine had a sad face. They walked in silence and were close to the diner and Lorraine turned to Lucy and said, "Lucy, don't say anything about this to anybody."

"Of course. It's none of anybody's business and if

you want anybody to know anything, you'll tell 'em."

"Right. Let's put on our diner's faces. Big smile!" And she drew a smile in the air close to her lips with her index finger. "Big smile equals big tips."

"Here we come, you cheap bastards!" said Lucy and both laughed. They entered the diner from the back door arm in arm and could see the nearly empty diner. They were called "The Gold Dust Twins" by Thomas and this is how he greeted them this morning.

The girls greeted everyone with their smiles. Thomas said, "I have coffee all ready for you girls." And his eyes lingered on Lorraine, so that she blushed. This didn't escape the stares of Stavros, who loved Lorraine like a daughter, but he knew of a beautiful Greek girl he wanted Thomas to marry. Everyone knew Thomas had different ideas and he had let his father know many times, in clear language, that he would choose his own wife; this was not Greece but the United States of America. Thomas never told his father that he had eyes for Lorraine, but it was obvious to everyone.

However, Lorraine never encouraged Thomas. She was friendly and respectful to him because he was the boss' son, but never allowed him to think she was the least bit interested in him. That made him yearn for her all the more. She didn't know this. Stavros observing all this simply shook his head; how do you stop the water cascading from the broken dam?

It was very busy now and Lorraine didn't see Walter enter the diner. He was alone. He sat at the counter on the stool next to the wall and that allowed him to watch Lorraine almost unnoticed. Lucy, passing by glanced at him, then turned and looked again in surprise. He didn't see Lucy who thought he was watching Lorraine as a hungry dog watches another stupid dog with a bone in his mouth that is going to be dropped any minute. Lucy didn't know if she should tell Lorraine but when she looked at her friend, she saw that Lorraine had just put eyes on Walter. Lucy wondered if there was going to be an eruption or not. *No, Lorraine is always in control and she knows what to do.*

Walter ordered coffee from the counterman and as he drank it very slowly, he kept his eyes on Lorraine, who was very aware of him. When he saw Lorraine walk in the back, he thought it might be her break and left his spot and went outside to walk to the rear of the diner. There he saw her. She had not seen him and was leaning against Stavros' car drinking iced coffee.

He walked up behind her and said in his low baritone, "Hello, Lorraine."

She turned swiftly, surprised and shocked; she had no idea who it could be. When she saw him, she tried not to show her pleasure. Quietly, she said, "I told you I never wanted to see you again. Didn't you think I meant it?"

"Yes, I thought you meant it, but I'm here to apologize profoundly, profusely, most humbly."

"Oh, stop it. You sound so clownish."

"Lorraine, I really mean it. I'm sorry I said that to you. I can see you're a girl who deserves respect and I promise you I'll give it to you."

She regarded him silently. He stepped closer to her. She was aware of his nearness, she smelled his cologne, and she stepped back. "Don't come any nearer. I told you I never wanted to see you again and I meant it. I don't like people thinking I'm not a lady simply because I'm a waitress. It's a good job; it's an honest job; it's hard work."

He came closer. "I know. That's why I came here to apologize. I could have waited until some days passed by but I wanted to see you now and tell you how I felt."

"Okay," she was starting get nervous and he noticed it. "You made your point. And you're not supposed to be in this area. They don't like it." She tilted her head toward the diner.

"Well, can we continue this conversation later? Like can we have dinner tonight so we can talk more? There's a great place where they have dining and dancing. I'd like to take you there. Whadaya say?"

She didn't answer; she looked around as though the answer would fall from heaven or some other secret place. Then she looked at him again, "I already made plans with Lucy."

"But, I'm sure if you tell Lucy you'll be with me, she'll understand."

"I don't do that to my friends. Do you think that's nice?"

"No, you're right, it's not nice and it's very selfish of me." He stepped closer to her, and touched her red pony tail. "Is this your real color?"

"Of course, it is."

"How could it be? Italians don't have natural redheads."

"Ha! That's how much you know. Italians have natural redheads, blondes and blue eyes and green eyes. We're just like everybody else."

He smiled; he was making headway with this doll. He recalled they had a similar conversation last night but played dumb. "Really?"

She realized what happened and nodded her head. "Oh, I fell right in your trap. That's one for you. But, I still won't go out with you. I gotta get back to work." She turned and walked toward the rear entrance of the diner.

"Okay, Lorraine. I'll see you."

Without turning around, she said, "No, you won't!"

Inside the diner, which suddenly seemed so wonderful and different, Lorraine went to her tables where diners were recently seated. Stavros didn't give them breaks as in an office. The waitresses took their short brakes when their tables were empty. Lorraine seemed to be walking on air, even though, she thought she'd never see Walter again. He'd come to apologize and he seemed sincere. She was pleased that he had come to apologize; he was a gentleman. Maybe she would see him again. Who knows?

For the rest of the day, she worked like a demon, but a smiling demon. Lucy noticed and knew why. Then she thought of Joe, but, no, she didn't feel for Joe what Lorraine felt for Walter.

Lorraine didn't know that Thomas has seen her talking to Walter; he never said a word about it to anyone.

At the end of their work shift, the girls left together, talking, giggling and planning to go to the church dance.

"Lucy," Lorraine began, "I know you saw Walter at the diner."

"Yes, I saw him and then I saw you look at him. He left the diner when you went out back. I suspected he came out back to see you."

"Yes, he did. He apologized for what he said. He knew he was out of line. But I told him I didn't want to see him ever again." Then she was quiet for a moment and seemed to calm down. "I think he wants to see me again. I want to see him...but I'm afraid."

"Why are you afraid of him?"

"I'm not afraid of him. I'm afraid of myself. I like him; he has those big blue eyes and I'm afraid that if I see him again and if I keep seeing him, I'll...I'll...well, you know, I may fall in love with him. I get a strange feeling with him. I can't describe it. I just have this feeling that it won't turn out right. Maybe I'm crazy."

"Oh, Lorraine, I think you're just worried about normal things and you can't put your finger on it. Don't worry about it. If you feel safe going out with him and you really want to go out with him, then go. That's the only way you'll find out if you're not meant for each other."

"Lucy, very deep. Thanks for helping me think straight. Now, I'll probably never see him again." She chuckled, "Well, anyway, tonight, we'll go to the dance and have a good time…if those dopey guys ask us to dance."

"You're so right. Well, here's our corner. I'll see you later. I'm hungry because I never touched the irresistible apple pie, thanks to you." She laughed. They parted.

"See you later." Lorraine said and waved.

She opened the back door and immediately saw her mother. "Hi ya, Ma. Hmm. Everything smells good."

"Hello, sweetie. How are you?"

"I'm fine, Ma, and looking forward to going to the dance tonight with Lucy. Woo woo, we've got new dresses. I'm sure we'll knock the boys dead." And she did a little rumba around the table.

"Not dead. Dead men don't ask you to dance."

"Oh, I never thought of that, Ma." She chuckled and went into the downstairs bath and washed her hands and came out to set the table. They were just having a light repast because on the weekend, Lena cooked Italian style; they had their big meal at midday.

Lorraine went to the fridge and removed provolone, prosciutto, mozzarella, black olives and fresh tomatoes and arranged everything on platters. Then she went to the bread box and removed a large round loaf of crusty Italian bread, from Russo's Bakery, which she commenced to slice and she put the slices in another platter. Lena had made a *frittata* which she brought to the table began calling the men of the family, who were in the living room watching a soccer match. They arrived, all three arguing at the same time about which player was the best. Then they looked at the table, ceased arguing and sat down quietly.

The boys asked Lorraine what her plans were for tonight.

"Lucy and I are going to the dance at St. Anthony's. Usually the boys stay on one side of the room and the girls stay on the other side. Sometimes never the twains meet. We have new dresses and are hoping to attract a couple of live wires." She laughed weakly, as she stuffed a piece of provolone in her mouth.

"Well," Vinnie intoned solemnly, "I hope you find live ones at least."

"Oh, thanks, Vinnie," Lorraine said as she spooned some of the *frittata* into her dish. "Sometimes we feel going to a church dance sort of puts *mal auguri* (evil wishes) on us. We really don't have any luck even dancing; the guys seem fearful; like if they ask us to dance, they think tomorrow we go for the furniture."

"Yeah," said Joe, drinking his wine, "I know how that feels but you gotta blame the parents of the girls. They're the ones who question the girls."

"How do you know this?" Vinnie asked.

"Well, you remember sometime last year when we went to the dance at the Y? Well, I met a girl there and then we had a date. The next time I called her, she said her mother had a nice bedroom set all picked out. I hung up fast. There's no way am I gonna have some dopey girl's dopey mother push me into marriage. I didn't even like the girl that much."

"But, Joe, you called her after the first date," Lorraine said, trying to get some information from the male side of the big problem.

"Well, yeah, I called her…maybe for another date…you know, just to give us a chance to get to know each other. But, when I heard that, I told her goodbye."

"Maybe it was her way of saying she liked you and wanted to see you again," Lorraine said.

Joe looked at her as though a light went on. "Yeah, well, it was the wrong thing to do. Geez, it's 1959, I thought that went out with World War II. Some people just don't keep up with the times." And he put some *frittata* on a slice of bread topped with a slice of provolone and mozzarella and bit into it.

Vinnie watched and listened to this interesting conversation and put his two cents in. "Do you realize, little brother, if you had let your then future mother-in-law choose your bedroom set, she would have been sleeping between you and your future wife!" And he burst into a loud laughter, which spread around the table.

"Oh, yeah?" said a pissed off Joe, "I would have sent the girl to you. You're the one who needs parental supervision. I remember that Irish blonde who trailed you at the dance and—"

"Okay, Okay, cut the crap. And the girl wasn't Irish. I think she was French."

"Agh, cut the bullshit! You don't even know what she was. I just know that you made a hasty retreat."

Lena said, "Boys, boys, at the table! Bad language! Stop it now."

But they were all laughing. "Sorry, Ma," said Joe. "We'll behave."

"Yes, all of youse behave," said Carlo. When Carlo finished saying this, the entire family burst into laughter. He looked around at each of them, bewildered. "What you all laugh at?"

Lorraine, who thought her father was brilliant, said, "Dad, it's not 'youse'. It's 'you'. The plural of you is you."

"Agh, this English language make me crazy. I try so hard and I always make mistake."

"But, Dad," Lorraine said, "you're doing beautifully. English is difficult for even the natives to speak."

"You mean the natives in the Tarzan pictures?"

Everyone tried to suppress their laughter but it was no use.

"No," said a smiling Lorraine. "I mean the people who were born here in America. You know, native as in *nato*, born."

"Ah, yes," Carlo said, "I understand. Lorraine, you have made it very clear. *Nato* means born, so native means one who is born in a particular place or country. Is right?"

Lorraine and the rest of the family smiled. She said, "Absolutely perfect Dad. Now you see how many English words come from ancient Latin."

"Yes, I do. *Molto interessante,"* Carlo said, proudly.

Chapter Four

Lorraine ran upstairs after their supper, brushed her teeth, showered and dressed. Although she thought of Walter and was sort of disappointed that she would not be seeing him tonight, nevertheless, she hummed. She was just glad to be going out to a dance with her friend Lucy. Even if she didn't dance, she would put on a happy face and hope for the best. Anyway, Lucy is always fun and a really good friend. They met on their corner at the appointed time and walked to St. Anthony's.

As normal girls do, they gabbed, giggled and walked arm in arm and hoped they would have a good time; at least not spending an evening which would make them gurgle with displeasure.

"Lucy, how are your feet? Any pain?"

"No…not much anyway. And if I get to dance, I'll welcome the pain. I think tomorrow I'll go buy flat heeled shoes, ya know, the kind you wear. Oh, and guess what?" Lucy's eyes were bright with pleasure and anticipation.

"I can't guess, Lucy, so tell me."

"Lorraine, I lost one pound. Yeah, isn't that great? I promise to keep it up and I haven't mentioned it to anyone at all. I can't believe I can keep my own secrets." She giggled and squeezed Lorraine's arm.

"Lucy, that's great. I'm so happy for you. When you reach the weight you want, we'll go out and buy you new clothes. Won't that be great?"

"Oo, yeah, I can't wait. I'm gonna save all my tips for new clothes only."

"Good. Get a little cardboard box and make a slit in the cover so you can drop all your change in it."

"Wow, Lorraine, what a good idea." They were approaching St. Anthony's school. "Oh, look at all the guys standing outside. Oh, I hate this; we'll have to pass all those dopes and listen to their remarks."

They passed the boys and Lucy was right, they heard all sorts of remarks. One was particularly offensive and Lucy turned and growled, "Don't even think of asking us to dance, you creep!" All the boys laughed.

The girls walked faster and entered the gym, which was lit very brightly. They greeted other girls they knew and walked closer to the band and they tapped their feet to the rhythm of the music; it was a cha cha. Within a few minutes, a dark haired young man approached Lorraine.

He looked into her eyes, tipped his dark, curly head a bit and said, "Good evening, Miss. Would you like to dance?"

Lorraine, who was talking, stopped in mid-sentence and after a moment of looking into his eyes, said, "Yes, thank you, I would. Excuse me, Lucy."

"Sure," said Lucy. And she watched them as they approached the dance floor and he deftly put his arm around Lorraine's waist.

On the dance floor, dancing the cha cha, they didn't speak much. Then they heard a soft, slow, very romantic song. They continued to dance and he said, "My name is Humphrey Pennyworth. What's yours?"

A surprised look spread on Lorraine's face. "No, you can't be named Humphrey Pennyworth." Then they both laughed.

"No, you're right, I mean, yes, you're right, I can't be named Humphrey Pennyworth. I just wanted to see if you were paying attention. My name is very ordinary; Martin Ranieri. Everyone calls me Marty. I hope you do, too."

"Well, Marty, my name is Lorraine Martini. What a coincidence that your first name and my last name are similar."

"Wow, yeah, that's amazing. And your last name

tells me you're Italian. I thought you were Irish."

"Oh, so does that mean this is our last dance?" They laughed.

"I hope not. Now, your friend, there, looks Italian. I would bet that her parents are from Naples."

"Almost right. Her father comes from Sorrento…or a little town outside Sorrento. I don't remember where her mother is from."

"Are both your parents Italian?"

"Yes, they are and you're not gonna tell me that you're surprised that I'm a redheaded Italian, are you?"

"No, I'm not because I have redheaded cousins. I know Italians are very diverse in their coloring." He was quiet, just looking at her face and thinking. "Do—do you have a boyfriend?"

"No." Lorraine was startled at such a direct question coming without a cough or a chuckle, and didn't offer any further information. She didn't like the way the conversation was going and she felt uncomfortable in his arms. He seemed to be tightening his hold on her waist with each word. The more he spoke, the more she doubted his sincerity. *Was she supposed to fall into his arms? Nothing doing!* As soon as the music stopped, she thanked him for the dance and made a quick get-away.

She saw Lucy standing almost in the same spot, which made her think Lucy didn't dance at all. She arrived at her side and spoke, a bit out of breath, "Lucy, I don't like that guy."

"But, why? You both were dancing beautifully together. I thought something nice was happening."

"No. I can't put my finger on it. I just got a queasy feeling and wanted to be away from him. I hope he doesn't come back here." Lorraine looked toward the spot Marty was and saw he had disappeared.

Lucy happened to look toward the dance floor and

said, "Uh oh." She turned her face away and faced Lorraine. "I think he's coming this way. Let's walk a bit."

Lorraine didn't look around but agreed. "Let's go to the Ladies Room, he surely won't follow us there, if that's his intention."

The girls entered the Ladies Room and met some of their friends. One was particularly upset because a guy named Martin had held her too tightly and made suggestive remarks. The poor girl was almost in tears. Lorraine and Lucy never said a word but they knew whom she was talking about and left the room.

Lorraine said, "Lucy, let's try to avoid that guy. I guess I wasn't the only girl he gave the creeps to." And she let out a loud breath. Lucy agreed with her. They went to the dance floor again and joined the "circle" of observers.

A young man came to ask Lucy to dance; without letting him see, she made eyes at Lorraine and went with him to the dance floor. Lorraine smiled at her friend's humor and she felt a tap on her shoulder and heard, "Would you like to dance?" She turned and there to her surprise was Walter. She gasped.

"Oh, y—yes," she said. She went into his arms and they danced very smoothly together. Lorraine couldn't believe it. At first they didn't speak.

Walter looked into her eyes and holding her gently, whispered, "I can't believe my good luck at finding you here."

Lorraine didn't speak. She looked into his steel blue eyes and looked down. He liked that.

"I—I don't think you knew I'd be here," Lorraine said softly and shyly.

"No, I didn't but I'm sure glad I came tonight. My buddy, Bob talked me into coming here. I resisted for more than an hour. He kept insisting the dances here are great because they have a live band." He looked toward the portable stage and listened for a moment; then he looked down at Lorraine's beautiful freckled face.

"I've been thinking about you since I first saw you." He whispered this so softly and intensely that Lorraine felt her face reddening and getting warm.

Lorraine was silent.

"Are you still mad at me?" Walter asked.

Lorraine looked into his eyes, and then looked away. He asked her again but this time he added a gentle nudge to her back. It made him seem familiar and she was puzzled. She looked again at him and whispered, "No—no, not anymore."

He smiled at her and said, "I'm glad. I've really been thinking about you and hoped that you wouldn't be mad at me anymore. I do apologize again for any offence I gave you."

She smiled, "Thank you. I accept your apology."

They danced silently and close until the music changed to a lively Latin beat, which they enjoyed together and never missed a beat.

After the set was over, Walter held Lorraine's hand and they walked away from the dance floor. They gazed at each other and he squeezed her hand, sending messages, which she understood. It frightened her. She liked him.

He said, "Let's get out of here."

"But, what about Lucy? I came with her."

"Well, I don't want to be alone with you and Lucy. I really want to get out of here and be alone with you."

Those words thrilled Lorraine. "I—I'll talk to her." And she searched for Lucy. She saw Lucy talking to the guy who had asked her to dance and headed toward her. What could she say to her friend? She didn't want to offend Lucy. Would she understand? Lorraine really wanted to be with Walter. She walked up to Lucy and knew immediately that Lorraine was about to drop a bomb.

"Excuse me, Lucy, I need to talk to you."

"Sure," she said and turned to the young man and said, "Will you excuse me a minute, Dave?" Before he could answer, the girls walked a few feet from him and conversed.

Lorraine had a strange expression on her face. "Lucy, I—I want to ask you a favor."

Lucy was preparing herself. "Sure, what is it?"

"Well, listen, I—Walter is here and he asked me to dance and we've been dancing for a while. He wants to leave and he wants me to go with him. Do you mind? I know we never do anything like this, but—" and she was talking fast because her heart was beating furiously; she didn't want to offend Lucy but she wanted to be with Walter.

Lucy smiled; her hurt was masked for the moment; hurt for her friend because now she was afraid for Lorraine. Lucy didn't trust Walter and couldn't explain the reason to herself, so how could she tell her friend; but, she didn't mention this to Lorraine.

"Hey, don't worry about me. Sure, go ahead and have a good time." She smiled. "But, be careful. Okay?"

"Sure, Lucy. You're such a pal. I'll call you tomorrow."

"Okay."

Lorraine squeezed Lucy's arm and turned to look for Walter. He was standing by the entrance which will now be the exit for him and Lorraine. He had a lopsided smile on his face and he broke into a full, triumphant smile as he saw Lorraine walking quickly toward him. She had an unmistakable expression on her face; it was good for Walter!

"Lucy's okay with this. She's such a good friend." Lorraine smiled; her heart was beating. They started to walk toward the exit and Lorraine retrieved her light coat.

"Oh, what about your friend, the one you came her with? Did you tell him we're leaving?"

"Oh, sure," said Walter confidently. He had lied to her. He had come alone looking for adventure and seeing Lorraine was just a lucky streak; he really did like her.

Outside in the lovely starry night, he took her hand and guided her to his car.

"Walter, do you live close by?"

"Yes, I do, but Bob and I didn't really know where we were headed until he saw the church and the crowd of people and decided this was a good place to spend a few hours." He looked at her; his steel blue eyes searching for her soul. "And look how fortunate I am; I saw you." Most of what he said was a lie; the part about his being "fortunate" was true.

His hand tightened on hers and she smiled. She thought, yes, how fortunate we both are.

At the car, he opened the door for her and then went to the driver's side, got in and started the car. It was a big car; late model and she thought he must have a good job in order to pay the installments. Then she changed her thoughts. She sat close to him and it thrilled him. They drove around a bit and Lorraine asked, "Where are we going? Please, let's not go to the diner where I work."

He looked at her, "I had no intention of going there. When we're off, we don't go to the places we work, if we can help it." And he smiled at her; she smiled back.

He drove down a dimly lit block and parked. "I just want to be alone with you. I've been thinking about you since the moment I saw you." He put his arms around her and pulled her close. Huskily, he said, "I want to kiss you." He did. He parted her lips with his tongue. She, at first pushed him away but he didn't let go of her and continued to kiss her in that manner. She wasn't accustomed to it and struggled but he held her tightly. Then she stopped struggling and yielded her mouth.

"You're lovely," he breathed. He kissed her again and his hands began to roam over her body.

She pushed him away. "Stop it!"

His arms were still around her tightly and she felt helpless. "Let go of me. You can't do this to me!"

"Do what? I'm only kissing you. We're making love. Well, we're not going all the way but this is how I make love." He kissed her again and his free hand touched her breasts. Lorraine tried to stop him but it felt strange to her; she was feeling urges she never felt before.

"Lorraine, I love you."

"I love you, too, Walter." She was surprised at his words and utterly astonished at her own. "Walter, please stop. We can't do any more of this."

"I guess you're right, baby." And he did something Lorraine had never seen before but had only heard of. She felt awkward. She felt afraid. She didn't know what to do or what to say, so she remained quiet. She looked away.

Later, he turned to her and smiled slyly.

"Lorraine, can you come out with me tomorrow night?"

"Yes," she said, in almost a whisper, because she was frightened.

"I'll pick you up at eight o'clock. How's that?"

"That's fine." She said quietly.

He knew how she felt. She wasn't the first girl that witnessed this. He smiled smugly.

"I'll take you home now." And that's how he found out where she lived and would be at her house the following night at the appointed hour.

Chapter Five

Sunday morning, Lorraine had gone to mass and didn't realize that she was praying very fervently. She couldn't sort her feelings. She loved Walter; she told herself that. But, she was also afraid. He'd acted as though they had been sweethearts for many months. Did he respect her? She didn't know. Should she tell her mother? OW, no, that's not the thing to tell her. She was troubled and didn't know to whom she could speak of this incident. What does she do?

When she returned, she looked at her mother. Does her mother know these things? Still, she couldn't bring herself to mention it. She set the table. Lena came into the dining room.

"Ma," Lorraine said.

"Yes, honey. What is it?"

"I have a date tonight."

"Really? Nice. Do I know him?"

"No, we met at the diner."

"Oh, what's his name?"

"His name is Walter. I don't know his last name. I'll find out tonight."

"Is he Italian? With that name, his people might come from Northern Italy…way, way up there in the mountains; the Italian Alps, they're called."

"I know." Lorraine had responded very quietly.

"Lorraine! What's the trouble? Is he nice or is he mean and disrespectful?"

"No, Ma, he's not mean or disrespectful. He's nice, as a matter of fact. It's just that I don't know him that well and I think we love…well, we like each other a lot."

Lena looked at her daughter, a smile breaking her face. "Agh, come on. Tell your mother the truth. You love him. Beh, I know how that is…you don't know a boy that well or that long and you just fall in love. The lightning bolt. I've told you about that many times."

"Yeah, I guess that's what it is. He's coming here at eight o'clock. I guess that's late for a date, but then it's Sunday night and tomorrow's work."

"What does he do?"

"I don't know. We haven't talked much." And she remembered what had happened last night and thought they should have talked about that instead of…of.

"Well, you go and have a good time. But, remember," her right hand came up, index finger extended, "he must not put his hands where they don't belong." And she walked back into the kitchen.

That worried Lorraine; Walter was a freakin' octopus. Walter was persuasive and he made his feelings known in a dramatic way. When Lorraine thought of his kisses, she melted inside. Her ovaries did a *tarantella,* a very lively Italian dance. She was scared.

After dinner, Lucy called and said she would like to go for a short walk with Lorraine, who was only too happy to oblige.

They met on the corner and Lucy knew immediately Lorraine had big things on her mind. "Hey, Lorraine, what's up? You look like you have all the world's problems on your shoulders."

Lorraine had a pained look on her face. "Oh, Lucy, I don't know if I'm coming or going."

"That son of a bitch! I knew he was trouble. What did he do? What happened last night?"

"Well, we parked on a dark street."

"You parked on a dark street!! With that guy? Are you crazy? Do you want him to deflower you?" Then Lucy realized what she'd said, immediately regretted it, and mumbled, "Oh."

Lorraine noted what Lucy said, but didn't

acknowledge it, "Yes, I think I'm crazy. I'm crazy about him and he's crazy about me."

"Oh, God, tell me about it. NO! Don't tell me anything. Oh, Lorraine, you look like you're… . You didn't do anything… anything foolish, did you?"

Lorraine laughed nervously, "Of course, we didn't. What a thing to think." But Lorraine was embarrassed as though Lucy knew what lewd acts took place last night. She knew!

Lucy looked intensely at Lorraine and said, "Lorraine, I'm gonna say something and I don't care if you get mad or offended. You're my best friend and if anything happened to you, something bad, I don't know what I would do. I—I don't trust Walter and no, I'm not jealous. He's not my type and he's not yours, either. You just don't know it yet. I—I think you're dazzled by him. There's something about him that—that doesn't feel right to me. Please—please be careful because I think—I think he can talk you into doing what you don't want to do. I'm sorry if I—I offended you." Her chin trembled and Lorraine saw this and was touched.

Lorraine looked down at her hands; she didn't know how Lucy knew. "Lucy, you haven't offended me and he—he hasn't talked me into doing anything I don't want to do. I'm puzzled. I don't know what to do. I—I just don't know what to do."

"Then don't do nothin'… if you know what I mean. Keep your distance."

Lorraine said nothing and then very quietly, she said, "I have a date with him tonight." She sounded almost remorseful that she'd made a date with him.

Lucy could only look at her. She knew her friend was in love… hopelessly in love. She would watch her friend and pray for her. But she knew she couldn't save her friend.

***

That evening, when Walter came to pick up Lorraine, he was introduced to the family. Lorraine detected the coldness from the family. Carlo was very cold to Walter. Lena was fearful. Vinnie and Joe were icy. Both brothers were muscular and had worn tight fitting polo shirts, just to show their muscles in case they thought Walter was bad news for Lorraine. Although they didn't say anything to Walter, their eyes went to Lorraine and she understood immediately that Walter was in grave danger… excuse the word "grave."

At an opportune moment, Lorraine said she and Walter would be going out and they all bid each other good evening. They rode around for a while and then Walter found a dark street on which to park; a dark street included many big trees that would obscure the street lights; a perfect hunting ground for a rapist!

Lorraine and Walter indulged in heavy petting on their first date. Walter's kisses were so dense that they left Lorraine gasping for breath. Walter wanted to have intercourse with Lorraine but she was frightened and offended that he would think she would actually do it.

"Come on, Lorraine, I know you want to do it as much as I do."

"Walter, we can't. Please stop." Her fear was palpable. He understood immediately. "You must stop. If my father finds out what you want to do, he'll kill us both!"

"Well, I'm certainly not gonna tell him. Or do we have to get his permission?" He said this with such sarcasm that Lorraine slapped his face hard.

"What kind of a girl do you think I am? You think I'm easy, well, you're wrong. Take me home, now!" She faced forward, but her anger was very apparent.

"Maybe you should take yourself home!" And he opened the door and pushed her out of the car.

"You son of a bitch! I hope you drop dead!" She turned and began walking, her shoulders squared and her head held high.

He watched her go. And though he was mad at her, his heart strings were tugged. It was then he realized he really loved her. He would not let her walk home alone; he got out of the car and ran after her. She heard him coming, turned and gave him a fearsome look and made a fist. "You take one more step and I'll give you a kick that'll send you to heaven!"

"Look, I'm not letting you go home alone. I apologize. I love you."

"You're crazy. You don't love me. You love yourself and don't come near me"

"Lorraine, I'm telling you the truth. I love you. I want us to get married."

"Don't come near me, you bastard. I hate you. I hate you!" She turned and walked swiftly toward the corner where she could catch a bus and go home.

Walter ran to her, swung her around and under her protestations, kissed her again and again, murmuring his love. Lorraine calmed down and finally returned his kisses. They stayed locked in their embrace, on the sidewalk of that dark street.

Then Walter heard her sobs and knew that he had deeply offended the most gracious girl in the world. How sweet she was. Her perfume embraced her and now him, too. He would marry her and they would be happy. She was the one girl for him, he knew that.

She stopped crying, but the sobs and sighs kept escaping her. She looked up at him. "Walter, did you really mean it when you said you loved me?"

He held her tenderly and responded in a voice laden with love, "Yes, I did."

"And—and did you mean it when you said you

want us to get married?"

"Yes," he smiled at her. "I meant every word. I love you and I want us to get married."

"But, Walter, we really don't know each other that well. We only had one date."

"That's all I need." He kissed her.

They began to date. Lorraine's family became accustomed to seeing Walter several times a week to escort Lorraine around town. While Lena had reconciled herself to a new son-in-law, Carlo and his sons still frightened Walter with their stares and muscles. Somehow, they knew Walter would never marry Lorraine and they were prepared to cripple him.

Walter had exhibited excellent control and never offended Lorraine again. It made her love him more. What she didn't know was that Walter was deathly afraid of the overabundance of the obscene muscles on the men in Lorraine's family. So, very wisely, he guarded his health by exercising great control and respect for Lorraine and her entire family.

Loraine had still not met Walter's parents and she had reminded him of it several times. Each time she had, he stuttered and tried to change the subject and gave her some flimsy reason that a meeting couldn't take place. She began to worry. Finally, Lorraine put her foot down.

"Walter! Am I gonna meet your parents or not? I haven't even met your sister. You've met my whole family, including my grandparents, who are crazy about you."

"I know, I know, honey. It's just that my parents have a busy social schedule."

Lorraine simply gave him a sidelong look.

"Don't look at me that way. I know, I know, Honey, you're right. You have to meet them. I'll do as you say. I'll tell my parents we have to set up a day for you to meet them. Oh," he said, with some relief in his voice, "you'll love them. They are great."

Finally, on a cold Sunday, in late November, Lorraine was invited to dinner at the Walter Hadley home. She was very excited and planned to bring lovely gifts. She pestered Walter, who could hardly hide his nervousness, as to what she could bring. She wanted to make a great first impression. The Hadley family was well-to-do. Walter, Senior, was the son of a man who started his electric business when Walter, Senior was a baby. The business had prospered and they moved from their tight little home to a large home and then to a still larger one. This is the home, Walter, Junior and his family lived in.

On that Sunday, Lorraine dressed in her best outfit, which happened to be green, the color that made Lorraine look very Irish. Walter came to pick her up and helped her bring the gifts to his family.

One of the maids opened the door when they arrived. Lorraine was dumbstruck. The house was huge. She gave the maid a very warm greeting, almost kissing her, the way Italians do when they enter a home. Walter gave her a nudge; kissing maids was left to the young man of the house, under the stairs; only if the maids were young and comely. Walter didn't tell this to Lorraine; she didn't have to know this.

They went into a living room, which was so huge; Lorraine didn't know in which direction to look. Walter guided her. Mr. and Mrs. Hadley were seated at the far end of the room in two thickly upholstered chairs, reading the newspapers. Lorraine thought of her mother, on a Sunday morning, she was busy cooking, no maid in sight; only the daughter to help.

Walter, holding Lorraine's hand, gently leading her, and in the other hand, a package, "Mother, Dad, we're here." As they approached the unapproachable, Lorraine's knees began to shake. She felt the blood drain from her face but forced a smile.

Walter said, through his stiff smile, "Mother, Dad, I want you to meet Lorraine Martini. Lorraine, this is Mother and Dad."

"How do you do, Mrs. Hadley. Mr. Hadley, I'm very pleased to meet you." She almost curtsied, but, luckily, she caught herself in time.

Mr. and Mrs. Hadley rose and came to meet Lorraine, their hands extended. "How very nice to meet you, my dear." Mrs. Hadley said. "My, what lovely hair you have."

Shyly, Lorraine thanked her.

"Won't you sit down, my dear?"

At that, Lorraine began to feel at ease. "Thank you very much, Mrs. Hadley. What a lovely room this is."

"Oh, thank you so much. Mr. Hadley and I gathered much of these furnishings on our many trips to Europe and the Orient. Our decorator was astonished at how I put all these items together to create a bit of harmony." She laughed remembering that her decorator almost had apoplexy, but she didn't say this to Lorraine.

"Well, you certainly did a wonderful job." Lorraine said. And, yes, as she looked around at the furniture and the paintings on the walls, she had to agree with Mrs. Hadley. Yes, she had to agree but in Lorraine's heart of hearts she thought the entire layout looked like a furniture store.

"Son, what are all these packages?" It was his bulbous nosed father who asked.

"Oh, well, Dad, these are gifts from Lorraine. This is how she and her family do things."

"Oh, really," said Mrs. Hadley icily. "That's interesting. Shall we open them now?"

"Oh, whenever you want, Mrs. Hadley." Lorraine was unsuccessful in hiding her nervousness. Her knees shook and her voice was unsteady.

Mrs. Hadley smiled stiffly. She had no intention of opening any gifts at this moment. "Where do you live, Lorette?"

"It's Lorraine, Mrs. Hadley. And we live in Astoria."

"Oh, yes, I've heard of it. Isn't that where the Triboro Bridge starts or ends?" She laughed, "I suppose it depends on where you're starting out from." She looked at her husband and made sure he laughed at her joke.

Lorraine was beginning to understand why Walter had not arranged a meeting sooner. She looked at his face; poor Walter, he was miserable.

"Tell me, my dear, that red hair of yours is striking, from which forebear did you receive it?"

Lorraine breathed a bit deeply before responding. Then she said steadily, "My redheaded forebear was and still is my little grandmother, who was born in Southern Italy."

It was as though Lorraine had struck Mrs. Hadley; whose eyebrows rose.

After a moment, the maid entered to say dinner was ready. Mrs. Hadley, recovered herself and said, "Ah, dinner is ready. Emily, please serve." She came to Lorraine and took her arm, trying to be chummy, and they walked into the dining room. Mrs. Hadley said, "I'm sorry you won't meet my daughter, Abigail. She's still at the University and will not return until Christmas. We call her Gail; she insists on it. She has a terrible temper and we give her leeway so that we have peace. She has red hair, as you do. Everyone blames the temper on the red hair. Do you have a temper, my dear?"

Lorraine, who was beginning to understand this lady, gave Mrs. Hadley her strongest look and said, very clearly, "Only when I'm provoked!" Her dart had not missed its mark.

They all sat down to dinner. Lorraine couldn't tell how the dinner was prepared and cooked; it consisted of roast meat and vegetables. She didn't like the taste; it was bland. It would never go over in her house. She could just imagine her brothers, Vinnie and Joe eating this dinner. "Yeah, Vinnie eat some meat. Joe help yourself to the green stuff! Oh, yeah!"

The dinner was quiet at times, the only noise being the silver utensils hitting against the lovely China. There were stares revolving from one to the other. It wasn't the noisy dinner Lorraine was used to. She looked at Walter and felt sorry for him. What a bunch of stiffs, Lorraine thought, you could die and no one, not even the dead, would know that somebody had died. Her mind didn't go into the future because she knew that Mrs. Hadley was not only her enemy, but a fierce Ice Empress. She felt she wouldn't see Walter very often after today. Her heart sank; she wanted to be with him the rest of her life and she knew he felt the same. But…

***

When Lorraine, unsmiling, arrived home, Lena, all excited, asked many questions. Then she realized her daughter was not forthcoming with descriptions of any kind.

"Lorraine, *figlia mia,* what's wrong. Did they mistreat you?"

"No, Ma, they were very cordial."

"Cordial?" Lena asked, a deep frown on her forehead. "What is this cordial? They should welcome you with open arms. You are a very good girl and you're beautiful, too. What are they expecting?"

"I don't know, Ma. They have a maid and a cook and I don't know how much help."

"Really?" Lena asked, her eyes opened wide with wonder.

"Yes, Ma, the maid opened the door and the cook cooked this awful dinner. It had no taste."

"You didn't tell them that, did you?" Lena was concerned; her eyes wide open with fear.

"No, of course not, Ma, but it was tough sending all that bland food down my gullet. Whew!" Lorraine wanted to go upstairs and started in that direction when her father came out of the living room to speak to her.

"Lorraine, you have nice time?" He asked her very gently and studied her face knowing the answer even before she made a response. He felt her pain.

"Yes, Dad, I had a nice time. They were very cordial to me. They—" She flung herself in her father's arms and tried to suppress her tears. She was unsuccessful.

Carlo held his daughter tenderly in his arms but his heart was beating fast. "I go there and talk to them. They are not better than we are. This is America! They told me when I become citizen, I and my family are as good as anybody else. I believe them."

"No, Dad. Please don't do that. Please let me handle it. I'm not going to let Walter suffer because of me. I know his parents don't want me for his wife." She could no longer speak. Her parents understood. They wouldn't say anything to prolong the pain and wouldn't say anything to remind her that they didn't approve of Walter, no reasons given.

Lena came close and put her hand on her daughter's shoulder. "*Povera figlia.* Poor child." She kissed her daughter's temple and sighed.

Lorraine controlled her tears, broke away from her father, looking at him with love and understanding in her eyes and then she went upstairs slowly and quietly. "Thanks, Dad."

Later, Lena and Carlo were sitting together, speaking in whispers, as though Lorrain could hear their words while she showered. "Carlo, what do we do now? She feels so bad; she's making me cry." Lena wept and put her head on Carlo's big shoulder.

"I don't know. I know from the beginning he's not for her. Joe and Vinnie know, too. They never like him. They told me."

"I know," Lena said. "I remember the looks they gave that boy. But, I could see he really loves her.

"But, the parents, they don't like our daughter." Carlo shook his head and shrugged his shoulders, utterly mystified. "Everybody loves her. I never met anyone who didn't like her. And Bruno Forti, every time I see him, he tells me he wants his nephew to marry Lorraine. I tell him she must choose her own husband, not like in the old country. I want my daughter to be happy; she's a good girl and works hard. The Madonna will hear our prayers."

"Yes, darling, you're right. The Madonna will hear our prayers. Lorraine is the best." She sobbed. Soon, both became quiet, looking at the television, not watching anything.

Chapter Six

In Walter's home, there also was an episode. Mrs. Hadley rebuked her son. "Walter, how can you bring that girl into our home with the intention of—of marrying her?"

"Well, Ma—"

"Ma! Ma! Is that what you learned from that girl from Astoria? I am 'Ma' now?" And she made a noise with her mouth and turned away in disgust.

"I'm sorry, Mother. I didn't mean to say that. That's how Lorraine addresses her mother and she loves and respects her mother."

"Well," Mrs. Hadley puffed, "you will absolutely NOT address me in that manner. And I do not care about her relationship with her mother. I'm not the least bit interested." She brushed some imaginary hair from her forehead.

"Yes, Mother. I beg your pardon. It won't happen again."

"It certainly will not!" There was ice in her voice.

Walter looked from his angry mother to his father, whose face was screwed up into a furious glare. He knew he was outnumbered.

"Mother, Dad, she's a good girl."

"I don't care in the least." Mrs. Hadley said, who raised her eyebrows and looked away.

Walter looked at his mother a moment, and then began again. "Mother, Dad, she's an excellent girl and I love her very much."

"But you hardly know her." Mr. Hadley said. He had to add his words so that his wife would not think he liked or approved of the girl; the redheaded, Italian girl from Astoria. Although if truth be told, he found her charming; her innocence and honesty, which he appreciated, were traits he hadn't seen for a long time.

"Dad, we've been seeing each other for a couple of months and we've gotten to know each other pretty well."

"But, what kind of a family does she come from?" Mrs. Hadley insisted on knowing.

"She comes from a very good family."

"What does her father do?" Mrs. Hadley asked.

"He's a construction worker, built like a Mack truck, and he provides well for his family. He was born in Italy, has become a citizen and speaks English well enough to be understood."

"Well enough! Probably speaks 'dese' and 'dose'. What about the rest of the family?"

"Mother, he doesn't speak like that. Lorraine has two brothers who are skilled mechanics."

"Awk! Do they bring grease in the house? Good heavens, Walter," addressing her husband, "we'll be the laughing stock of all our family and friends."

"Mother, please stop it. They don't bring grease in the house. Mrs. Martini keeps a spotless house. They are a friendly, warm, caring family and they work hard. I'll tell you, they bring in the money. They want for nothing."

"Oh, really. I want to see for myself. Please ask them to invite us for dinner."

"No, Mother, I don't think I'm going to do that. It seems contrived on your part and you'll be going there with the intention of insulting them." Walter was surprised at his courage; very rarely did he stand up to his mother.

"But, how do you know? I want to go there to become acquainted with them. After all, you love her you say and want to marry her. I have every right to see with whom my son wants to ally himself with."

"No, Mother. I won't have Lorraine and her family disparaged or humiliated because of your uppity ways. I want to marry her; not ally myself with her!"

"Oh, Walter!" She gave her husband a pleading look, who came swiftly to her side and put his arm around her waist. He harrumphed and said, "Son, your mother is right. You must think of your future. This girl will not fit into your future. She has no connections and you know that's important for your future. We know that."

"Dad, I love her and I want to marry her."

"Oh," wailed Mrs. Hadley, who began to faint.

Mr. Hadley held his wife so that she wouldn't fall to the floor, "Walter, Walter help me get your mother to the couch." Walter, Junior, came quickly to assist his parents. His face showed anger and impatience. This wasn't the first time an episode like this happened. A few years ago, there was another girl his parents didn't approve of and she was long gone. He didn't want that to happen to Lorraine.

After a few minutes of wrist massaging, and clucking by her husband, Mrs. Hadley was revived.

She spoke through short breaths. "Walter, you can marry whomever you please. You are an adult. However," here she looked at her son with great strength and Walter, Junior knew he was cooked. "if you marry this girl, you will hurt us beyond measure. We will have to banish you from our home and our family. We will have to cut you out of our wills. You will not succeed your father in his factory and you will not inherit his position in his factory; something for which you've been groomed for many years. We're counting on you to continue our dynasty. We'll be old before you know it and we need you to fill Father's position. You cannot fulfill your destiny with this girl from Astoria. Please consider what I've said. You know how serious this is and how we need you, Walter. You're our only son, our only hope, and not only do we depend on you but your sister, who's so frivolous, also needs you. You know she won't amount to anything so that she can support herself. We don't know if we can ever arrange a suitable marriage for her. You'll have to give her a position in the office, no matter what it is, just so she can claim a salary and all the rest of the benefits. Walter, I'm imploring you to reconsider your choice for a wife. She must fit in with our own society." Then she spoke softly, and embraced him, "Darling, I know that I can count on you to do what's right. You know we love you tremendously and have given you the best of everything; education, travel and more."

Walter, Junior, was lassoed and he knew it. But, he loved Lorraine. What will he do now? He had promised to call Lorraine after the dinner to tell her the honest comments his parents had made. What could he tell her; how could he embellish the truth. There was no way it could be done and he knew there would be no smooth sailing.

What Walter didn't realize was that he, being naturally shallow and self-indulgent, didn't love Lorraine as deeply as she loved him.

"Yes, Mother. I know. I'll—I'll stop seeing Lorraine. I'll tell her that I don't love her, even though I'll be lying. And, you know, she'll know it. Both our hearts will be breaking. Just give me the time to let her know and let her down easy. It may take a couple of weeks. Is that okay?"

Mrs. Hadley was smooth. "Of course, darling. Take all the time you need. It's necessary for this girl—this young lady to understand completely and accept a clean break. Don't you think so, Walter?"

Walter, Junior, looked at her, then cast his glance down, nodded and turned to go to his room.

Mrs. Hadley smiled and looked at her husband to emphasis her victory and great accomplishment. Mr. Hadley could only look back at her and not make any sound or twitch his face; as he wanted to do. He knew his son would suffer as he had suffered with his insufferable wife. His heart was breaking for his son. He thought of his own youth. He had fallen in love with a girl of the lower class and his mother had done exactly as Mrs. Hadley had done. He had to leave her and Miss Martha Maude Benson was introduced to him by his parents, who ordered him to marry her because she came from a high class family with great connections and lots of money. Six months after the wedding; the Benson family lost their fortune; but Martha Maude was settled and was not in trouble as the rest of her family who quickly became leeches to poor Walter. Martha Maude turned out to be exactly like his mother. It's a terrible thing when a man marries his "mother."

Young Walter was in his very large room. He looked around at all the paintings on the walls. Everything in this room had all been selected by his mother. He had no pictures of his friends. All the pictures were of family, grandparents on both sides and of himself when he graduated the academy. The furniture had also been selected by his mother; very uncomfortable. He couldn't come home and jump on his couch because it was not done in the Hadley home.

By contrast, Lorraine's home was warm and inviting and comfortable. He realized that's what he found so attractive and amazing about it. The men of the house removed their shoes when they entered and walked around the house in their stocking feet. No one gave cries of disgust or fainted at that sight.

But, what can Walter do? He knew his limited qualities. No industry attracted him. His present job was a farce. It was a temporary job until his father could fit him in someplace in their factory, which Walter knew, due to present circumstances, would soon occur.

Walter was feeling so low and melancholy; he threw himself on his bed, not caring that he hadn't removed the bedspread and he had his shoes on, yet. He was hoping his mother would come into his room to see the brazen Walter lying on the satin embroidered bedspread, made in the Far East and that had cost a fortune. He lit a cigarette and threw the match on the floor because there were no ashtrays in his room because Mother didn't approve of smoking.

He thought of Lorraine and wondered how he could break the news to her. He knew he was trapped and not strong enough oppose his parents. He hated himself; he was a shit. But, hadn't he detected a sort of approval of Lorraine in his Dad's eyes? Oh, maybe not. No one was strong enough to stand up to Martha Maude. She should have been a general in the war! Or maybe a matron in a women's prison. That put an evil smile on Walter's face. He thought of a bunch of tough prison broads ganging up on Martha Maude and kicking the shit out of her.

Walter picked up the phone to call Lorraine. He didn't know what he would say; he just wanted to hear her voice, maybe he would gather some strength from her warmth. But do you call your love, knowing she's hoping to hear some words of love and approval and stab her? Even if it is via phone, it will still hurt!

"Hello," Lorraine said. Her voice was a bit plaintive. He was affected by this and wished he could be there to take her in his arms and tell her he loved her and wanted to marry her, no matter what Martha Maude said. But, no, he couldn't get those words out of his mouth. Martha Maude's destructive, awful words were still fresh in his brain.

A subdued Walter answered, "Hello, sweetheart."

Lorraine, glad to hear his voice, knew immediately that things had changed. She wouldn't push him.

"Are you okay, Walter?" Her voice, though soothing, still showed a bit of melancholy and pain. Walter was affected.

"Yes, I am. Everything is per—fine. Are you okay, too?"

"Sure, I'm fine. I—I hope I didn't embarrass you in front of your parents."

"Honey, you could never embarrass me." His voice caught in his throat and Lorraine heard and her heart pinched.

"Walter, I don't know what it is, but I'm very tired. Do you mind I cut this call short? I think I need to take a shower and get into bed. Maybe I'm coming down with something. I don't know what it is." Her voice was unsteady and her chin trembled.

Walter, relieved somewhat, because he didn't know what to say, said, "Sure, sure, honey. Do that. I'll call you tomorrow. I hope you feel better. Maybe you should go to the doctor." And he realized he should shut up because he was belaboring the situation and accomplishing nothing. He said, "Goodnight."

"Goodnight." She had used the extension in her room and looked at the phone for a long time and then hung up silently. She lay down and the tears kept coming. She knew instinctively that Martha Maude has succeeded in destroying two young people. And she thought, when will he let me know? Hours later, she fell asleep. Her fears that things would change and she would never see Walter again would come true. She would soon see their dates, which were two or three times a week, come to one a week.

***

The telephone rang. Lorraine didn't awaken. Lena answered the phone downstairs.

"Hello."

"Hello, Mrs. Martini. How are you?"

Lena couldn't place the voice. "I'm fine, thank you. Who's calling please?"

"It's Paul. Paul Rimini. Do you remember me?"

"Ah, yes, Paul. How are you, honey? I haven't heard from you in a long time. You sound wonderful."

"I'm fine, Mrs. Martini and I'm glad you remember me. How's your family?"

"We're all fine. How's your mother? I saw her a couple of weeks ago in the A & P. I was so glad to see her, we talked and talked. But, you didn't call to talk to me. Vinnie and Joe are not home now."

"I know. I just saw them. We had a good time talking and drinking beer. Oops, maybe I shouldn't have told you that." And they both laughed. "I wanted to talk to Lorraine. Is she home?"

Lena's face frowned. What does she tell him? Well, she'll have to tell him a partial truth. "Uh, Paul, Lorraine is—she—is upstairs. She's not feeling well. I think she's asleep. Do you mind if I don't call her? I'll tell her you called. Is that okay?"

"Sure, Mrs. Martini, that's fine. I hope she feels better soon. Please tell her I called; just want to say hello and I'll call her tomorrow night, probably about eight o'clock. I might call her earlier, depending on when I get home. I have a job interview in Manhattan."

"Oh, you left your job in New Jersey?"

"Yes, I did. My parents need me here, so I'm trying to get something similar here in Manhattan. We'll see what happens. Thanks so much, Mrs. Martini. Tell Lorraine hello. Goodnight." He sounded so cheerful that Lena wanted to tell him to wait and she'll call Lorraine, but then she thought better of it.

"Goodnight, Paul and I'm glad you're back."

Lena put the phone down and looked straight ahead, her mind was rushing; she smiled. She went back into the living room, her smile still on her beautiful, freckled face. Carlo saw her; a puzzled expression quickly filled his face.

"*Beh, che e`?* What is it?" He asked her quietly, not

angrily.

"Well, it's really nothing—but it might be something."

"Well, tell me!" Carlo demanded.

"Honey, do you remember Paul Rimini, that handsome boy who studied engineering and went to live in New Jersey to work?"

"Paul Rimini, the boy with the big nose is handsome?"

"Of course, he is. Honey, you're a man and you see him with male eyes and not female eyes. To us girls, he's handsome. Hm-mm." And she rolled her eyes heavenward and did a bad imitation of Mae West.

"Yes, the eyes of a mother who wants her daughter to marry as soon as possible. She should not be an old maid. Well, Lorraine is not an old maid and I don't want you to push her to get married. And I want you to listen to me."

"Carlo, sweetie, you know I always listen to you and I don't want Lorraine to rush into marriage but this boy, Walter, *oh, che nome brutto*, what an ugly name, he didn't seem like he is sincere. And you saw your daughter's face tonight. His rich parents don't want him to marry our daughter, like she's a shit."

At this, Carlo lost his temper. "My daughter is not a shit!" he shouted.

"Sh, sh, you'll wake up Lorraine. Of course she's not a shit, just because we're not rich."

"Who says we are not rich!"

"Sweetheart, you know what I mean. Our pictures will never get into the society pages in the newspapers."

"E che me ne frega!!! I don't give a fuck! My daughter can marry anyone she wants; anyone who will treat her like a lady and she is a lady."

"I know, I know. Calm down, you crazy Italian."

She went and sat on his lap and he seemed to calm down immediately, especially since Lena gave him a face sucking Italian kiss!

Carlo looked at his Lena; she returned his look. It was a look that was all too familiar to them and yet, it was as exciting as the first time they looked at one another. They went upstairs and after making sure that Lorraine was asleep, they walked quickly to their room.

Chapter Seven

As Carlo and Lena lay in each other's arms, quiet and comfortable, Carlo said, "Tell me about Paul."

"Oh, he said he's looking for a job in Manhattan. He's come back to Astoria because his parents need him. What a good boy."

"Never mind that; did he ask to speak to Lorraine? Or he want to speak with Vinnie and Joe?"

"No, he had already seen Vinnie and Joe and he asked to speak to Lorraine and I told him she wasn't feeling well. I didn't know what else to say; I didn't want to tell him about Walter. He said he would call tomorrow night." She looked at her husband, concern in her eyes. "It's up to Lorraine to tell him about Walter. Paul will call tomorrow night."

Carlo stared at the ceiling and muttered, "Well, that's good. Let us hope that he has a genuine interest, an honorable interest in Lorraine." He turned to his wife and shook an index finger at her. "And don't be annoying and try to push them together. Leave them alone. You promise me that?"

"Yes, my love, I promise not to be *la mashada*, the nosey body. But, you know, I feel better about Lorraine already. I think it's a sign from the *Madonna.*"

"Yes, I think so, too." Carlo said quietly, pensively.

They heard their sons come home and they both thanked God for their safe return and they fell asleep.

The sun rose on a beautiful Monday morning. Lena, as usual, was in the kitchen, coffee already on the stove and some bread already toasted and buttered in a dish and more bread in the toaster. "Come on, get up, everybody. The toast is getting cold and will soon be like shingles. Then don't blame me!"

She heard various voices answering her call and

invitation. Soon all were tumbling down the stairs. She looked heavenward. Her family hadn't changed. They were all adults but when they responded to the call for a meal, wherever they were, it was like a herd of elephants in a stampede. She smiled in happiness. Typical Italians, she thought.

The men were busy talking about sports.

Carlo said, "Agh, you don't know sports. You must know soccer; the most beauteefoo game in the world."

At this the boys laughed and kidded their father. "Dad." said Vinnie, "that's a sissy's game."

"Yeah, you think so. You have never played it. One must be on the run always. It builds muscles. You see my legs? Very strong and muscular from always running after the ball. It's not like baseball, where everyone waits for the pitcher." He made some silly motions of people shifting their weight from one leg to another, waiting for the pitcher to make up his mind, which caused his sons to laugh and slap their father on the back.

"Well, we gotta wait for the pitcher. He's the crucial player," Vinnie said, a smile on his face.

"Ah," Carlo waved his hand, "shut up and eat!"

Lorraine was very quiet. She sat and ate only toast and drank her coffee. Her parents stole glances at her.

Joe, the youngest son, said, "Ma, Dad, guess who we saw last night."

Carlo said, with a brandishing of his fork, "Ah, I know. It was Paul."

The boys looked at their father in surprise. Vinnie asked, "How did you know, Dad?"

"Ah, I am *un stregone,* a big witch." He smiled, teasing his sons.

Lorraine looked at her father, a slight interest in her eye. She remembered Paul as a very sweet, respectful, large nosed young man. She also remembered that he'd had a crush on her, but she brushed that out of her mind. She didn't care. Her life was a shambles; she knew she would soon be rejected by the one she loves because his mother thought she was unworthy of him.

She looked down at her coffee, silent, feeling alone.

Lena and Carlo exchanged glances, which the boys noticed, but knew they should remain quiet at this time. More small talk ensued and soon everyone was finished breakfast. The men left the table, kissed Lena and left for work. Carlo kissed his daughter and stroked her face; his love was evident; his concern was deep. He blinked his eyes repeatedly as he walked toward the door. Big, tough Carlo couldn't take his daughter's hurt.

Lorraine didn't have to leave for work for another half hour and she began to help her mother clear the table.

Lena stole glances at Lorraine of which Lorraine was oblivious. She wanted to say something to her mother; ask her something, but she didn't know what to ask. No words were issuing from her mouth, although, she had a dictionary full of words in her head.

Lena asked, "Lorraine, are you all right? You seem a bit distracted, annoyed, angry…I don't know, something. Do you…I don't know what to say."

"Well, Ma, there's not much to say. I spoke to Walter last night and he sounded…I don't know how to describe it. I…I think that we're—we're finished."

Lena had a sad look on her face. "Oh, I'm so sorry." She embraced her daughter. "Maybe he'll call you again." She was actually content that they were finished; if they were really finished, but she still hurt for her daughter.

"Oh, he'll call me again. I'm sure of that." Her voice sounded so plaintive that Lena's heart hurt.

"How can you be sure he'll call you again?" Lena's eyes had that inquiring, worried look that mothers have toward their children.

"Because he didn't tell me we're finished. He gave me the idea that he'd call again. I don't think he has the courage to tell me his family doesn't think I'm good enough for him."

"But, you are good enough—maybe too good for him." Her face was creased into a frown because she felt her daughter *was* too good for Walter.

"Ma, you should see their house! It's five times bigger than this house. The furnishings, though they don't really match, are extremely expensive. I noticed that. The mother is so—so la de da. Walter calls her 'mother'. Imagine if Vinnie, Joe and I called you 'mother'! You'd faint! So would the whole neighborhood."

Lena smiled; she wanted to laugh; her children calling her "mother," indeed. Then she thought that it would be nice. "Well, what's wrong with you kids calling me 'mother'? I think I like it."

"Oh, Ma, it's not really like us." Then she looked at her mother as she brought the dishes to the sink. "Ya know, Ma, I think you're right. But, of course, if we did that at this time in our lives, it would seem like putting on airs. It would seem unnatural. But it seems so natural for Walter. If I married him, I'd have to call her 'mother'. I don't think I'd feel comfortable doing that. Maybe she would insist on my calling her Mrs. Hadley."

"Well, maybe Walter's mother is putting on airs." And Lena continued to clean the table.

Lorraine looked at her mother, a pensive expression on her face. "Ma—Mother, I think you're right! I think that Mrs. Hadley is the phoniest person I've ever met."

"Does that make you feel better?"

"No." Lorraine's eyes filled with tears. Lena embraced her daughter, murmuring sweet words to her daughter. "Wait a few days. Calm down. See if he calls and what he says. But, if his mother…"

"Ma, I don't want to think what his mother says. I—I don't want to hate her, but I'm close."

Lena couldn't think of anything else to say, so she said, "You know who telephoned last night, for you?"

"Who, Ma? Walter? Did Walter call? Why didn't you call me?" There was excitement in her voice; excitement for Walter, who couldn't tell Lorraine he didn't care what his mother said; he would marry her because he loved her. And that's that!

"No, my love, Walter didn't call. It was Paul."

"Paul? Paul Rimini? Oh. I wonder why he called. I'm sure he called for Joe and Vinnie."

"He had already seen them last night and he called because he wanted to speak to you."

"Well, why didn't you call me? And I wonder why he wanted to speak to me."

"I didn't call you because you were sleeping and I would not wake you because you looked as though someone had kicked the shit out of you last night."

"Wow, was I that bad?"

"Yes." Lena's heart was breaking, which was so obvious to Lorraine.

Lorraine looked at the clock. "Ma, I'd better get going. I don't want to be late. Do I look beaten up?" She had a wan smile on her face.

"No, sweetheart, you don't. And be strong! Don't let Walter destroy you! He's not the only fish in the sea, as they say; another stupid saying. Paul is going to call tonight. Go to work. Don't be late. Make money. Ciao."

"Ciao, Mother." Lorraine had a small smile on her face, which disappeared the moment she faced the door.

Lena smiled. She watched her daughter go out the door, and then she went to the window to watch her daughter walking to the corner to meet Lucy. How beautiful and adorable her daughter was. And what pain she was in, all because a stupid woman didn't think Lorraine was good enough for her son. *Rich people!!! Pah*! And she swung her hand as if to slap someone. She turned and went to do what she normally did on a Monday morning.

While she did her chores, she thought, *why can't things be as simple as when I met Carlo. The lightning bolt hit both of us at the same time. I resisted him because my friends called him a greenhorn, but I couldn't help myself. Carlo told me the night we met that we would marry. And I believed him.*

The telephone rang and broke her reverie.

***

Lorraine waited for Lucy, looking up and down the avenue, as if to see someone special, and in a few minutes she saw Lucy walking toward her. It was a nippy morning and while Lorraine always had the neck of her coat open, Lucy was always bundled. Lucy felt the cold immediately.

"Lorraine, aren't you cold? I'm freezing. I didn't want to get out of bed. My mother said she would get the broom." And she smiled her beautiful smile at Lorraine.

Lorraine smiled at her friend. She didn't want to drag Lucy down. But, she never could fool Lucy, who had big, brown eyes and when she questioned, her eyes grew big.

Lorraine was aware and said, "Lucy, I went to Walter's house for dinner yesterday."

"Oh, no. Don't tell me. Okay, tell me. They treated you like shit!"

"No, they didn't. They were cordial."

"Awk! Cordial! I'd rather be treated like shit!"

This made Lorraine laugh. She had to agree. When you're treated like shit you could respond but when "cordial" is the word, you just have to be quiet…cordial. Oh, how brutal!

The girls walked arm in arm, silent for the moment,

then Lucy said, "What are you gonna do?"

"Well, I can't do anything now. I'm gonna wait until Walter calls me. I'll see what he says. Then I—we—I don't know what." She shook her head sadly.

Lucy stopped walking which caused Lorraine to stop; she looked very seriously at Lorraine. "Lorraine, please don't do anything stupid like eloping with him. I gotta be honest. I don't think he's the one for you. But, I want to support you in anything you do, except elopement. That's too cruel to do to yourself and your family."

"Lucy, how did you get so smart! I love you like a sister and you've always been honest with me. I think that's why I love you so much. I really appreciate a good friend like you." Lorraine smiled wanly at her dear friend.

Lucy was embarrassed, she smiled and said, "Agh, come on. We've known each other practically since we were born. And, yeah, I love you like a sister. Neither of us have sisters, I guess that's why we feel like this about each other. We can't talk about these things with our brothers. I know my brother couldn't be bothered."

"I think our brothers are very concerned about us, but I wouldn't say anything to my brothers, either. I can see they don't like Walter. Neither does my father."

"Well, that tells you that you'll have lots of trouble with the men in your family."

"Walter has one sister and she's away at college. Now, I'm sorry I didn't continue with college. I should sign up again." And she looked straight ahead of her not believing her words about signing up again. She had envisioned herself already married to Walter, living in a lovely house, with two or three babies. That dream went poof!

Lucy said, "There's the diner. God, it's already full. Stavros is gonna have a fit, even though we're not late. Let's hurry."

Both girls increased their speed and entered the diner using the front door even though Stavros didn't like it; he preferred the help to use the rear entrance. He saw them, didn't say a word, but they knew he was glad to see them. The girls walked swiftly to the back, removed their coats, greeted everyone and dashed to the front to take orders.

They began working, smoothly and efficiently and after the lunch crowd had left, the girls, a bit bedraggled went to the rear to decide what they would have for lunch. To their surprise, Thomas had prepared his specialty; grape leaves stuffed with broiled lamb strips and spices that only the Greeks know how to mix.

"You girls worked so hard today. I prepared this myself for you both. Come and sit at my table in the back. I'll join you for lunch." Thomas said. He was beaming. He had made up his mind he would tell Lorraine today how he felt about her.

Lorraine and Lucy was speechless and hungry, they sat down, smiling and surprised. Thomas brought the dishes, fresh warm bread and coffee. "I hope you girls like warm bread. Some people don't like it."

The bread filled Lucy's eyes with glee. "Those people who don't like warm bread are just plain nuts. Don't you agree, Lorraine?"

Lorraine smiled at Lucy and said, "You're absolutely right, Lucy." Then she looked at Thomas and said, "Thomas, what a lovely thing to do for two working girls."

Thomas, love in his eyes, said, "Well, you girls really worked hard this morning. There were no complaints about the service today." His eyes lingered on Lorraine, waiting for approval.

Stavros walked to the table, "What do you call this?" he teased. "This table is reserved for the president."

He tried to stop smiling; it wasn't possible.

"Dad," said Thomas, "you'll agree the girls were excellent today. They deserve the president's lunch."

He earned a slap on the back of his head, "Agh, shut up and eat!"

Thomas laughed and they all began to eat and talk. Lorraine, though she was still hurting and was pensive, was able to get into the jovial mood. Lucy watched her and was glad. She knew Thomas had eyes for Lorraine and he wasn't a bad choice.

The phone rang and since everyone was busy, he answered it. The girls kept on eating and talking. Lorraine noticed that Thomas' face froze as he spoke. He left the phone open, came back to the table and whispered to Lorraine, "Lorraine, phone for you." And he sat down. He was quiet and his face betrayed an unhappy feeling.

Lorraine grew worried, "Thomas, who is it? Is it my parents?"

Quietly Thomas said, "I don't know. It's a man."

Frightened, Lorraine quickly got to her feet and answered the phone. "Hello?"

"Hello, Lorraine?"

"Walter! Is anything wrong?"

"No, honey, nothing's wrong. I jush wanted to talk to you."

Turning away from the stares of Lucy and Thomas, and not wanting to show them she was disturbed, Lorraine said, "Walter, you shouldn't be calling me here. I'm busy. Walter. Walter, are you okay?"

"Yesh, I'm okay. I wanted to shpeak with you. I gotta go. I'll call you tonight."

"Walter. Walter. Are you there?" All was quiet and then the dial tone sounded.

Lorraine was ill at ease and after a moment she went back to the table. Lucy and Thomas stared at her and she felt their gazes and blushed. She would not talk about it in front of Thomas. He was aware of that and he said, "I'll clear away the dishes. Anyone want dessert?"

None wanted dessert; the slightly festive occasion was halted and ruined by Walter's call.

Lorraine worked like a zombie for the rest of the afternoon. Thomas regarded her frequently. He was feeling at a loss. He knew he could never entertain the idea of courting and marrying Lorraine. He could see that she had someone else in her eyes. This is the day he would tell his father that he would marry the beautiful Greek girl Stavros had chosen for him.

At the end of their work shift, Lorraine and Lucy made haste to leave. But, Thomas asked Lorraine if he could speak to her for only a moment. He led her to the office and closed the door gently. He looked at her as only a love sick man could look at the girl he loves, who doesn't love him.

"Lorraine, I won't keep you but a minute. I just—I just want to tell you—you something. You know that my father has chosen Effie Tsanos for me to marry and I've been resisting him. I told him that I am already in love with someone else. But, this other girl doesn't know that I love her and she's has someone else in her eyes."

Lorraine seemed a bit distracted and puzzled that Thomas should be telling her this. It was none of her business, but if she had not been so troubled in the last couple of days, she would have seen the light.

"Lorraine, it's you that I love. I know—I know, I shouldn't be telling you this. It wasn't my intention to trouble you and I know that at this time, you have some problems. I could see it in your face. I just want you to know that I won't be any trouble to you. I'm going to tell my father that I will marry Effie. She's a good girl—but she's not Lorraine Martini." He looked tenderly at her, took her in his arms and kissed her sweetly. She didn't struggle. She was too shocked to do anything. She didn't rebuke him. Her eyes filled with tears and wordlessly, she put her hand on his face, then turned and left. Her heart hurt for Thomas as they were sort of in the same boat.

She closed the office door as quietly as Thomas had and she caught up to Lucy. They walked in silence at first. "Lucy, I can't believe what's happening to me."

Lucy looked at her friend. She was puzzled but waited for Lorraine to speak.

"Thomas just told me he loves me but is going to marry the beautiful Greek girl his father selected for him because he knows I don't love him."

"Holy shit, Lorraine. I don't believe it. You've got problems."

"Well, Thomas has not presented himself as a problem, so that's okay. But, he made me cry anyway." She couldn't control a few more tears streaming down her cheeks.

Then Lorraine, who knew that Lucy was dying to know but wouldn't ask, not to hurt her friend, said, "Lucy, that call? It was Walter. He sounded drunk. His speech was slurred. And somehow Thomas knew it was a personal, troublesome call."

"Oh, no."

"Yes," Lorraine said quietly. "Walter said he would call tonight. I don't know what he's going to tell me." And after a few moments of silence, she said, "Remember Paul Rimini?"

"Oh, yeah. I do. They used to call him 'shnozzolla.' He's been gone a long time."

"Well, he called and told my mother he's back in Astoria; his parents need him and he said he would call me tonight. I guess tonight's gonna be a busy time for me." She shook her head slowly. "I think I wish both wouldn't call me tonight. I don't feel like talking to anybody. What a day! I simply can't believe it. One guy tells me he loves me. The other guy promises to call me tonight and I'm sure he's gonna give me the air. And now Paul Rimini is going to call me tonight. My God, it's too much!"

"Lorraine, you gotta talk to them. You don't know what either of them will say to you." She had a frown on her face, trying to give Lorraine a bit of courage; but she, herself, didn't know what to say. They reached their corner and both left each other. Lucy regarded Lorraine and said, "Will you call me tonight?"

"Sure."

Lorraine entered the back door that led right into the kitchen; heavy with the fragrance of Lena's cooking. "Hello, Ma, I'm home." She kissed her mother and went upstairs to wash. Lena looked after her daughter; she had a lot to tell her and she wanted to say it before the men came home.

"Lorraine, come down quickly."

Hearing this Lorraine stopped at the steps and returned to the kitchen. "Ma, what is it?"

"The telephone has been ringing and ringing."

"Well, who was it?"

"It was Walter. He's been calling so many times and he's drunk. I wanted to tell him to go to hell, but I didn't, I knew you would want to speak to him."

The phone rang. Lena said, "It's probably that drunk calling again. Lorraine, I don't like it. He obviously has no respect for you or for me." The phone rang again. "You better get it. And be careful what you say. If he's drunk, tell him to call tomorrow. If Dad gets the phone and hears a drunken Walter, no telling what will happen." Lena's anger showed on her face.

Wordlessly, Lorraine went to the phone and picked it up. "Hello?"

"Uh…uh—"

"Who's calling?"

"Lorraine, ish me, Walter."

"Walter, what are you doing? You called me at work and you know I can easily get canned. They don't like us to get personal calls unless it's an emergency. What is it? Are you in trouble?"

"Yesh. I mean, no. I mean, I don't know what I mean. Yesh, I know. I gotta shee you tonight. Can I come over now?"

"Walter, you're in no condition to go anywhere. You're drunk. You can't let my family see you in like this. Please stay home and go to sleep. I think that's what you need. Call me when you're not drunk!"

"I'm not drunk, honey. I gotta shee you tonight." He hiccupped.

"No, Walter," Lorraine said quietly, her eyes going heavenward. "Please do as I say. I don't want to see you in this condition. Call me when you feel better." And she hung up the phone. She ran upstairs and flung herself on her bed. What a mess this was. She didn't know what to do or think. She loved Walter, but a sober Walter. A drunken Walter wasn't lovable and she knew that his parents had something to do with his inebriation. She was embarrassed that her mother had to take Walter's many drunken calls today. Thomas had told her he loved her. And tonight, Paul Rimini will be calling. What does he want? She felt a bit dizzy.

"Lorraine. Lorraine, come downstairs." Lena called urgently.

Lorraine heard her mother and immediately rose from her bed, smoothed her hair and went down to the kitchen. She really didn't want to talk about this anymore than she had to.

Lena looked at her daughter, saw she was disturbed

and said, "Sweetheart, please set the table. Everybody will be home soon. I don't want them to see your face like that. If Walter calls when we're eating, take it upstairs in your room. I'm sorry that Walter called, but I didn't know what else to say to him. He should be ashamed, drunk and calling and insisting that you were home and I wouldn't let him speak to you!"

Lorraine's long face changed to surprise. "Ma, you didn't tell me that. He was insistent? How—how do you know he didn't believe you?"

"Well, he insisted and I kept telling him you were working. Then he hung up and didn't call anymore."

"That's probably when he called me at the diner."

Surprised, Lena said, "He called you at the diner?"

"Yes, Ma."

"Oh, God. This boy is crazy. Did you get in trouble?"

"No, I didn't. I didn't stay long on the phone. And he called when Thomas, who took the call, had prepared a lovely lunch for Lucy and me; we were all sitting together and it was kind of nice. He said we deserved it because the diner was extra crowded and we kept up with the orders; we gave good service. I was sort of embarrassed because I don't want the bosses to know anything about my personal life." She looked at her mother and added quietly, "I think Thomas likes me." She didn't want to tell her mother what Thomas had told her today. It was too much for Lorraine to hear, she could imagine her mother hearing this. She'd go nuts. Better to leave it as "likes" instead of "loves."

Lena's eyes lit. "Well, I'm not gonna ask if you like him. You obviously don't…in that way, I mean. Is he nice?"

"He's very nice. Looks like a typical Greek; dark and handsome and smart."

"And you never encouraged him?"

"No. I don't know why. He's sweet, too, but I just didn't go for him. I don't know, maybe I'm nuts. His family owns a diner; I would never go hungry." She laughed and made her mother laugh, too.

"Well, come on," said Lena, "let's get busy setting the table. We can talk more about this when the men leave the table."

"Sure, Ma." Lorraine said, somewhat relieved and comforted by her mother's words and manner. Lena was a super mom and Lorraine always knew it.

Tonight they were having roast chicken, a large one, roasted potatoes, asparagus and a large salad of mixed greens. And wine on the table. A dinner like this was consumed with gusto and delight. The men never stopped talking about sports but they were acutely aware of Lorraine's demeanor.

Vinnie, the oldest brother, looked at Lorraine and said, "Hey, Red, what's goin' on? You look like somebody stole your puppy."

Lorraine looked up from her dish, "It's nothing, Vinnie, really. Just work; we were so busy today."

"Oh, I thought it was something silly, like Walter getting drunk!"

"What! How did you know?" Lorraine was upset because it was brought out in front of the whole family and at the dinner table, yet.

"He passed by the shop today. I told him to go home and sleep it off. I don't know if he got home safely or not. Lorraine, I hate to say this but I think he's trouble. Drunk as he was, he still looked down on Joe and me. I don't like it. I don't know what you feel for this guy; I think you like him, maybe you even love him, but, he's trouble. I don't know what his problem is but if he has to get drunk to find the solution, I feel sorry for him." His eyes never left his sister's face and when he finished speaking, he looked at his dish. He knew his father and Joe would agree with him.

Lorraine looked down at her dish, then abruptly rose and ran upstairs to her room.

For a moment, the family was very quiet. Then Carlo spoke, "Vinnie, why did you speak like that?"

"Dad, somebody's gotta say something. She thinks she headed for the altar and we all know this guy's a shit. He may be rich, but I'm sure when he's in his drunken fits, he'll beat her. If he does that to my sister, I'll beat the shit out of him!" And he left the table in anger.

Carlo looked at Joe. "Joe, you feel the same?"

Joe took a breath, a very serious look on his face said, "Yes, Pa, I do. Lorraine deserves only the best. Nobody should look down at any of us." And he took a slug of wine and calmed down. "Just because we're not high class or have college educations or have an American name, that doesn't mean we're dumb or callous. You and Mom taught us manners and I'm proud of you."

Vinnie returned to the table. "I'm sorry I burst out like that. We have only one sister and we treat her like a queen. And she is a queen. No rich guy, who thinks he's too good for her and thinks he's doing her a favor with his presence, is going to make my sister cry." His breaths came in loud spasms.

Carlo looked at each one of his family. "Well, I feel the same. I don't like his attitude; whenever he came here to pick her up for a date, he was always with his nose in the air. *Che siamo, cafoni?* What are we, low class? Okay, I don't speak good English, but I am an honest man and a hard worker. Nobody in my family goes without shoes on their feet or food in their belly. We have a nice house. This is a nice house, isn't it?"

They all nodded.

Lena, a worried look on her face said, "Well, we're

all in agreement. But, what can we do. She has to see this with her own eyes. And maybe she won't because he's good looking and rich."

"Well," Carl said, "we didn't bring up our daughter to concentrate on good looks."

"Sure," Lena said, "we didn't, but look at the movies. All the leading men who are romantic are good looking. Look at Robert Taylor and Tyrone Power. All really good looking. I know we should not judge people on their looks but we do." And she thought of Paul, with the big nose.

The telephone rang. No one moved.

Chapter Eight

Lena put her hands on the table and pushed herself up to her feet. She thought it was Walter calling again, her face showed annoyance and she was ready to tell Walter to take a hike! She answered the phone. "Oh, hello Paul. How are you?" And she made motions with her hands and sent her eyes heavenward. "Yes, just a moment. She's here." She let the phone hang by the wire and went to the stairs, "Lorraine, Lorraine, telephone."

Lorraine quickly wiped the tears away from her cheeks, "Yes, Ma, thanks, I'll get it here."

She picked up the extension and when she heard her mother hang up the phone downstairs, she said, "Hello." She was angry with herself because she thought her voice gave her weeping away.

"Hello, Lorraine. It's Paul. I hope you remember me. How are you?"

"Oh, yes, I remember you, Paul. I'm fine, thanks, how are you?" She took a tissue and wiped her nose.

"You sound like you have a cold." At this Lorraine's lips tightened against her teeth and she was glad he couldn't see. "Your mother told me last night you were sick. I hope you're feeling better."

"Oh, yes, I am," she lied, but it didn't bother her because it was only a little lie and little lies don't count.

"Lorraine, I was wondering if I could see you tonight. I know it's a work night and I promise not to keep you out late. I thought maybe we could go for coffee. Just to talk, ya know."

"Well, ah, I don't know. I'm still in my uniform."

"Okay, can we make it another night?"

Lorraine thought *what a sweet guy.* Then she said, "Well, okay, if it's just coffee and talk. I'll just change."

"Oh, that's great. How about I come to your house

in thirty minutes? Is that enough time for you or do you want me to come later?"

"Thirty minutes is fine, Paul. Goodbye."

"Goodbye."

Lorraine went quickly into the bathroom to wash her face; she didn't have time for a shower. She put on fresh make-up and went into her room to change. She didn't want to wear something too dressy. She picked out a dark gray suit and a black sweater and the correct accessories.

After she thought her eyes looked normal, she went downstairs. Lena had cleaned the kitchen and the family was in the living room, watching the news on TV. Lorraine appeared at the entrance of the living room, a bit shyly, she said, "I'm going out with Paul Rimini. He'll be here soon. We're just going out for coffee. Please don't make a big fuss and don't mention Walter. I'll be home early." She stopped talking and tried to breathe normally. Then she thought how stupid of her to give her family instructions on how to act.

Nobody made an inquiry or answer. However, she detected satisfied looks on all the family. She turned, sent her eyes heavenward, but made no comment.

The doorbell and the phone sounded at the same time. Lena pushed Lorraine toward the door, whispering that she would take the phone. "Go out and enjoy yourself. Paul is a nice guy."

Lorraine, for once, happy her mother pushed her, went to the door, but also wanting to answer the phone because she was sure it was Walter. It was.

Lorraine opened the door and there stood a smiling tall Paul. Lorraine tried to keep her attention on him, she greeted him shyly but her ears were on her mother who was talking to Walter and telling him that Lorraine wasn't home. She hung up the phone and greeted Paul. The men of the family all came to the vestibule to greet Paul. And before it could turn into a bull session, Lorraine said, "Shall we go?"

"Yes, yes, goodnight everyone," a smiling Paul said.

And they left the house and walked toward Paul's Chevy. Once in the car, Lorraine looked back at the house, hoping her mother would call her back because Walter had called again. But, no such luck. She turned to Paul to make small talk. And that's what it would be because she was in love with Walter.

Paul drove, turning to look at her and turning again to look at the road. "You look so different, Lorraine. I guess the three years I was away made a big change in both of us. I probably look different to you, too."

She looked at him and said, "Yes, you look more mature. I guess that's the way it is with both of us. You know, three years can make a big difference. I think I was sixteen and in high school. And you had just finished college, if I remember correctly." And she thought to herself, *why am I talking so much? I don't even want to be here with this guy. I want to be with Walter.*

He told her about working in a huge office in Newark, New Jersey. He liked it but he liked Astoria more and he missed his parents. He went on and on about his plans and she didn't listen until he told her that he thought of her often. Then she looked at him with a raised eyebrow.

"You thought of me? A silly teenager with a face full of freckles?"

"Yes, I did. Weren't we all silly teens?"

"I never thought you were…or even my brothers. I thought because you all were older than I, you were all sophisticated, ya know, tough and sophisticated."

Paul laughed and pulled into a diner parking lot. "This looks like a good place."

"Oh, yeah, it's good. This is where I work!"

"Oops, we'll make a hasty retreat." And he backed out and went to another diner.

It wasn't difficult to find a diner in Astoria and before many minutes had passed, Paul found another one. It had no parking lot and they had to park around the corner and walk back. As they walked back, Paul forced himself to talk. Lorraine, ever the well-mannered young lady, listened and nodded.

They were seated in a booth by the window and soon a waitress came to take their order; coffee and apple pie ala mode.

While waiting, Paul looked at Lorraine with a lopsided smile on his face. He told her of the area in which he lived in Newark, New Jersey. It was a lot like New York. And he looked at her, knowing she wasn't all that interested; in fact, he knew she hadn't heard a word he said. He put on a serious face and said, "I killed three men!"

She immediately looked up from her pie, eyes wide, inquiring.

He smiled at her, "I thought that would get you."

"Oh, I almost believed you. I'm glad you didn't do any such thing."

They both returned to their pies and coffee. Lorraine looked at Paul and said, "Ya know, something about you is different. I can't put my finger on it. It isn't only that we both matured by three years; you look different."

He smiled and said, "I had a nose job." And he turned profile, like Rudolph Valentino, very worldly.

Lorraine gazed with interest. "Why, your nose looks great but why did you do something so weird? I mean, you were okay before."

"Well, it wasn't a case of vanity. You see, I was with a girl, very much like you, red headed, too. We'd gone to some gathering, I don't remember what, and a guy she'd dated only twice came to her and said something really objectionable and we came to blows. We just kept punching each other and we didn't realize right away, but we broke each other's noses. We started to laugh. We were so bloody; we went to the ER together. The ER doctor told us both our noses were badly broken and we should consider plastic surgery because this was a good time to do it and we both had large noses. So we did. Not at the same time, or course, but we thought it was a good idea to take advantage of at that time. The plastic surgeon, who thought our story was so funny decided to give us a cut rate, and he warned us not to fight anymore and if we did, we should not get our noses broken but break the other guy's nose and send the new patient to him. The guy I fought, his name is Ben, became my friend and whenever we see each other, we put up our dukes." He looked down at his coffee cup and then up at Lorraine. "I'm kind of glad that happened because I couldn't take any more ribbing from the neighborhood kids anymore. That's one of the reasons I took a job in another state; not that I didn't get the ribbing but it made it more tolerable because they were strangers to me. And I didn't expect to spend the rest of my life there. Getting a normal size nose gave me a lot of courage to pursue my career. And other things." He smiled slyly at her at this last statement.

She pretended she didn't understand. However, Lorraine's smile showed she enjoyed the story. "Paul, I always thought you had courage. I remember one New Year's Eve you came home with my brothers to wish us happy holiday and you kissed me. I'll say you had courage; kissing me in front of my parents and my brothers."

"I remember that kiss," he said quietly. So did she but she didn't want him to know it. He had already been giving her looks that kept no secret of how he was feeling.

There was a slice of silence. Paul looked at her and said, "Lorraine, you're even more beautiful than the last time I saw you."

Her brown eyes peered at him, "I don't think so, I have more freckles than the last time I saw you."

"I love freckles." He smiled as he said this. He had beautiful, white, straight teeth.

She just shook her head. "Paul, it's getting late and I have to be in early tomorrow morning. Do you mind if we go now?"

"Oh, I'm sorry, Lorraine, I should have been watching the clock. Sure let's go. I've got another interview tomorrow morning so I've gotta be bright eyed and all the other stuff."

On the ride home, Paul continued to make small talk. Then in front of her house, he stopped the car, got out and came to the passenger side, opened the door and took her hand. Lorraine wasn't accustomed to this and she found it pleasant.

At the front door, Paul took her hand and said, "Lorraine, I had a great time tonight. I mean, we didn't do anything special and I didn't take you to a special place. But we sat and talked. It was nice. You're wonderful." He had a remarkable smile, which he lavished on her.

All this sweet talk was making Lorraine nervous because Paul didn't know about Walter. But, he did know; she didn't know he knew.

"Oh, no, I'm not wonderful," and she wished she could disappear.

"Lorraine, do you think we could do this again? Maybe go to dinner, or the movies or dancing? Huh, what do you say?"

Lorraine looked up at his brown eyes and pulled at her hand and he let it go. "I—I don't think so. You see, I'm seeing someone or maybe I'm not—" She could contain her tears no longer. She had turned away and let them come. Paul put his arms around her and held her close.

"You poor kid. I'm sorry, I really am."

She looked up at him and there was a moment of silence and thoughts; he kissed her. She didn't fight his kiss, neither did she participate; she remained weakly in his arms. He understood, she was not leading him on.

"Lorraine, could we, I mean, this relationship you speak of sounds—sounds not too strong. I won't pressure you. I just want you to know that I'm here. Could we be friends, like, if you need someone to talk to or take you someplace, we could do that. Am I being annoying or does is sound okay to you?"

Lorraine, wiped her eyes with a tissue, suppressed a sob, and said, quietly, "Yes, Paul, I think it would be nice. I never had a boyfriend, two words, before and I think it would be nice. Okay. Sometimes we could get together and have coffee. But, if you meet someone special, don't hesitate to let me know. Look for a brunette this time."

They laughed and he kissed her forehead. He had his folded index finger under her chin, "Goodnight, Lorraine. Don't get too hurt."

"Goodnight, Paul, and thanks so much." His words had touched her heart.

She entered the house from the front door. Inside, she looked for her parents and found them in the kitchen savoring some strong espresso. Lorraine marveled that her parents could sleep after drinking such sleep stopping liquid.

Lena looked up at her daughter, "Hello, Lorraine, did you have a good time?"

Carlo also greeted his daughter, throwing her a kiss. "Ciao, bella."

"Hello, Ma and Dad." She came to each of her parents and kissed them. Her mouth was turned up at the corners ever so slightly. “Yes, I had a nice time. Paul is a good guy.”

Lena and Carlo exchanged looks. Lorraine was already on her way upstairs, “Goodnight. I’m going to call Lucy.”

“Okay” said Lena, shrugging.

Carlo said, “Why you shrug?”

“Do you realize she didn’t ask about the phone call from Walter?”

“Ah, yes, that’s true. Do you think Paul is making her forget *Gualtiere*? (Walter)”

“Maybe. Who knows? You Italian guys have that charm. Do you remember when we met?”

“Ah, my love, I’ll never forget. I think all your girlfriends are jealous of you.”

“That’s what I love about you, Carlo. You’re so modest. *Chitrool!* My friends told me not to waste my time with a greenhorn like you.”

Carlo’s eye widened, “You never told me that.”

“Well, did I listen to them?”

“No.”

“There you are!” And she smiled at him and when he finally caught on, he smiled, too.

***

Upstairs on the extension, Lorraine called Lucy.

“Hello.” Lucy said.

“Lucy, it’s me, Lorraine.”

“Lorraine, I was thinking about you. What happened tonight? I hope nothing terrible.”

“Well, not much, really. Well, I’ll tell you; it was really crazy. I was upstairs in my room, crying and the phone rang and my mother told me to pick up. It was Paul and I sounded like I had a cold. Paul asked if he could see me tonight and because when he called the other night, my mother told him I was sick, he thought I really was sick. He suggested just a cup of coffee and talk. Then he said maybe he could come over some other time and I thought, well, I might as well see him. What have I got to lose and it's not a real date. So, I told him to come over. I decided to change and just as I got downstairs, the telephone and the doorbell rang at the same time. I was gonna answer the phone but my mother motioned me to get the door, actually, she pushed me, and she'd get the phone and so that's what happened and it was Paul at the door and Paul and I went out to have coffee and pie."

"Well, that's some story; are you out of breath yet?" And they both laughed.

"But, Lucy, that's not the end of the story."

"What! Well, tell me."

"When we got home, he kissed me and—"

"What! He kissed you—like a romantic kiss or a friendly kiss?"

"Well, I think it was more romantic than friendly—or maybe it was friendly—no I think it was more romantic. I don't know. I can't even think straight. He's nice."

"Oh, Lorraine, I'm so happy. Is that it? Nothing more?"

"I told him that I was—I—I'm crazy, I started to cry, I—that's when he took me in his arms and kissed me. I told him that I was seeing someone—that I wasn't seeing someone and he took me in his arms and comforted me. Then he asked if we could be friends and it sounded so marvelous—I mean it—I almost peed my pants. I never heard anything so sweet in my life. So, I said yes and I have a boyfriend, two words."

"Lorraine, that sounds so wonderful. I think he handled it so great and you are magnificent the way you handled it"

"You think so, Lucy? OH GOD!"

Lucy almost lost her marbles. "LORRAINE! What

is it, are you okay? LORRAINE!"

"I just remembered. When I came home, I didn't even ask my mother what Walter said. I gotta go downstairs right now and ask her. Lucy, I'll see you tomorrow. Goodnight." And before Lucy could answer, which would have been, "Shit on Walter!", Lorraine slammed the phone down and ran downstairs.

"Ma! Ma!"

"Lorraine, what is it?" Lena was just as agitated as Lorraine.

"Wasn't that Walter on the phone when Paul rang the doorbell tonight?"

Lena's eyes went heavenward, "Oh, God, I thought you fell down the stairs and broke you neck. Yes, that was Walter, drunk as before. He's crazy. He wanted to come here even if you weren't home. I told him again and again, you were out. I didn't tell him that you were out with a young man. It's none of his business. The way he treats you, when he calls I should tell him to go to hell and slam the phone closed."

"But, what did he say?"

"I really don't know, his speech was slurred. And I didn't want Dad to really know what he was saying, not that I could understand him. I could only make out that he would call you again and I don't know when."

"Okay, Ma. Thanks. I—I think he'll call tomorrow. I'm going upstairs. Goodnight, Ma and Dad." She turned and went upstairs. Tomorrow is a working day.

Lorraine showered and got into bed and tried to read a book. It was no use; sleep wouldn't come. Why didn't Walter call again? She couldn't call Walter because she was a little hesitant. She didn't want his mother to answer the phone. But, she decided to screw up her courage and call. She dialed his number.

"Hello?"

"Hello, Mrs. Hadley?" (Oh, crap!)

"Yes, this is she speaking. Who's calling please?"

"Mrs. Hadley, it's Lorraine. How are you?" (You bitch!)

"I'm well, thank you. I hope you're well. And I know you're calling for Walter. Walter is not at home. He's in the hospital and—"

"In the hospital?! Mrs. Hadley, what happened? Is he all right? What happened?"

Mrs. Hadley, who was already a piece of ice turned into mountain of ice. "Young lady, you're the cause of Walter's hospitalization."

Agitated, Lorraine said, "What! What happened? How did I cause it? I'm confused. I'm sorry he's hospitalized. Please tell me what happened."

"He said when he told you he didn't love you and didn't want to see you anymore, you became belligerent and hostile. You—you struck him! And when he drove away from you, he was blinded with tears… a result of your behavior toward him and he drove off the road. Thank heavens, he wasn't badly hurt. He's in the hospital for observation. I think you understand that the two of you are to have no further communication." And she hung up the phone.

Lorraine was aghast. This was the first she was hearing of something so horrible. She thought, *how could all this happen in the short time between his calling here, the moment I left with Paul, and when I came home. Something's wrong. I didn't strike him; I didn't even see him! I'm gonna call the hospital.*

She ran downstairs to get the telephone directory. Lena noting Lorraine's fast movements, asked, "Lorraine, what is it? Has something happened?"

"I don't know, Ma. I just called Walter and spoke to his mother. She said he was involved in an auto accident and I want to find out if he's in the hospital, as she said." Then she ran upstairs carrying the directory and when she was safely in her room, she looked up the hospitals in the area. There were only two and she dialed the emergency room of the first one and she was informed that no Walter Hadley had been admitted.

At the second hospital, the Emergency Room nurse said, "Yes, we had a Walter Hadley here. He was admitted. He had an accident; slightly injured while driving drunk. He has been released. That's all the information I can give you."

"Thank you very much. You say he wasn't badly injured?"

"That's correct."

Each hung up the phone. Lorraine sat on her bed thinking. Lena knocked on the door and opened it a bit. "Lorraine, can I come in?"

"Yes, Ma, come in."

"Did you call the hospital?"

"Yes, I called two and the second one said that Walter had been admitted and released. He wasn't badly injured and was driving drunk."

"There, you see; I told you he was drunk when he called."

Lorraine looked dejectedly at her mother. "Ma, I know you wouldn't lie to me; you have no reason to do so. His mother told me that he was with me and supposedly when he told me that he didn't love me and never wanted to see me again, I struck him and that caused him to drive off the road and have an accident. That's so crazy. His mother lied to me. I didn't even see Walter tonight. You and Dad know that. Why would she lie to me?"

"Because she's a fangoolin, snobby bitch!" an angry Lena almost shouted. "And she's a liar and trouble maker. Maybe Walter told her that story to make you look bad...like that was necessary to convince his parents. Lorraine, honey, please listen to what's going on. They don't like you because they think you're low class and vulgar. And they think the same of all of us."

Lorraine looked at her mother, her mind working and then she said, "I don't think so, Ma. I know Walter wouldn't say such a thing. Walter lo—" She couldn't finish her thought. She looked away. Lena hurt for her daughter.

Paul's words came to her mind. "Lorraine, don't get too hurt."

But it was too late; Lorraine was hurting as she'd never been hurt before. She looked at her mother and said, "Ma, I don't know what to do. Mrs. Hadley lied to me. Walter hasn't called me and I don't know where he is. Mrs. Hadley hung up the phone when she finished telling me those lies."

"Lorraine, try not to think of this. Try to sleep now." Lena was concerned about her daughter and wanted her to rest.

Lorraine rose from her bed, and embraced her mother. "Ma, thanks. You're the best. Thanks for not telling me what a dope I am."

"I would never call you that; you're not a dope. I know what it feels like to fall in love with a guy who turns out like—like—well, like this situation." Lena didn't know what to say; she just held her daughter and then said softly, "Sweetheart, go to sleep now. You're tired. Sleep and maybe tomorrow things will be different. Maybe in the sunshine, you'll see things differently." She kissed her daughter and Lorraine nodded to her mother because she couldn't speak. She got into her comfortable bed, which wasn't comfortable tonight, and couldn't sleep until well past four a.m.

Chapter Nine

Before eight a.m. the following morning, Lorraine was waiting for Lucy on their designated corner. It was cold; they were in the first week of December. The stores had Christmas decorations in the windows and many had the crèche. Lorraine thought this was going to be a sad Christmas for her. She blinked her eyes to keep back the tears, but some flowed out of her eyes.

"Good morning, Lorraine. How are you? Oh, you have a tear on your cheek. Are you crying?"

"No," she sniffled, "it's the cold."

Lucy, who knew, said, "Oh. Yeah."

Lorraine knew that Lucy knew, but they walked on silently, each with her own thoughts.

Lorraine said, "Lucy, have you started your Christmas shopping yet?"

"Yeah, I did. I already got my parents gifts. And I know what I want to get my grandmother, so tonight I might go to Steinway Street and do some shopping. Wanna come?"

Lorraine tilted her head to the side and said, "I don't know. Maybe. I'll let you know." Then she told Lucy what Mrs. Hadley had told her.

"Oh, what a rotten thing to say. You see! She thinks because you're a waitress, you're far below her. This is America, where we're all supposed to be free and equal. She doesn't know anything. She's mean. Oh, Lorraine, I'm so sorry. You don't deserve to be treated like that."

"I know. But they're rich. What can I do? And another thing; I haven't gone to college like her daughter. They think because I haven't gone to college I'm dumb."

"Yeah."

"You know, Paul said something very profound to me last night. He said, 'Lorraine, don't get too hurt'."

Lucy said, "Wow."

They arrived at the diner and went to work.

At lunch time, Lorraine looked for Walter. She was hoping that he would appear but he never did. Her days were miserable.

And she didn't hear from him until Christmas Eve, when he called from his home in which there was a Christmas party.

"Hello." Lorraine said.

"Lorraine, it's me, Walter."

Lorraine was stunned and for a moment she didn't speak; she couldn't speak.

"Hello, hello, Lorraine. Lorraine, are you there?"

"Yes, Walter, I'm here." She didn't know if she should shout with joy or slam down the receiver because he was a slimy coward.

"Lorraine, I—please forgive me for not calling you sooner."

"Well, that's okay, Walter, I thought you were in a body cast and were totally helpless."

After a few seconds of silence Lorraine knew he was repentant, he said, "Listen, honey, I know you have every right to be mad at me—"

"Mad! Gee, I'm not mad. I called your home weeks ago and your mother told me that I struck you and that caused you to have an auto accident and she gave me to understand you were seriously injured. That was a blatant lie! I hadn't even seen you that night. And my parents can attest to that fact. You called here as I was on my way out. And your silence led me to believe that you were deceased! And now you call me! Have you come back to life because you're rich and too good for me?!!"

"Honey, please, let me explain. Please, I love you and I miss you. Please, listen to me."

"Well, speak and make it fast because I'm busy."

"Lorraine, I have to see you and speak to you in person."

"Well, in a case like that," she said, sarcasm dripping from her voice, "you'll have to come to my home. And I don't advocate that unless you're suicidal."

"Oh, Lorraine, please, honey, this is so hard. Please don't make it harder."

"Yes, you're not used to hard situations. What's all the noise I hear? I hear music and people laughing and talking."

Walter looked over his shoulder as though he didn't know what she was talking about. "Oh, it's only a little gathering. My parents have invited some of their friends for a little Christmas party; nothing big, just a little party."

"Oh, really! Do you have a female companion there; someone suitable?"

Fuck! How does she know? "Of course not, honey. I'm just wandering around the guests; I'm stag. I'm lonely for you." The last sentence he said with a bit of exaggerated feeling.

With all her heart, Lorraine wanted to believe it. "Yes, I'm sure." He detected a bit of melancholy in her voice and milked it for all he was worth.

"Well, I am. Funny, like I'm alone in my own house at my own party. I miss you, baby."

She started to feel sympathy for him, like his unhappiness was coming through. "Listen, Walter, we have guests, too. So, I'll talk to you another time. Merry Christmas."

"Lorraine, Lorraine." But she had hung up the phone and run up to her room because she didn't want her family to see her upset and weeping. But Lena saw, though she didn't follow her daughter upstairs. They had guests and none of them saw, except Paul.

Lorraine was mad and sad at the same time. She

wept, wrung her hands and paced her room, which was little in comparison to the room she imagined Walter had. Then she fixed her face went downstairs and mingled.

Lucy came to her and said the pastries Lorraine and her mother had made were delicious. She also told Lorraine that since she had lost fifteen pounds and looked fabulous in her new dress, she'd only had one...or maybe two pastries…small ones.

Lorraine smiled and said, "Lucy, I'm proud of you and you do look gorgeous. Come with me." The girls went into the den and Lorraine closed the door and proceeded to tell Lucy about the phone call.

Lucy frowned. "Lorraine, he's a bastard for treating you the way he did. Don't think about him; that's wasting time. He's not worth it. You deserve someone good and he's not good." Then she smiled, "Did I tell you Vinnie told me I look wonderful? Now, don't get hysterical, I haven't given him any encouragement, I swear."

Lorraine smiled at Lucy, knowing that Vinnie didn't need encouragement; Lorraine had always suspected that Vinnie had eyes for Lucy and why he didn't make a move before perplexed her.

They walked out together, arms around each other's waist. Someone had put dance music on the phonograph. Paul walked up to the girls and asked Lorraine if she would like to dance. Lorraine seemed refreshed and said, "Yes, Paul, I would like to dance. Excuse us, Lucy."

Paul said, "Excuse us, Lucy."

Lucy was very happy and then Vinnie asked her to dance. When the music was slow, Paul and Lorraine slow danced together, as did Vinnie and Lucy, smiles on their faces.

Despite her disturbing phone call, Lorraine managed to put that in the back of her mind. *Why shouldn't I enjoy myself? All our friends are here, dancing, eating, laughing and having a good time. It's Christmas. Paul is nice.* She looked up at his face and accidentally stepped on his toe, and she said, "Oh, I'm sorry Paul. I don't mean to cripple you."

"Don't worry, Lorraine, those are only little taps; they don't hurt a bit. OW!" And he grimaced. They laughed. Paul had the ability to make Lorraine laugh. "I made sure that I wore my oldest shoes...I think they're twenty years old."

"Oh, get outta here!" Lorraine said. Paul swung her around and then the slow music came back on the phonograph and they slow danced. Though Lorraine felt comfortable dancing with Paul, her thoughts went to Walter. Yes, he was treating her like a low class whore, but she loved him and was sure that he loved her. But, what would life be like with him with his parents dead set against her because she was not of their class. But, Mrs. Hadley was a liar! Didn't that action show that she was not better than Lorraine, who never lied? She thought that much of the future with Walter would be turbulent. How could it not be? His mother was a powerful busybody. She sighed and Paul looked at her, knowing he wasn't the cause of her sigh. He held her close and his chin was against her temple; he hummed. He promised himself, one day, she would sigh for him.

Someone at the party suggested they all go to midnight mass; then one by one, everyone decided it was a good idea. Soon, they all trooped out of the house to walk to St. Joseph's Church. They were all a bit late and mass was very crowded with the C & E Christians; Christmas and Easter, and the entire group was standing in the back. Paul and Lorraine managed to stay together; he held her hand and she was very self-conscious about it; after all, they were in church. Lorraine noticed that Vinnie and Lucy were together, also. Some of them received Communion together. After mass, they all returned to Lorraine's house, Carlo and Lena, since they had to stay around to sort of chaperone the young people, wished they would all go home.

The young people continued to dance, eat and drink. Lorraine made fresh coffee. Finally, they called it a night and there was much friendly kissing and promises to see each other soon or the next day.

Vinnie was quick to go to Lucy and asked her, "Lucy, can I walk you home?" He smiled a most beautiful smile. She felt a tingle of surprise and pleasure at the prospect.

"Of course, Vinnie. That would really be nice." They got their coats and off they went. Vinnie didn't want any hangers on. He'd waited for this opportunity for a long time. As they walked along, Vinnie held Lucy's hand and said, "Lucy, I noticed—I noticed that you—you lost a little bit weight."

Lucy was shy, smiled a bit and said, "Yes, I did. I lost fifteen pounds. And it was Lorraine who helped me. She's my best friend."

"Wow, fifteen pounds. Don't lose anymore, you look great." He looked down at her lovely face and smiled. Lucy felt thrills and wondered if this conversation would have any consequences.

When they arrived at Lucy's home, they didn't say goodnight immediately. Vinnie talked a bit and Lucy could detect that he was shy. She loved it; thinking she caused the confident Vinnie to stutter. He stopped stuttering because he was kissing her. She trembled. At the end of the kiss, Vinnie, still holding her close, said, "Lucy, I've wanted to kiss you for a long, long time."

"You have?"

"Yes, I have. I've been thinking about you a lot. I said to myself, 'myself, I think Lucy needs a boyfriend and

I am the one she needs.'"

Lucy laughed at his theatre, then she smiled, and she had a beautiful smile, "Vinnie, you're kidding me, right?"

"Wrong. I—I want you to be my girl. Is that okay with you?"

"Well, gee, I don't know. I'm sort of in shock." Now she was getting scared.

"This will remove you from your shock." He kissed her deeply. Lucy was enthralled.

"Vinnie, I don't know what to say. This is all so new and unexpected."

Vinnie smiled at her, took a little curl from the side of her face and said, "Repeat after me; Vinnie, I love you."

Lucy's eyes widened and she said, very softly, very shyly, "Vinnie, I love you."

"Lucy, I love you, too." And they kissed very beautifully and long.

"Oh, Vinnie, I never thought this would happen."

"Neither did I, baby. You will marry me, woncha?"

"Yes, I will. I will. Kiss me." He did.

***

Joe had gone with some of his friends to another friend's house. Carlo and Lena were in the kitchen tidying up. Paul was the last to leave; he and Lorraine were at the front door talking.

Paul, holding Lorraine's hand said, "Lorraine, can we see each other tomorrow night? Maybe have a little dinner." She hesitated. She was thinking about Walter and the hope that he may call her. She said, "I don't think so, Paul. I—I have to work tomorrow and I probably will be tired and all."

Paul, trying to hide his disappointment, said, "Sure, you're right. It's been a busy night and you'll need your rest." He turned to leave, then turned back to Lorraine abruptly, took her in his arms and kissed her deeply.

Lorraine gasped. "Paul, I—I—"

He kissed her again and left.

Lorraine felt something but she denied it. What was happening to her?

***

Two days later, Walter called Lorraine at the diner. "Walter, you can't call me here. It's my place of employment and they don't want us to accept phone calls unless it's an emergency."

"But, honey, this is an emergency."

"Walter, stop doing this. I don't want to get fired."

"Why! Are you in love with the Greek God!!"

"Walter, that's not true and it's not your business." He could feel the anger in her voice and picture her left eyebrow raised, a sign that she was really angry.

"It is my business. I love you, you're my girl, and I want to see you."

"Walter, I—I have to go."

"I'll call you tonight."

And they ended their telephone conversation with Lorraine looking about to see who was paying attention. She noted that Thomas had seen her hang up the phone. She was uneasy; she didn't want to lose this job. The pay wasn't that great but the tips were fabulous and she had decided to attend a community college at night with those proceeds.

Later that night, Walter called. "Lorraine, honey. I gotta see you. I really miss you."

Lorraine was uneasy even though she had answered on the extension in her room and her parents didn't know whom she was talking to. She wanted to keep this call a secret because her family was still very concerned about her and Walter.

"Walter, I'm sorry. It's obvious your parents don't

approve of me. I don't want you to suffer because of me. I'm not going to see you anymore." Though she wanted desperately to see him and hold him in her arms and tell him how much she loved him and missed him.

"But, Lorraine, you can't do that. Please. I love you. Don't you love me?"

"Walter, I—yes, love you, but it's obvious your parents don't like me. Your mother said such lies about me and I'm innocent." Her voice became subdued, "Didn't it bother you that she said all those lies about me?"

"Well, yes, it did, honey. Of course, it did. I know how you feel, honey, and I don't know why she did that. Actually, we spoke about it and she repents and says she likes you."

"Really?" Lorraine's heart skipped a beat; this was wonderful news. Maybe she and Walter would have a future together. She wanted that so badly.

"Yes, and she said when she sees you, she's going to apologize and help you plan for our wedding. Doesn't that sound great? In fact, Mother had tears in her eyes; she's so happy for us." Walter looked heavenward; he couldn't believe all the shit he was telling her and his good fortune that she believed it. He felt himself puff up with glee. He'd always gotten the girls because of his light blue eyes. He'd been getting girls since he was twelve years old. What could stop him now?

"Gee, Walter, I can hardly believe it."

"Well, you can believe it, baby doll. It's true. You don't have to worry that my parents have a terrible control over me; they don't."

"Wow," said Lorraine.

"So, can we get together for New Year's Eve?"

"Of course, darling, of course."

"Listen, we've been invited to a friend's house for a party. We'll have a great time. How does that sound to you?"

"It sounds wonderful. I can't believe it. I can't wait. What time should I be ready?" He could picture her smiling her beautiful smile, her freckled face lighting up and showing those gorgeous white teeth.

"It's gonna start late, around eleven or eleven thirty. There'll be food and drinks, so don't have dinner at home. I can't wait to see you and hold you in my arms and kiss you. I'm glad we got past our little misunderstanding."

"I am, too, Walter. I'll be ready. And I can't wait until I see you. I missed you a lot, sweetheart."

"Me, too, bye."

"Bye."

***

As soon as she thought it was safe to tell her parents, Lorraine, who was still fearful, told them she had a New Year's Eve date with Walter. Her parents looked quizzically at her.

Lena spoke up before Carlo could. "Lorraine, why do you have a date with Walter? I thought, we thought, that you didn't think of Walter anymore. His mother told lies and he didn't get in touch with you. What is this?"

Carlo spoke, too, "Lorraine, I don't like you to see him anymore. I don't trust him."

"But, Dad, Ma, he said he loves me and wants to marry me. He said his mother is sorry she said what she did and is going to apologize to me. And—and she even wants to help me plan our wedding."

At the beautiful words, "plan our wedding," Lena gasped. She wanted her daughter to get married but she had a feeling that this is not the boy for her daughter. And if any mother was going to be involved in planning Lorraine's wedding, it was going to be Lena and no one else! She shook her head sadly, "No, *cara mia,* my dear, I don't see a wedding for you with this boy."

Lorraine was angry, "So, what are you now, Ma, a fortune teller? You can see the future?"

Lena raised her hand to strike Lorraine but stopped in time. She was shocked that she would hurt her beloved daughter because of this worthless, rich boy. She turned away and a sob caught in her throat. Carlo went to Lena and embraced her and gave Lorraine a warning look. Lorraine was thoroughly ashamed of herself. She'd never insulted her mother so. She was able to gasp, "I'm sorry, Ma. I'm sorry, Dad." She turned and ran up to her room.

It was still two days from New Year's Eve and Lorraine thought of Walter and then of her parents. Were they right? Sometimes Lena had visions or feelings that would come true. *Oh, this is nonsense. Spooky things like that happen only in the movies. But what about the time Mama had a feeling of foreboding couldn't put her finger on it and then she received news that her father had been hit by a car and was near death. Thank God, he didn't die. Oh, I won't think of that. I love Walter and he loves me and it's our life together that's important to me.*

Lena and Carlo were wrong. Lorraine wanted to see Walter very badly and she counted the hours to New Year's Eve. She even told Lucy that she had a date with Walter and she would have a wonderful time. And the appointed time arrived, it seemed, sooner than expected.

Lorraine was very excited and rushed home from the diner as fast as she could. She showered, shampooed her hair, brushed her teeth and didn't have dinner because Walter said they would have food at the friend's house they were invited to see the New Year come in. She dressed very carefully, making sure her dress was unwrinkled and her jewelry matched. She turned and turned in front of the mirror until she was satisfied that she looked perfect. Her naturally curly hair just wouldn't stay put, and she gave up trying to keep it tamed. The doorbell rang. She jumped. She knew Walter was going to come here to pick her up, so why did she jump? Nerves. Why nerves; she was going to be with the man she loved. What was that nagging feeling she felt; nagging and uncomfortable? *Oh, stop it!!*

Lorraine took one more look in the mirror and thought she looked horrible. But, she had no time to change. She decided to go downstairs because she was sure Walter was here. As she slowly descended the stairs, she was assured it was Walter; those steel blue eyes were staring up at her. He had a corsage in his hand.

Lena had a cross look on her face and said, "Lorraine, Walter is here." And she brought her lips to the side of her face.

Lorraine said, "Yes, I see, Ma…mother. Good evening Walter." She extended her hand; which he took and held close to his heart.

Lorraine turned to her parents and said, "Mother, Dad, we're going to Walter's friend's house. We'll have something to eat. So, I'll see you about one a.m. Happy New Year," and she kissed her parents and brothers.

The men in the family had scowls on their faces. Walter shook hands with all of them to wish them Seasons Greetings. All the men squeezed his hand quite hard in an effort to warn him to be careful. They didn't want to voice their thoughts because they didn't want Lorraine to hear. Carlo didn't care who heard, who felt embarrassed or who would get mad.

"Walter, I want you to be careful…careful driving. Don't drink so much that you cannot drive carefully. And take care of my daughter; I do not want her to get hurt." The last was whispered menacingly, all the while squeezing Walter's hand hard so the message got through. Walter had a painful smile on his face.

Walter was fearful. Carlo was over forty but possessed bulging muscles that would scare a bear!

"Yes, sir, Mr. Martini, I'll be very careful and I'll take care of Lorraine. You can trust me."

Carlo, who didn't trust Walter and showed his feelings, gave him a warning look and said, "Hmph, make sure. If you drink too much, call me, and I'll come and pick up Lorraine."

"Oh, Dad," said an embarrassed Lorraine, "there's no need. We'll be okay." She looked at Walter and gave him a reassuring, dazzling smile.

***

They arrived at the friend's house around eleven o'clock. Most of the people present where already bombed out of their skulls. Lorraine noticed that the majority of the crowd were young people. She didn't see anyone who looked or acted like a parent. Lorraine wasn't a drinker but as soon as they entered, her coat was removed and a drink was shoved into her hand. Lorraine was introduced to everyone, their names quickly forgotten as hers was. Lorraine, who usually didn't drink, watched as everyone drank with no terrible results. She drank, too. She didn't realize she was drinking on an empty stomach.

They danced and ate little snacks and drank. Lorraine tried to refuse the drinks saying she wasn't a drinker and would get drunk. Walter assured her she wouldn't and laughed and forced her to drink and mix drinks. Lorraine began laughing and laughing. Other young men asked her to dance. She was surprised because they all were with their own girls, but it's a party, it's happy time. She danced with others, casting her eyes at Walter, who was talking quietly with a friend, a drink in his hands, which he sipped often until it was all gone. He went to the make shift bar to replenish his drink.

At midnight, champagne was served. Lorraine drank with the rest of them, thinking she was okay. She laughed and laughed. Walter took her upstairs to one of the bedrooms, locked the door and put Lorraine on the bed. He began to kiss her. She laughed. He put his hands on her breast. She laughed. He started to undress her. She laughed. She was completely nude. She laughed. He gave her a drink and she laughed. He was undressed. He gazed at her lovely nakedness, kissed her and he said, "Now, I've got you!" He was on top of her, laughing. She laughed and laughed. He fucked her and fucked her.

She was quiet and the drunken Walter, who could still think in that condition, realized that Lorraine had passed out. He finished and lay beside her, satisfied that he had accomplished what he intended to do from the moment he saw her, and in a few moments, he too, passed out.

Time passed and she woke up. Lorraine was fully dressed and so was Walter. She had no idea what had occurred. Her head was fuzzy, her mouth felt dry as a desert. She looked around and realized to her horror, she was in bed with a sleeping Walter. She sat up quickly, too quickly because she felt dizzy.

"Walter," she croaked out. "Walter, we fell asleep. Wake up." She nudged him strongly.

Walter awakened at her call and wondered what had happened. He looked at Lorraine and remembered, but he kept a few details to himself. He laughed, embarrassed, and said, "Gee, honey, we must have drunk so much and fell asleep on the bed."

"What time is it? I don't see a watch. I don't hear any noise from downstairs. The party must be over." Suddenly she realized it must be very late. "Walter, what the hell time is it?? I have to get home. My father's gonna kill me!"

"Agh, he won't kill you. It's New Year's and he's probably drunk himself."

"Walter, you don't know my father. Come on, let's get out of here!" Real fear was in Lorraine's voice.

"Let's stay a bit more." Walter cajoled as he attempted to embrace her and pull her down on the bed.

"Are you crazy! My father has probably called the police. What time is it?" Her fear, so evident, didn't make a dent in Walter's mind.

"It's early, honey. Who cares what time it is? We don't have to go now." He was still enthralled with what had happened; with what he had done to her and he smirked at the fact that she didn't know and he wouldn't tell her. It was his delicious secret.

"Walter, my father is gonna kill both of us. Take me home now!" She got up from the bed and looked at a smiling Walter, who wouldn't take her seriously. "Walter, you don't know how much trouble we're in. Get up, now, and take me home." Lorraine was scared. Walter had promised to take care of her. "You got me drunk. Why? What did we do? WALTER! WHAT DID WE DO!" There was fury in her eyes, which he found irresistible.

"We didn't do nothin'. We drank and we passed out. That's all, I swear it. Lorraine, you don't have to worry about anything. I wouldn't hurt you. I love you."

Lorraine was slightly appeased. "Then let's go. Take me home. I don't feel well. I think I'm gonna—" she ran to the bathroom and vomited. Now, Walter was getting worried. This wasn't part of his plan.

When she exited the bathroom, wiping her mouth with a tissue and glaring at Walter, she said, "Walter, if you don't take me home now, I'll go myself, but before I do—" she lunged at him, scratching and punching his face. "You son of a bitch, if you did anything to me, I'll—"

Walter, fearful, laughed and tried to embrace her, not out of love, but to hold her fierce arms by her sides. "Okay, okay, I'll take you home." Then he looked at her like a naughty boy, "You know, I love you."

Lorraine turned away from him. She had a bad

physical and instinctive feeling about Walter. Softly, through her teeth, she said, "Take me home now!"

He took her hand and led her downstairs. People were sprawled all over the place, passed out or sleeping or both. This made Lorraine worry all the more. She was scared. He got their coats, helped her on with hers and they both walked unsteadily to the front door. It was still quite dark outdoors. On the ride home, neither spoke. When they arrived at Lorraine's house, she had her key in her hand and quickly got out of the car. She didn't say anything or look at Walter, though he tried to say something to her. She ran as quickly as she could up the walk, unlocked the door and let herself in as quietly as she could.

"Lorraine, is that you?" Lena said sleepily, obviously trying to stay awake until her daughter came home.

Lorraine answered as well and quietly as she could, "Yes, Ma, it's me."

"You okay?"

"Yes, Ma, I'm okay. Goodnight and Happy New Year." She was lucky she finished speaking because she thought her voice was beginning to tremble and that would have brought Lena and Carlo out of their bed.

Lena fell asleep.

Chapter Ten

Lorraine ran up the stairs, scared and worried. She felt in her heart something had happened; but what? What could happen? She was with Walter? She was safe. He loves her. But, what was that gnawing feeling she had? She couldn't know what it was. She only knew that she had a guilty conscience and she didn't know why; the Catholic Italian upbringing!

She wasn't going to take a shower; it was late. She washed her face, brushed her teeth and sat on the toilet. When she finished urinating and wiped herself, she saw blood. She looked at her panties; blood. *Oh, I got my period. I wasn't due until next week.* She cleaned herself, changed her underwear and put on a clean napkin and went to bed.

She couldn't sleep. Many strange visions came to her. She was feeling uneasy and didn't know why. Finally, she slept. The next morning, she still had the queasy feeling she attributed it to a hangover; the first she ever had. But, when she wiped herself after urinating, she found bits of pink stuff on the tissue paper. It wasn't blood, she instinctively knew that. Was it something she ate? She felt the blood rush to her head. *What is all this?* She felt a throbbing in her head and her heart beat fast. She looked in the mirror and said, "What happened last night? Did Walter…? No, he wouldn't do anything to hurt me. He loves me." The mirror gave no answer. She shook her head slowly, fearfully. She had a feeling that something had happened, but how could it? Uncomfortably, she couldn't remember anything. She let out a loud annoyed breath!

She took a shower, dressed quickly and went downstairs. Maybe a change of scenery would clear her head; clear her head of the thoughts that assailed her. She wasn't reassured and couldn't shake the strange feeling.

Maybe the sight of her mother would bring her some comfort.

Lena was in the kitchen alone, making scrambled eggs and toast. "Ah, good morning, my love. Happy New Year," she said to Lorraine. She kissed her daughter.

Lorraine had a sudden feeling of worthlessness but tried to hide it. She also greeted her mother with a smile, a kiss and a Happy New Year. She began to set the table and one by one the men in the family came down to breakfast.

Joe said, very quietly, "Good morning everybody and Happy New Year. Ow!" He put his hand to his head.

They laughed because they knew he was feeling what he drank last night.

They all greeted him and wished him Happy New Year and many more. "Please, stop shouting, folks. Can't you noisy Italians speak in a normal tone of voice like Medigons (Americans)?"

This caused more laughter. Everyone was talking at once, except Lorraine. Lena noticed but didn't say anything. Carlo looked at his daughter, "Lorraine, what time did you come home?"

"I—I don't know, Dad. When I came home I went straight upstairs and never even looked at the clock." That was the truth. She avoided his eyes and that made him wonder.

"Were you a little tipsly?"

"Tipsy, Dad, and no, I wasn't." Lorraine considered it the truth because at the time she wasn't. If Dad had asked about earlier, Lorraine would have lied to her father for the first time in her life. She knew she was drunk because she didn't remember going upstairs to a strange bedroom with Walter. Her face betrayed her feelings, she thought. So she remained quiet and continued to eat her breakfast.

Her brothers looked at her, too, thinking she looked a bit haggard and worn out. This was a very unusual look for Lorraine. While she wasn't usually bouncy at breakfast, this silence was definitely abnormal.

The telephone rang and Lorraine answered it. She was surprised to hear Lucy's voice; she had expected it to be Walter.

"Happy New Year, Lorraine. Did you have a nice time last night?"

"Oh, Lucy. Happy New Year to you, too. Yes, I had a very good time last night." She knew she lied and she felt bad, Lucy was her best friend and you don't lie to your best friends, even if it's to save your ass. "Did you have a nice time?"

Lucy had a puzzled look on her face; Lorraine was asking her as though she didn't know that Lucy was with Vinnie. "Lorraine, Vinnie and I were at my house. We had a good time and we missed you. My mother made those pastries that we used to call 'bellies' because they're filled with sweet ricotta and then fried. They were delicious and I gave some to Vinnie to take home to you and your family. Did you see them?"

Lorraine began to get nervous; she looked all around, then she spied the pastries on the counter. "Oh, I see them. I haven't tasted them yet. They look really good and I love them."

Lucy tried to sound casual. "Lorraine, do you know that Vinnie and I are—" She stopped talking because she knew that Lorraine wasn't listening to her. "Lorraine, is anything wrong?"

"No, no. Everything is fine."

"Lorraine."

"Lucy, please don't worry. Nothing's wrong. Listen, I gotta go now. I'll talk to you later. Okay?"

Lucy was subdued.

Lorraine walked away from the telephone, knowing she needed to speak to Lucy but now was not the time.

***

In the first weeks of the New Year that followed several major things happened. Vinnie and Lucy started going "steady." This brought pleasure to both families but especially to Vinnie and Lucy. Lorraine was thrilled, though she couldn't really show the extent because she was absorbed in her own horrible, puzzling thoughts. Lucy was concerned because she knew that Lorraine was thrilled at the idea but had not spoken as much as one would have expected.

Walter had not called Lorraine and she was confused and decided several times to call Walter. He was never available; the maid always told Lorraine that Mr. Walter was absent from the house and she didn't know when he would return but would give him the message. He never returned her calls. It was mystifying to Lorraine, who remembered that Walter had told her he loved her at the party. What was happening?

It was after dinner, at the end of January and Lorraine called Lucy and asked her to meet her at a certain diner, one which they didn't frequent.

Lorraine was morose. When Lucy saw her, she immediately asked, "Lorraine, what is it? You've been out of sorts since the beginning of the year. I'm worried about you."

They were sitting in a booth near the window, from which Lorraine peered. She slowly turned her head back, put her hand on the side of her brow. "Lucy, I'm late."

"Late for what?" Then she understood and said, "Ooohh. Lorraine, how? You must be mistaken. Please don't worry about it. You can't have done… done… done…"

Lorraine looked at her friend, who all thought would soon marry Vinnie and be part of the family. "Lucy—Lucy, you're my best friend. I love you and I've been deceitful toward you." She looked away to hide her tears, which began to fall abundantly. She quickly took her napkin and wiped her eyes.

Lucy sat quietly, a concerned frown on her face; she reached for Lorraine's hand and held it tenderly.

"Lucy, I—I'm pregnant."

Lucy gasped; instantly her hand tightened on Lorraine's hand. Lorraine, who would never do anything to sully her reputation; Lorraine, who would never give in to a man just because he wanted to, Lorraine, who had so much self-respect and honor she could have thrown it away!

"Lucy, the party I went to with Walter?"

"Yeah," Lucy whispered, breathing hard, and kept holding Lorraine's hand because she knew now Lorraine was about to tell her awful happenings.

"I don't even know where the house was located. There were a lot of happy, young, drunk people. They gave me drinks. I told them I didn't drink but they said I should drink because it was a party; it's the New Year. I planned on holding the drink but Walter urged me to drink, saying it was weak and I would be okay. I *trusted* him. Lucy, *I trusted him.*" She stopped to wipe away tears. She turned her head from side to side. "I can't believe I was so stupid as to get caught in a trap I couldn't see coming. But—but I was so happy to be with Walter. I thought we would get married. I thought our troubles were over and everything was settled. I thought all wonderful things were going to be happening."

Lucy's eyes filled, too.

"I don't know how much I drank. We ate, we danced, and we drank. Other guys asked me to dance. I danced with them and then they gave me a drink. I remember laughing. At midnight, we drank champagne. I don't know what happened after that. I woke up in a strange bed next to Walter, who was sleeping. I was fully dressed and so was he. I don't remember a thing. But, I had this feeling that something was wrong. You know, how my mother gets those feelings and they come true. I had to threaten Walter to take me home. He wanted me to stay longer. And when I got home, I saw blood on my panties and I thought I had my period. I should have been so lucky!"

"Oh, Lorraine, I'm so sorry, I really am." Lucy wept for her friend.

"I can't believe that I could have been so stupid! I, who never threw myself at a guy before should fall for Walter's schemes and tricks. He told me his mother regretted offending me and was going to apologize and help me plan the wedding." She looked at nothing, a dejected, resigned look on her face. "For all we know—"

"We're still dumbbells." Lucy finished.

They were quiet for a while.

"Lorraine, what will you do now? You're gonna show soon. Have you given any thought to that?"

"Well, I'm not gonna get in touch with Walter, that's for sure. It's his baby but I will never tell him. He doesn't deserve such happiness!"

"Happiness?"

"Yes, the more I think of it, ya know, having a baby, the happier I get. I don't know why. But, then I think of the moment I have tell my parents. They're gonna be so disappointed in me, and I don't blame them. The first word that will come to their minds is *puttana*, whore! And it isn't my fault. My parents told me they didn't like Walter. My father said he didn't trust him. I thought because Walter said he loved me, he really did. I trusted him not to let anything bad happen to me. I don't know how I could have been so stupid. I hate myself, bringing shame to my family." Lorraine covered her face with her hanky, a sob escaped her heart. Then she took a deep breath and calmed down a bit.

"You know, he raped you and you could have him arrested."

Lorraine's eyes widened. "Oh, no. I'd never do that."

"Why?"

"Well, I wouldn't, that's all. I don't want publicity. I don't want anyone to know what happened. I'll have to make a plan. Maybe I can go someplace where nobody knows me and have the baby...*my baby*. Not his. I don't want to have anything to do with Walter. I don't want his parents to get any ideas that they have a claim on this baby. I don't want any of them to know about this baby."

"Lorraine, I don't think they'll ever do such a thing. They want nothing to do with people like us." Lucy had so much compassion for Lorraine.

Lorraine looked at Lucy with love, "Yes, Lucy, I think you're right. But, I still don't want Walter to ever know."

"He'll never hear anything from me. I'll never betray you."

Lorraine's chin quivered. "Lucy," she managed to say, "You're the best friend anyone could ever have."

"I know. And so are you to me."

And they both shed a few tears.

Lucy thought a moment and watched Lorraine's face before she broached the subject. "Lorraine, you—I mean, you could get married."

"What! No. Nobody will marry me."

"Well, there's Thomas. He evidently loves you. He's always looking at you."

"No. Thomas would never marry me now. First, I don't love him; I like him. Then there's tradition, ya know? The Greeks are like Italians; they don't want their sons to marry pregnant girls, especially if the baby belongs to somebody else. And I can understand that. So, I want to avoid all that controversy. And besides, I told you that he was set on marrying the Greek girl. No, I wouldn't do that to Thomas. He doesn't deserve that. He'll be happy with his Greek girl."

"What about Paul. I see by the way he looks at you, he loves you."

Lorraine looked at her in surprise. "Really?" Then she thought of his kisses on New Year's Eve and thought maybe Lucy was right. "Well, yeah, maybe he has feelings for me, but I couldn't do that to Paul. He's a good friend and I would never put pressure on him. He may not want to marry me or even see me or be near me. I can understand that. I want to keep him as a friend but I truly think things will change when he sees me with a big belly."

Lucy's big eyes almost filled with tears. "Oh, Lorraine, I wish I could do something to help you. I really do. I love you like a sister; maybe more since we don't have any sisters ourselves."

Lorraine looked at Lucy with love and compassion. "Lucy let's do what the kids used to do, make ourselves sisters. We'll cut our fingers and join blood…Nah, I might get sick!"

Lucy smiled and said, "Done!"

But, they didn't do it.

***

The next few weeks were turbulent for Lorraine. She had morning sickness, which she tried to hide from her mother, and since Lena was always downstairs in the kitchen making breakfast, it was easy to do. Lorraine was getting frightened and nervous because soon she would begin showing and would have to tell her family. What would they do to her? What would they do to Walter, even though she'd never name him, they knew he was the only male she'd been with except for Paul, and no one would suspect him or expect him to betray Lorraine. He made no secret of his respect for her. Walter still hadn't called her. And Lorraine made up her mind that she wouldn't call him, no matter what! She wanted no contact with him at all.

One Sunday, very close to March, she read in the Sunday newspapers of Walter's engagement to a girl from a very prominent family. Lorraine didn't panic, or scream or fall apart. She was upset, but she detested Walter for the coward he was and she knew that Walter was out of her life forever. She regretted that their baby would be a constant reminder of him and without a father, but she consoled herself with the thought that Walter would never know of this baby.

Lorraine faced her mother one day when they were alone in the house. "Ma, I have something to tell you."

Lena looked at her daughter, a smile on her face as though she just thought of a joke. "I know. You're pregnant!" And then she said, "God forbid." And she made the Sign of the Cross. But the look on Lorraine's face told her she was correct.

"NO!!!" Lena screamed. "NO. *Puttana!!* NO. Lorraine. No. Tell me it's not true."

Lorraine couldn't speak, she just nodded. She put a paper napkin to her mouth and she dropped into a kitchen chair, sitting sideways with her shoulder leaning on the back of the chair.

"But, how, when? You brought shame on the family. You ruined your life. You stupid girl! Who's gonna marry you now? What will people say? Lorraine, tell me it's not true. Your father is gonna kill you! Then he'll kill me." She held her palms upward and waved them up and down in her anxiety and fear.

"Why?"

"Because I'm the mother of a *puttana!* Then he'll kill your brothers."

"Why?"

Lena screamed, pulling her hair, "Because they are brothers of a *puttana.* Then he'll kill himself because he's the father of a *puttana.* Oh, *Madonna Santissima,* please, don't let this be true."

Lorraine's eyes filled with tears. "So, he'll wipe us all out. Well, that solves the problem."

Lena realized how terrible all her words sounded to her beloved daughter. She dropped into a chair; she made the Sign of the Cross, put her hands in a prayerful position on her breast and said, "Lorraine, how could you bring shame on all of us? What are people gonna say?"

"What about the shame on me? Is that all you can say? Are you worried about what people will say more than my feelings?" Lorraine was getting angry, now. "Who cares what people say? It's my life. I didn't go and get myself deliberately pregnant. I was raped."

Lena wept, "Lorraine," she was starting to come out of her hysteria. She embraced her daughter so tightly, Lorraine was comforted. "Lorraine, what happened? I know my daughter; she's not a *puttana*, she's a good girl. How could this have happened?" And she wailed.

"Ma, I'm sorry. I don't know how it happened. I trusted Walter and—"

"And your father didn't trust him. Oh, God, when he hears this, he'll kill Walter. We have to keep this from him, but how?"

"I don't know." Lorraine wept. "I'm sorry, Ma. I should have listened to you and Dad but I was so in love with Walter and now, I realize he didn't love me. He got me drunk at the party and I passed out. You know, I'm not a drinker, and we woke up in a bedroom, fully dressed. I was unconscious throughout the whole ordeal. I knew for sure when I didn't get my period and got morning sickness." Lorraine looked pleadingly into her mother's eyes. "Ma, I need your help. Please, help me. I never want to see that bastard again. If I do, maybe I'll kill him myself. I don't want him to know about the baby."

"What! He must know."

"No! I absolutely do not want him to know. If anyone tells him, I—I—I don't know what I'll do. I'll leave and you'll never see me again! Everyone has to listen to me on this; everyone has to be on my side."

"But, Lorraine, he's the father. He should know and offer support and maybe marry you."

"Ma, get the marriage idea out of your head. I will never marry Walter. He's a coward and a bastard! I have no respect for him and no love. I couldn't marry anyone while I have those feelings."

Lena rocked herself in her chair and all she could say is, "Oh, *Gesu, Gesu aiuto.* Jesus help."

Lorraine, who was gaining strength from her mother's weakness, said, "Ma, that's enough. I'll tell Dad this evening and if he wants to throw me out of the house or kill me, so be it. I'm completely innocent, stupid, but innocent."

Lena looked at her daughter, who made so much sense and nodded weakly. "I'll be here when you tell your father. I don't want him to do anything to you or Walter. I want you to stay with us."

"No, Ma. I can't stay here. I want to go somewhere where I'm not known. I don't want to shame anyone, especially now that Vinnie is seeing Lucy."

"But, Lucy is your friend."

"I know and I know she'll understand my feelings."

"You told Lucy already."

"Yes. I'm sorry I told her first but some things can't be told to parents right away. I needed to gather courage to tell you. I hope you understand and forgive me."

"Of course, I forgive you. I want to help you.

You're still my daughter." She looked at her hands, and then she rose from her chair, with a loving, compassionate look on her face, she came to her daughter and embraced her. The two women wept and held on to each other tightly. Lorraine kept apologizing again and again.

"Ma, please forgive me. I—I'm so ashamed. But, I—I'm innocent. I made a mistake to trust Walter. Please, Ma, forgive me. I love you and Dad and my brothers so much and I'm so ashamed. Please help me."

Lena, quietly said, "Lorraine, these things happen. Walter is a coward and a son of a bitch and I don't blame you for not wanting him to know. I think you're right and I will insist that we all respect your wishes. Do you want something to eat?"

"Ma," Lorraine said, looking at her mother with love and gratitude, "you're the best and I love you."

"I know. I love you, too, and I'll always support you." Then a thought came to her. "Lorraine, I know! I'll call Gooma Nancy."

"Who's Gooma Nancy?"

"Ah, she's a wonderful, wise old woman. You remember her; she came here when you were about five years old. She's a natural blond. Everyone thought she was Irish. She'll know how to advise us. Leave it to me."

"But, what about Dad and the boys? How do we tell them?"

"With great care," said the wise Lena.

Lena prepared a delicious dinner. While it was in the oven cooking, she called Gooma Nancy. "Hello, Gooma Nancy, it's Lena Martini. How are you?"

"Ah, Lena, how wonderful to hear from you. I'm fine, thanks, Lena, how are you and your family?"

"Well, we're fine. Except—we—" Lena broke down and cried.

Gooma Nancy's soothing voice said, "Lena, honey,

take your time. Breathe. Good, now tell me what's bothering you."

"Gooma Nancy, you remember my daughter, Lorraine, don't you?"

"Of course, she's the beautiful redhead, like you. So?"

"Well, she was seeing this boy, a rich boy, and—and—"

"I think I understand. She's pregnant and he doesn't want to marry her."

"Well, yes. She doesn't want to marry him either. She doesn't even want him to know about the baby. She's a thick head."

"Like you, Lena." Gooma Nancy smiled and even though Lena couldn't see it, she knew.

"Yes."

"Does Carlo know?"

"No, Lorraine just told me today and I thought of you because she wants to go somewhere where she's not known. How could I let her go someplace alone and without her family and be far away from us? I thought you might have an idea."

"Okay, this is what I want you to do and you tell me if it's a good idea. Or rather, if Lorraine thinks it's a good idea. We have to tell her and get her opinion; after all she's an adult and we can't make plans for her without her knowledge and we need her consent. You can tell Carlo that I need someone to help me. I never advocate lying to husbands and fathers because it always makes a bad situation worse, but in this case, you may need a little time for you and your daughter to get used to the idea of her being pregnant. Then, maybe, when a little time passes, it will be easier to tell the father of the girl. Sometimes, it's not. But this is the chance you take. There are not too many options. And pregnancy has the habit of continuing to the delivery of a wonderful baby. This is what you have to keep in mind; the wonderful baby!

"Lorraine can stay here with me until she either gives birth or you folks think of something else, like maybe take her home whenever you can live with an unmarried, pregnant girl, which will be a little difficult considering the circumstances. You really have to have a lot of compassion for this girl. I take it she wasn't a willing partner in this event."

Lena listened, nodding her head, looking at Lorraine, who didn't know what the conversation was about. "You're right; she wasn't willing. All right. I'll tell Lorraine and I'll call you back either later tonight or tomorrow. Is that okay?"

"That's fine, Lena. Be sure that Lorraine feels comfortable about it. There's a room here for her. She'll have all the privacy she needs. I recommend she get a job someplace close to our home. I'll take good care of her. My son and daughter-in-law, I'm sure won't mind Lorraine's being here. I'll simply tell them that Lorraine is sort of helper. They'll understand. How does that sound to you?"

"Oh, Gooma Nancy, that sounds wonderful. I'll tell Lorraine."

"Lena, why don't I speak to her; that may be better."

"Oh, yeah, yeah, that's a good idea. Hold on. Lorraine, come here, Gooma Nancy wants to speak to you."

Lorraine shook her head but Lena made faces and shook the phone at Lorraine.

Lorraine, frightened, took the phone and said, "Hello, Gooma Nancy. How are you?"

"I'm fine, Honey, how are you?"

"Well, I have a little problem." And she held back a sob.

"Lorraine, I just told your mother that, if you're

agreeable, you can come and stay here in our house. You can be introduced as my helper. How does that sound to you?"

"Well, it sounds good. But, I don't want to impose on you or your family."

"Sweetie, it's no imposition. My son, Gabe, and his wife, Ida, are two great people. There's a room upstairs; it used to belong to my grandson, Steve, who recently got married. I'm sure he won't mind if you occupy it. Talk with your mother, make plans and call me back. Okay? Whatever you decide let me know. Okay?"

"Gooma Nancy, that sounds fine. Ma and I will talk. Of course, tonight there will be a volcanic explosion and I might not survive, in which case, my problem will be solved."

"Nah, nah. There won't be an explosion; maybe loud talking but everyone will survive. Take it easy and call me. Okay?"

"Yes, Gooma Nancy. Thank you so much for your kindness. Bye."

"Bye, sweetie and *coraggio.* Bye."

Lorraine looked at her mother, a slight smile on her face. "Ma, she sounds so nice."

"She *is* nice. People go to her when they have problems and she is so wise, she's able to give them good advice. She's a doll."

"Ma, could it be that people are in a distraught state of mind when they go to her and she's easily able to help them?"

"Yeah, um, well, um I guess so. She's also very funny. She makes everybody laugh."

"Well, that's a good trait, too. Now, what about tonight? Could she come here to referee?" Lorraine laughed nervously.

Lena said, "Lorraine, maybe we shouldn't tell Dad

and your brothers anything. Maybe you should simply go to Gooma Nancy's house and I'll tell Dad that you...ran away."

"Oh, yeah, that's a good thing to say. You'll make it worse."

"Well, I can't tell you how scared I am."

"Me, too, Ma, but I won't lie to Dad. He doesn't deserve it and I'm not a liar. Here's what we'll do. Tonight, while you're having espresso, I'll tell Dad."

"No! He'll kill you."

"Ma, he won't kill me. He'll get mad and uncontrollable and we have to be careful then, but I'll handle him."

"You? The sinner?"

"Yes, Ma, keep reminding me, like I can forget! I'll talk to Dad. He's my father and he loves me. I'll have to remind him of that. Meantime, you stay on my side. Just keep agreeing with me. Okay?"

Lena was subdued because it was getting late and soon the men will be home and the next operatic act was approaching!! "Yeah," she whispered and made the Sign of the Cross. "Oh, *Madonna Santissima!"*

"Amen, Ma."

Chapter Eleven

Lena was a nervous wreck until Carlo came home. Then she turned into a stuttering machine.

Carlo looked at her and said, "Lena, what is it? You seem very nervous tonight. Has something happened?"

"No, no, no, no, Carlo, nothing happened." And she smoothed out her apron and looked at the stove. She didn't want to look at Lorraine. The boys came home talking about a smashed up car that they were going to work on. As they greeted their parents and sister, they knew something was up.

"Well," said Vinnie, "something's going on. Let us in on it."

"That's what I said, but Mama, she say nothing is wrong," said Carlo.

"Please everybody sit down and let's eat. Nothing is wrong." Lena was too nervous and it was obvious.

Lorraine, who had been silent, looked at everybody, said, "Mama's right. Let's all sit down and eat."

For some reason, everyone obeyed silently. But they still didn't pick up their forks to eat Lena's delicious chicken cacciatore. Everyone looked at each other.

Lorraine cleared her throat. Very quietly, she said, "I have something to say and I wish you all would please not lose control. I want you all to please remember that you love me and I love you all very much."

"What is it?" demanded Carlo.

Lorraine thought, *this is not going according to plan; we were supposed to eat, have espresso and then erupt.* "Dad, please don't lose your temper. I—I—I don't know how to say this so I'm just going to jump in." With words like that, she had everyone's attention and they were already disturbed. Lena, sitting next to her, took her hand and tears came to her eyes.

"Is somebody sick?" Carlo asked.

Lorraine looked fearfully at her father and whispered weakly, "Yes, well, no. Dad, I—I—" she couldn't continue. She covered her face in an attempt to cover her shame and fear.

All the men looked at Lorraine and then they looked at Lena, whose face was contorted.

Carlo's eyes narrowed. He thought of Walter. He rose from the table and brought his powerful fist down so hard, the dishes and utensils jumped. "*Ma, io l'ammazzo.* But, I kill him! He cannot do this to my daughter. He cannot come into my house and bring shame to you and to us! *Figlio di puttana. Sfacim! Devi morire!* That son of a bitch must die!" And he turned to leave, he was so distraught, he didn't know in which direction to turn. His family, in unison, went to him to hold him back and it took all of them to do it.

Lena screamed, "No! Carlo, no! Please, sit down. Please, honey, listen to me."

"Lasciatemi, lasciatemi, let go of me! I will kill him! He can't do this to my daughter. I don't care how rich he is, he's a scumbag and a shit! I will kill him and nobody will stop me!"

Lorraine expected him to explode but when she actually saw him do so, she began to cry. Lena, already crying, said, "Carlo, Carlo, calm down. Please calm down so we can talk. Please, honey, come and sit down so Lorraine can tell you and, please, don't do anything to her. You'll see she's an honorable girl. She's completely innocent. Listen to her, please. We have to take care of her; she's our daughter. We love her. Please, Carlo, listen to me."

Carlo, his face contorted in anger, looked at his wife as though she were a stranger, then he said, "I know my daughter is an honorable girl. I know she is innocent. I know who she is. She is my daughter!" He was breathing heavily, his mighty chest rose and fell. His fingers were bunched and he pounded his chest with them, the way Italians do, as he spoke his words "*Gualtiero*, Walter must pay. We are Italians but we are honorable; not low class Italians." He was breathing hard and Lena was afraid he would have some kind of attack.

Vinnie and Joe were silent; their lips were pressed to their teeth. They didn't speak because Carlo didn't need to hear them. They both were already formulating plans which they would consult with each other later, away from parents and sister.

Lorraine said, "Dad, thank you for your words." She wiped away her tears and blew her nose. She continued, her voice subdued, "I apologize for not listening to you and Mama. I really do. You both were right. Right now, I—I need support from all of you and that doesn't include revenge. I—I—I was so in love," she wept, "with Walter and I thought he felt the same. He told me he loved me and wanted to marry me. Now, I know he lied. He's a coward and a liar. I never want to see him again." She stopped talking to regain some composure and try to speak intelligently so that they knew how she felt and would be on her side.

Carlo, a bit calmer now, demanded, "Lorraine, how did this happen? Did he hit you or force himself?"

Her brothers, fists clenched, each said, "Yeah, we want to know because we…"

Lorraine held up her hand and that silenced everyone. She gained control of herself, sat down, her hands clutching a tissue, and began the story. "We went to his friend's house. There was food, drink, music, and young people. We drank and danced. We—we—were having a good time. Walter—he gave me a drink. I told him I didn't drink and he said the drink was weak and wouldn't affect me. We ate, drank and danced. At midnight, we had champagne. I guess I drank too much. I don't remember anything until I woke up, fully dressed on a bed. Walter was beside me, also fully dressed. I don't remember what happened in the interim." She turned away, ashamed and wept.

The men in the family knew what horror she went through and they sympathized with her and showed their love.

Carlo looked at his daughter, love and revenge in his heart, "Lorraine, don't worry about it. We know you; we believe you and we love you. We will take care of you."

"Thank you, Dad and all of you. I really don't remember what happened but I can only imagine and it's horrible. Please you've got to believe me. I know I've brought disgrace and shame to the family and if you want to kill me, throw me out, I'll understand. And maybe it's a good idea."

They all were saying, "No, no, Lorraine. We love you."

Vinnie said, "That son of a bitch raped her!"

Joe said, "We'll call the police and put him away!"

Vinnie, his eyes blazing said, "But, first, we'll beat the shit out of him!"

"No!" said a panicked Lorraine and they looked at her with question marks above their heads. "I don't want to call the police. I don't want publicity."

"You're gonna have plenty of publicity when you start showing a belly and no wedding ring," said Joe.

"I know. That's why I'm gonna go somewhere, sort of, to hide myself until the baby is born."

Vinnie said, "And you'll come back with a baby and nobody will know where he came from. Is that what you think? Do you think you can tell people you found a baby under 'Mrs. Wigg's Cabbage Patch'?"

"No, that's not what I think." She wiped her eyes. At this action, all the men in her family felt so much love and sympathy for Lorraine. Carlo came to her, wrapped his arms around her and held her close. He could not speak, his throat was constricted, and he rocked her. Suddenly, she was a little girl again, who ran to her father when she fell down and scraped her knee. He made it better with his embrace. She wept heavily. Her brothers came to her and gave her hugs and words of love and encouragement.

Lena sat, watched and cried. She was glad that all her men embraced her daughter.

After a few minutes when some of them quieted down, Vinnie said, "We gotta tell Walter about the baby. He has to know. He has to marry you and provide support."

"Yeah," said Joe, "he needs to do the right thing. He has to give the baby a name."

"NO!" shouted Lorraine. "I don't want him to know anything. I don't want to marry him. He's a coward and he's shallow. I despise him. I never want to see him again. Mama and Dad were right about him but I was blind. I'm not blind anymore. I'll repeat that; I'm not blind anymore and I never want him to know anything about the baby. It's my baby; not his and the baby will have my name; Martini. I want every one of you to swear you'll never tell him. Never speak of it to anyone."

"How are we gonna do that? Pregnancy is kind of difficult to hide." Vinnie said.

Lorraine said, "I'm talking about informing Walter about the baby. Walter must never, never know. I never want to see him again. This baby is mine, not his. Understand! Mama has called Gooma Nancy and she offered a place in her home for me to stay. We'll talk it over; all of us and come to a conclusion and then I'll speak to Gooma Nancy."

"Where does Gooma Nancy live?" Joe asked.

"I don't think I know her." Vinnie said.

Lena, excited that no blood was shed, said, "You all met her when you were little and then she moved out to the Island with her son and daughter-in-law. I spoke to her and she said Lorraine could stay there; they have a room Lorraine could use. She's most welcome to stay there. She'll be safe there. She'll be with good people. Gooma Nancy is well known for her intelligence and kindness. What do you think?" She didn't realize how fast she was talking.

The men nodded; they were satisfied, but they didn't like the idea of Lorraine being so far from them. But, this was a story that had to be hidden and then when Lorraine returned, *with a baby,* then all the busybodies will be busy and they could all go to hell.

Vinnie looked at Lorraine; he wasn't happy about the arrangement but had to go along with it to save face. But, in the end, no face can be saved!

They all sat down at the table. Lorraine was miserable but glad that the murder threats seemed to be extinguished. But, she could see the hatred for Walter on all the faces at the table, hers included. Slowly, they began to eat their dinner, which had grown cold; but that didn't stop them. They were all quiet, but their brains were working. This made Lorraine fearful because she knew the Walter problem had not been settled. She knew there was still danger because she was innocent and the family members must take revenge. It was the code!

It was decided for now, that Lorraine would go to stay with Gooma Nancy until after the baby was born or something else prompted her return to the family home.

When Lorraine was able to, she called Lucy and told her of the plans. Lucy was glad that no blood had been shed.

"Lorraine, I hate to see you go, but you know what

you're doing. I'm gonna miss you, my sister."

"I'll miss you, too, my sister. Lucy, thanks for your support and your love. I'll keep in touch with you. And I'm gonna quit the diner tomorrow. Of course, I'll tell them a lie, but it doesn't matter. They're not that important to me."

"Well, don't forget, you're important to Thomas."

"I know, but he's found a nice Greek girl, a virgin. You know, that's important. Nobody's gonna marry me now." Lorraine stifled a sound, realizing how deep the damage was. Lucy heard and she felt such compassion for Lorraine.

"Oh, Lorraine, I'll miss you and take care of yourself. If you want me to come to visit, let me know."

"Sure, Lucy, bye."

"Bye, sister."

***

That Friday, not wanting to waste any more time, Lorraine had quit her job at the diner. They were all stunned that she was leaving. They asked her why, did she want more money, and did she want shorter hours? But, Lorraine said she was going to college.

Thomas waited until he could speak to her alone. "Lorraine, it's the guy who came here once and called you a few times, isn't it?"

Lorraine could only look at him. She didn't answer.

"Lorraine, if you're in 'trouble', I will marry you. I want to marry you. I love you. I don't care what my father says. I love you."

"Thomas, I'm not in 'trouble'. And thank you for your kind words. But, please, don't worry about me. Really. I'm going to college." And then she smiled because sometimes when an Italian boy went to prison, it was said he went to college.

Thomas took Lorraine in his arms and attempted to kiss her. She broke away. "Please, Thomas, don't make it more difficult than it already is." She gave him a look that told him she was grateful for his offer. She turned and left the diner forever.

Thomas could only watch the girl he loves walk out of his life and he knew it was definite. Stavros and his brother watched Thomas' face when he re-entered the work kitchen. They were full of regret and sympathy for both young people, but they had no idea of Lorraine's problem because they knew Lorraine was a "good girl."

***

Arrangements had been made for Lorraine to leave for Gooma Nancy's home the following day, Saturday. She wanted to leave before she started showing and she could feel the swelling under her hands when she showered.

Lorraine had packed two suitcases until they bulged like her belly soon would. Gooma Nancy lived on the Island in Garden Square, a small village just over the Queens-Nassau County line. Vinnie would drive her there; the trip may take one hour.

The dinner on the night preceding her departure was somber. It didn't matter what Lena cooked, they could only eat a little bit. Carlo was mute. His jaw muscles contracted many times and Lena noticed and was very worried. Vinnie and Joe were nervous.

Vinnie said, "Lorraine, we don't want you to worry about anything. You need something, call us and we'll come running."

Lorraine, her throat constricted, nodded silently.

Joe looked at his sister, opened his mouth to say something, but nothing came out. Finally, he said, "Lorraine, Vinnie's right, don't worry about anything. We're behind you. We'll keep our promise. I'll make sure anybody who asks about you gets no information from me. And call us. Call us anytime. I don't have to tell you that we're all worried about you and not happy about your going somewhere else. Please be careful."

Lena was proud of her sons and she squeezed Lorraine's hand. She cleared her throat and said, "I spoke to Gooma Nancy this morning and she's looking forward to your visit. I know I don't have to tell you to be respectful to them. I raised you right." She *covered* her mouth, trying to suppress a sob. She cursed and hated Walter for bringing such unhappiness to her daughter and family. *Her daughter, innocent as she was, had to hide herself and be away from her family, while he's comfy with his own family, free of shame. How unjust.* She made a fist and shook it to God, and pulled her lips against her teeth. "I hope his eyes fall out of his head. May he never know a moment's happiness and never find a wonderful girl to marry. May his prick shrivel. I hope his mother's belly ruptures." She finished her litany of curses and sat there breathing heavily. The family could only watch her and though they didn't voice their agreement, they knew how she felt because they felt the same. It seemed as though their love for Lorraine seemed to increase, if that was possible.

Dinner was over; Lorraine went upstairs for two reasons. She packed some last minute stuff and she couldn't bear to watch the faces of her family. It hurt her. Lucy called her to say goodbye; but neither girl said much. They wept together.

***

The next morning, everyone had a quiet breakfast. Lena could only repeat what she'd said the night before. Carlo was still mute, but kept glancing at his daughter. He was hurting so bad and tried valiantly to hide it.

"Lorraine," he cleared his throat many times.

"Yes, Dad?"

"You remember who you are. You come from a good and honorable family. You have no cause to be ashamed." He could no longer speak; he drew in a sharp breath and lowered his eyes and he held his daughter to his heart.

"I—I know, Dad. I want you all to know I love you very much. I'm very lucky to have a family like you. I appreciate all you're doing for me."

There were murmurs from her family and she could feel their love and support and it gave her a tremendous amount of strength. She had not mentioned to any of them the article in the newspapers announcing Walter's engagement and wedding date. She thought none of them knew. But her brothers knew; they'd cut the article out and saved it.

It was time to go to Long Island. Vinnie brought Lorraine's luggage downstairs. The goodbye was the most difficult thing they all had to do. Tears were shed. Carlo cursed under his breath, he gulped and he forced a hundred dollar bill in her hands. Vinnie and Joe again told Lorraine if she needed anything, she should call them.

"Lorraine," Lena gasped, "we'll call you every day. Don't use their phone; it might cost a lot. We'll call."

Lorraine nodded.

Vinnie took her luggage and put it in the trunk of his car. He took Lorraine's hand, pulling her from her mother's arms, weeping and wailing, Carlo clutching his daughter to him, and brought her to the car. Joe hugged her even though he would be riding with them. The parents went to the front windows to look and wave to her. Lorraine looked at them, the car moved slowly away, kisses were thrown from each of them to Lorraine and she reciprocated to each of them. Vinnie made his way to Grand Central Parkway and was glad that traffic wasn't heavy. They rode in silence.

When the car was no longer in sight, Lena heaved a sigh and then gulped a few times. Carlo sat on the sofa, covered his face and cried like a baby. "My daughter, my daughter," he croaked. Lena had never seen Carlo weep like this and she couldn't hold back either. They wept in each other's arms. In his heart, Carlo vowed vengeance.

***

They arrived at Gooma Nancy's house. Vinnie looked at it. "Nice house," he said. "Who owns it, Gooma Nancy or her son?"

"I don't know. I guess you have to ask Mama."

"Are you scared, Lorraine?" asked Joe.

"No. Yes. I don't know. Oh, that must be Gooma Nancy at the door. Isn't she sweet looking?"

"Yeah, she does look sweet. Okay, I'll get the luggage," Vinnie said.

"Thanks, Vinnie."

Gooma Nancy came down the few steps from the porch and had her arms extended in welcome. "Hello, Lorraine. I'm so happy to see you. I haven't seen you since you were a little girl. How beautiful you are! How are you?"

"Hello, Gooma Nancy. I'm happy to see you, too."

"Hello, Gooma Nancy." Vinnie said. Joe said the same.

"Which brother is which, Lorraine?"

"This is my brother, Vinnie, the oldest. And this is my brother, Joe, the youngest."

"Hello, Vinnie and Joe. You're as handsome as your father. Come in, come in. It's still cold. How are Lena and Carlo? I haven't seen them in such a long time."

Vinnie answered because Lorraine seemed to be losing her breath.

"Oh, they're both fine, Gooma Nancy, and they send you their love and regards."

"Oh, thank you and send them mine, too. Oh, here's my son, Gabe, and his wife, Ida. Gabe, Ida, this is Lorraine and her brothers, Vinnie and Joe." They all shook hands and Lorraine was the recipient of many kisses. She felt better after this warm welcome.

Gooma Nancy asked them all to sit down and was about to make coffee but Vinnie begged off, saying he and Joe had to get back to work.

"Oh, don't tell me you work on Saturday, too." Gooma Nancy said.

"Well, we don't, but my brother and I are allowed to work in a space provided by our employer; we fix old cars. We do it for experience and learn from old wrecks because we want to open our own shop: The Brothers Martini, we fix wrecks."

"Of which I am one." Lorraine almost bitterly said, and instantly she regretted her remark.

Gooma Nancy looked at her, smiled and said, "Nah, nah, Lorraine, we don't want to hear that kind of talk. You're gonna be fine and we want you to be happy. Well," she turned to Vinnie, "I'm sorry you can't stay for coffee. Please give your parents my best regards. I'll show Lorraine around the house so she can be familiar; that's what I want for her."

Vinnie had a lump in his throat, he croaked, "Thanks, Gooma Nancy. I can't tell you how much we appreciate what you're doing for my sister. She's a good girl and never gave us any cause to worry."

He and Joe leaned down, because Gooma Nancy was short, and they gave her a hug and kiss and said goodbye to all of them, thanking them profusely. Then Vinnie went first to their sister, hugged her and whispered, "Lorraine, take care of yourself and don't worry about anything. We'll talk often on the phone and if you need anything, let me know." He held her closely and kissed her. When it was Joe's turn, he, too, told her not to worry. She could detect their troubled breathing and was affected by it.

The brothers turned quickly and left them. They didn't want anyone to see their tears. Yeah, they were big strong guys but they were Italian brothers who knew they had the best sister, who was suffering because of some rich, spoiled rotten guy.

Lorraine went to the door and watched him enter the car. They waved to one another. She felt lonely, almost deserted. *I hate Walter. I hate Walter.* She watched as her brother's car disappeared around the corner.

Wise Gooma Nancy noticed and understood. She came to Lorraine, put her arm through Lorraine's arm and said, "Sweetie, let's go upstairs to your room. My son will bring your luggage; don't you even try to carry them upstairs. Come on. My daughter-in-law is going to make veal cutlet parmigiana for dinner tonight. Do you like that?"

"Yes," Lorraine replied weakly, shyly.

"Ida is a good cook. I don't tell her that because she'll get very conceited and think she cooks better than I do. So, I tell her she'll never learn to cook the way I do. Or even her mother! Eh, Ida?"

"Whatever you say, Ma." And they all laughed.

Everyone was upstairs; Gabe had brought the luggage upstairs and left the room. Too many females congregated in one place scared him. The ladies teased him about it and he laughed on the way downstairs, glad to be away from them.

Ida said, "Lorraine, this is or was my son, Steve's room. He recently married. I don't know if my mother-in-law told you."

"Yes, I did. I assured her she'll have plenty of privacy. Lorraine, you can have the run of the house. We have a lot of books, if you like to read and we have a nice record collection. I have my own private collection of opera, which I keep separate from 'their' hands because they don't appreciate good music." And she laughed. "Do you like opera?"

"Well, I never really—I never really listened to it. I guess I could learn," she said quietly and shyly.

"Well, whenever you want to listen, we'll listen together and I'll tell you the stories…very lovely, very 'womantic'." And she smiled at Lorraine.

Ida, who had gone downstairs, called, "Ma, coffee's done. I've set the table. Come on down."

"We'll be right down, honey." Gooma Nancy shouted. She turned to Lorraine. "Ida is really a wonderful person and we love each other like mother and daughter. Her mother is gone and I miss her, she used to be my good friend. Ah, well, that's what happens. Come on down, sweetie, Ida made a very tasty pound cake for dessert. We'll have lunch first."

Lorraine followed, shyly and quietly. She was beginning to have second thoughts but she knew she could not stay in Astoria with a growing belly and no wedding ring. She felt miserable. She sat obediently at the table, ate sparingly, drank coffee but couldn't put Ida's delicious cake in her mouth. "Please excuse me for not eating the cake, which looks delicious. I just can't eat another thing now."

"That's okay, honey, pregnant women sometimes have eating problems. Don't worry about it, the cake will wait. I am not one of those old fashion fools who think an expectant mother should eat everything in sight and if she doesn't the baby will be born with a birth mark. I don't believe in those old fashion superstitions, which I call 'stupidstitions'."

Lorraine smiled, "I never even thought of that, Gooma Nancy."

Gooma Nancy chuckled, "When I was pregnant, I had to fight off all the fools who wanted to feed me. I would have been as big as a house if I had listened to them. I made many enemies but I didn't care. I don't take orders from fools. After the baby was born and there were no birth marks, they all became my friends again, but still, many were disappointed that my children weren't born with a 'mark', as they called it."

They passed a pleasant time and after lunch, Gooma Nancy perceived that Lorraine needed a nap and she insisted Larraine go upstairs. Lorraine obeyed; she went upstairs and entered Steve's room. She felt very strange to be in this room. There were still many things that belonged to Steve evident in the room. She went to the bed and pulled the blankets down and noticed that the bed had clean sheets. "Wonderful." She it said aloud, and then looked around in fear as though someone had heard her. She removed her shoes and lay down and fell asleep instantly.

Walter came to her and tried to take her in his arms and said, "Lorraine, honey, I love you and I miss you. Why don't you answer my phone calls?"

Lorraine said, "Walter, you don't love me and you're afraid of your mother. And your mother is a liar. And I don't want to have anything to do with you. This baby is mine. I love you." And she wondered how she could be so stupid as to tell Walter she loved him. Then she woke up, looking around a strange room, she almost fell off the bed in an effort to get out of a strange bed quickly. Then she remembered where she was and settled down. She was gratified that it just a dream, or was it a nightmare or a daymare, since it wasn't night?

She noticed a phone on the night table and she was tempted to call her brothers to come back and get her. Then she remembered why she was there; to hide. *A circus tent won't be big enough to hide my belly! The busybodies would know, they could tell. My family would be dishonored because Walter raped me. And who would believe me that he raped me. Oh, I hate Walter. She rubbed her belly as though she were caressing her baby.* And she was.

Chapter Twelve

Each day, Lorraine was feeling more comfortable and at ease. She kept the bedroom clean. She helped in the housecleaning whenever she could. Lena called almost daily and Lorraine felt regret that her mother felt sad and left out of a most important part of her life. After all, Lena is the grandmother, *la nonna,* of this baby. This is a time when a daughter, who would soon be a mother, should be close to her own mother. This was blamed on Walter and the more Lorraine thought of it; the more she despised Walter for cheating her out of another important and happy event in her life; one her own wedding and now this, the pregnancy of her first child.

Gooma Nancy and Lorraine, when they were alone one evening having dinner, asked Lorraine some pertinent questions.

Lorraine felt comfortable telling her of the rape. "But, Walter must know. It's his right. He must take care of you financially and in other ways."

"Gooma Nancy," Lorraine said firmly, "I do not want Walter to know anything about me or the baby. He has no rights. He raped me. Nobody will believe me when I say that."

"But, how do you know?"

"He comes from a prominent family. They're filthy rich and I will be accused of seducing him rather than the other way around, which is the truth. They consider us low class no class. They will probably say I want money from them, which I don't. I won't be ridiculed by his lying mother. I despise all of them."

"Ah, I see." And she looked at Lorraine with her thoughts swirling around her head. "I admire you, Lorraine, you haven't let this boy disgrace you or put you in a weepy position. You haven't allowed him to kill your spirit. You are strong. I like that. Stay that way! Well, what will you do with your life?"

"Well, I was thinking of taking some night classes at the community college. I have no idea what I'll study but once I get there, I'll see what they have to offer."

"Excellent. I have a suggestion and you think about it and if doesn't appeal to you, you can do something else. Studying Real Estate and Insurance may be a good idea for you. You don't want to give up your baby. When he's old enough, your Mom can watch him and you can open a small office. At first, of course, it will be difficult but if you persevere, you will be successful and independent, you'll make money and support yourself and your baby, and that's what you want. Live with your parents; I'm sure that would be what they want. The baby will grow up in familiar surroundings, loving surroundings, which is important for a child. He or she will have the love of your parents and your brothers. That's important. Family is important."

Lorraine smiled, "Ah, Mama said you were wise. And I remember seeing storefront offices like that in our neighborhood. Yes, that sounds like good advice; I'll do that. I also have to begin seeing an obstetrician."

"Yes, that's most important. Ida probably knows one. Oh, yeah, we'll ask my granddaughter, Gloria. She's pregnant. Oh, you'll love her when you meet her. She's beautiful like me." She laughed out loud. "Oh, I'm so conceited! Hey, I don't care; when you get into your eighties you can say all sorts of outrageous things."

"Gooma Nancy, I think you're wonderful and beautiful, too. I feel better already. Thank you for making me feel comfortable. I really appreciate that."

"It's my pleasure. Now, you'll have to excuse me. I want to shower and get into my bed. You can stay up as late as you wish; watch TV or read. Okay?"

Lorraine nodded and smiled. Gooma Nancy kissed

her and left. Lorraine was alone in the living room and the phone rang. She looked toward Gooma Nancy but she was already in the bathroom and Lorraine didn't know if she should answer the phone or not. She decided to answer and take a message.

"Hello?"

"Hello, Lorraine?"

Lorraine was puzzled; this was an unfamiliar male voice and how did he know she was here? "Yes, who's calling please?"

"It's me, Paul. How are you?"

"Paul! How did you know where to call me?"

"Now, Lorraine, don't get mad; don't lose your temper. I begged Vinnie to give me your number and when I told him we're good friends, he finally gave me the number. Is it all right if I call you sometimes; you know, just to talk, to be friends, which is what we are?"

"Well—well—I don't know Paul. This is a long distance call and maybe we shouldn't—because I—I—I haven't seen you in a while."

"That doesn't negate our friendship, Lorraine. Maybe I could come out to see you sometime. How does that sound?"

Lorraine was twisting the phone wire around her finger, thinking of what she could tell Paul, without giving him too much information. She wasn't going to tell him about her bulge. She was quiet, thinking of words to say.

"I could come out there this Sunday and we could go to dinner. Vinnie said you're a helper and thinks you have Sunday's free. Do you?"

"Paul, I really don't think it's a good idea." There was silence on the other end and Lorraine wanted to scream because she'd hurt her friend.

"Okay," a subdued Paul said, "maybe we could make it another time. I miss our talks, Lorraine. Don't think that because you're out there, you're impossible to visit. Okay? It's really not that far." His voice had become tender and sweet as though he knew but how could he know, her family had taken a vow and they wouldn't betray her, no matter what!

Softly, Lorraine said, "Okay, Paul. We'll make it another time. Thanks for calling. Take care. Goodbye."

Paul, throat constricted, said a husky, "Bye."

Lorraine hung up the phone covered her face and held back the tears. She'd hurt Paul and she hadn't meant to do so; she was saving herself the hard job of telling Paul about her misfortune and she didn't know how Paul would take it. She didn't want to tell Paul she was raped; it sounded so awful and a lot of people thought a rape could be prevented. Maybe he would think that. Her family knowing was enough. The more people who know a secret makes it not a secret. But Paul was nice and, yes, they were friends but this was difficult to tell him.

She went upstairs, decided to take a shower and go to bed. She brushed her teeth and when she had rinsed her mouth, she looked in the mirror for a moment. Then she said aloud, "You freckle faced fool!" In the shower she scrubbed herself as though she could scrub Walter out of her system and her mind. He was already out of her heart because he had caused so much unhappiness to her and her family; and Lorraine knew he didn't and never had loved her. For some reason, Lorraine was more concerned for her father than any other family member; he must always love and respect and accept her; if he didn't she would not be able to live. And she could see and feel how much he had been hurt by this situation. Maybe not taking revenge hurt more than taking revenge. But, that wasn't a good idea; there was trouble with the law to think about. No, it's better that they remained quiet.

In the following days, Lorraine had investigated the

local community college and found they offered a course in real estate. She would also take several other courses which would help her in her new career. Only one problem existed. There was no public transportation in Garden Square. What could she do? What a question for a girl with two brothers who were excellent mechanics. She decided to call them.

She called and Vinnie answered the phone. “Vinnie,” she said, “call me back immediately. I don’t want this call to be on Gooma Nancy’s son’s phone.”

Vinnie called back immediately. “Vinnie, how are Mama and Dad and you and Joe?”

“We’re all fine. Missing you. How are you?”

“I’m fine. I miss you all, too. I have a problem.”

Vinnie became frightened. “I’ll come there right away.”

“No, it’s not that type of problem. I’m gonna go to the community college and there’s no public transportation like in Astoria. Luckily, you guys taught me how to drive and I have a license but now I need a car. It doesn’t have to be new, just serviceable.”

“Well, that’s great. Joe and I have just the car. It’s a Chevy Bel Air which we bought very cheap because it was really messed up. We worked on the motor, gave it a new paint job and now it runs smoothly. It looks great now.”

“Oh, wonderful. Listen, I know you guys put out some cash for it and I will owe you. Can you wait for the money?”

“Agh, you don’t have to pay us. Just go to school and learn a lot. I’m so damn proud of you. You didn’t let a shit, oh, excuse me, like Walter knock you on your ass. Oh, again, excuse me.”

She laughed. “Vinnie, I needed that laugh. But tell me, how and when can you get the car here?”

“How about tomorrow?”

"Oh, that's wonderful. Oh, um, Vinnie," she said in a low voice, "Paul called me and said you gave him this number."

"Yeah? Was it all right? He really pestered me and he really wanted to speak to you."

"Did you tell him anything else?"

"No. I thought you would take care of it. Whatever you want me to tell him, I will. He's really concerned about you, Lorraine. I think he—"

"Vinnie, I haven't told him anything and I won't. He's my friend but that doesn't mean I have to tell him everything. I don't know what he'll think of me."

"He regards you very highly."

"I—I—think I know that but who knows what he'll think when he finds out I'm—I'm—"

"Believe me; I don't think you have to worry about that. And we haven't told him anything. That's completely up to you, Lorraine. Do you need anything?"

"Just the car and love from all of you. I miss you all, Vinnie, especially Dad. How is he?"

"Dad is Dad. He's very worried about you but we talk to him and he becomes quiet. I think he'll be okay. He misses you, too."

"Bye, Vinnie." Lorraine could speak no more. She was determined now more than ever to be successful, to keep her baby and to move back into her parent's home. And she would get a diploma or a certificate in Real Estate; whatever it took, she would do it.

Vinnie felt Lorraine's hurt. The first moment he could speak to Joe in private, they would make their plans.

Vinnie quickly told the family about the call and they were all happy about Lorraine's decision; it was a step in the right direction. She could have moaned and groaned but she was standing on her two feet making plans for herself and her baby. But that didn't surprise them; they knew Lorraine was a strong person.

Vinnie and Joe would prepare the proper papers for the car; they wanted to put the car in Lorraine's name; get her insurance and complete any other items that they could do for her.

Lorraine was convinced that Gooma Nancy was a wise woman. What Lorraine didn't know was that Gooma Nancy was also excellent match maker and she had Lorraine on her mind for her next "job," which due to the circumstances would be difficult. No Italian boy could bring an unmarried mother to his mother as a prospective bride. An eruption from Mount Vesuvius would be nothing in comparison to an *Italian Mamma.*

Vinnie and Joe delivered the car as promised. They were overjoyed to see their sister. They tried not to look at her obvious bulge; they were shy, but they realized that that little bulge was their nephew or niece. Lorraine was very pleased to see her brothers and the car and immediately jumped in to test drive it. Ah, her brothers were magicians; they had transformed an almost total wreck into the shiniest, smoothest running chariot. They gave her many kisses and hugs and much encouragement. They also gave her some money their father insisted the brothers be sure to give her.

When Paul had accidentally heard of their trip to bring Lorraine the car, he wanted to accompany them. But the brothers absolutely refused to let him come. They told him Lorraine could not have any visitors at this time and he was mollified. They would not do anything to anger their sister in this delicate predicament. They knew that Paul was in love with Lorraine. Vinnie and Joe knew it; everybody in the world knew it except Lorraine. But Lorraine was right, what would Paul think and do?

The brothers left shortly after delivering the car. Their parting was still sad and uncomfortable. They promised to call every day. Vinnie said, "We won't tell Paul anything but I'm sure he'll want to call you again. Maybe it's best that you tell him how busy you are, ya know, with school and all. Lorraine, please take care of yourself and the baby; our nephew or niece." He blinked his eyes to keep them dry.

"Yeah," said Joe, "we're gonna teach him how to play baseball."

Lorraine hugged and kissed her brothers, smiling at their words and thanking them profusely and sending love and kisses to their parents. As Vinnie and Joe drove away, she kept her eyes on them, one hand on her swelling belly and raised her other hand in an affectionate wave. They also waved back.

***

Lorraine was thrilled with the car and when she saw Gooma Nancy, who wasn't home at the time of the delivery, she almost danced and then offered to take her for a ride. Gooma Nancy accepted and they went to the store to buy some fruit. Gooma Nancy was pleased with Lorraine's happiness and ambition. She knew Lorraine would survive and persevere. Gabe and Ida also were glad for Lorraine.

In a few weeks, Lorraine had started the community college, made an appointment with the obstetrician and gotten a part time job. She was happy; learning and making money. It wasn't a lot of money, but she was able to offer some money for her room and board but it was refused. That's how she learned her parents sent a monthly check to Gooma Nancy, which she handed over to Gabe, who handed it over to his wife. What a good husband.

Her pregnancy progressed nicely; the baby kicked when he or she was supposed to. Gooma Nancy kept a sharp eye on Lorraine to be sure that she was happy and content. What was the statement from the famous dairy company? Contented cows make the best milk!

"Lorraine, I never asked you before; maybe it's none of my business, but what are your plans for the baby?"

"Oh, I guess we'll go back to my parents' house. I miss them and my brothers so much. Remember, you advised me to live with my parents. I guess it's a good idea for many reasons."

"Oh, I meant, the baby, without a father, do you want to—to keep it or—"

Lorraine's eyes opened wide. "Of course! I never thought about anything else but keeping my baby and raising him or her myself. I would never give him or her up for adoption, if that's what you're thinking. This baby is mine. MINE." Her eyes were fierce and she breathed heavily.

"Lorraine, please, I didn't mean to upset you. Please be calm. I'm glad to hear you say that. Many times, girls have no idea as to what to do with their babies, ya know, because—because of the circumstances. But, I'm glad you're so sensible."

"I plan to raise him myself. This is the only good thing that's come out of this relationship—if that's what I can call it. I never thought Walter would betray me or—or—"

"I know, I know. It isn't like the old days in Italy, where a poor girl was left in the family way and when her baby was born; she wrapped him up, put him in a basket and went to the local convent, rang the bell and hid behind a tree to make sure the nun who answered the door took the baby in."

"Is that true, Gooma Nancy?"

"Well, that's what people said. And it probably is or was true. After all, there was no local orphanage where these girls could deposit their babies anonymously. Sometimes life was tough in the old days."

"Well, even now, it's tough." Lorraine said thoughtfully, "Where can a girl put her baby up for adoption if she needs to do so? A better question is: how can she?" And she shook her shoulders, showing it was a horrible thought.

"There are agencies that take care of that kind of stuff." Then changing the subject, she said, "Come on, Lorraine, Ida is not home. We'll make dinner. Ida left a chicken in the fridge. Let's do something good with it."

And like two sisters, they began to cook. In this way, Lorraine learned cooking from Gooma Nancy, among other things. She learned to accept her situation with more ease. When she spoke to her mother, Lena could detect the change in Lorraine's demeanor and she was grateful.

***

At the Martini house, all they talked about was when Lorraine would come home. She'd been away for four months; she'd reached six months of her pregnancy. Carlo had never ceased to mention Walter's name with threats and curses following. His sons urged him to calm down and not think of seeking revenge. It would have brought so much trouble down on their heads since assault and battery were against the law. But, Carlo told them, "In my country, it would be okay if I beat up or killed Walter. Anyway, the police would not go out of their way; they weren't like the American police. He has brought dishonor to my daughter and to the rest of the family. Who will marry my daughter now? She's not married and is going to have a baby, an illegitimate baby! Walter deserves to die." And each time he said, "kill" or "die," his fist would come down hard on the table. And when he mentioned Walter's name, he cursed a blue streak!

When this happened, Lena would try to calm Carlo, but to no avail. He was bent on revenge. Vinnie and Joe looked at each other, knowing they would have to keep an eye on their father. Carlo was built like a tank. Walter was built like a weed. There would be no question as to who would be the victor in such an encounter.

Frequently Carlo would heave a nervous sigh, look at Lena and say, "When is Lorraine coming home? She is gone a long time. I want to see my daughter."

Lena would look despairingly at Carlo and say as softly and as calmly as she could, "Carlo, honey, she'll be back after she gives birth. It's only a few more months and she and the baby will be home with us. I know, I can't wait either. I miss her so." And a sob caught in her throat. Carlo would hold her hand.

Some air expelled from his mouth; he was impatient to see his daughter. He never stopped thinking about her; how she must be suffering away from her family and being pregnant and not married. His rage against Walter was worrisome at times.

At these times, when Vinnie and Joe witnessed their father's impatience, anger, hurt, and concern, they looked at each other, thinking the same idea.

***

In the Society Notes pages of the newspapers, there was an announcement that Vinnie and Joe had been waiting for; it was very interesting. It announced the Bachelor Party for Mr. Walter Hadley, the day, the time, and place. It was to take place the day before his wedding. An address was printed. Joe clipped it and put it in his pocket.

When he saw Vinnie later in the day, he said, "It's time."

Vinnie flashed a lopsided smile. "Excellent." He pounded his right fist into his left palm.

Late on the night of Walter's bachelor party, two young men dressed themselves identically in black from head to toe. They waited patiently in their black car across the street from the restaurant where Walter's bachelor party was taking place. It was close to three in the morning when slowly, Walter's drunken friends were exiting the building. There was much shouting, laughing and ribald jokes. Finally, Walter and a friend were the last ones to leave.

From nowhere, two black figures appeared. One punched Walter's friend and put him out of commission. Then the two black figures pulled a struggling, puzzled Walter into the alley and beat the shit out of him. They never said a word. Walter tried to tell them who he was, who his father was, and they would get into a lot of trouble. The assaulters never uttered a sound. They had blackened his eyes, punched some teeth out, and broke his nose. Blood dripped down his face and on to his rumpled shirt. Walter was left on the ground, unconscious. The two black clad figures completed their job in five minutes. They walked to their car and drove slowly away.

A short time later, a chef exited the side door and saw Walter's limp, bloody unconscious figure. He ran back inside and called the police who arrived within minutes. By this time, Walter had regained his senses and was a bit groggy. Slowly, he recalled what happened. His friend, who had been left in the front of the restaurant, hearing and seeing the police, struggled to follow them down the alley. He was shocked at Walter's appearance and asked, "Walter, who did this to you?"

Walter couldn't answer.

A police officer asked him questions; what his name was and what was he doing in this neighborhood at this hour.

Walter replied, as quickly as he could, "My name is Walter Hadley and I was attending a bachelor party for me with my friends at Gino's Restaurant. Henry, here, and I came out and suddenly," Walter, still a bit stunned, said, "there were five guys all dressed in black who jumped me. I don't know who they were. They never spoke to me, just kept hitting me. I tried to get them to stop. I know I hit one or two of them really hard. I think I broke someone's jaw."

One officer asked, "Were you conscious when they left you? Did you see which way they went?"

A piteous Walter said, "No, officer, I'm sorry. I was unconscious when they left."

"Okay," the officer said, "we'll take you to the hospital."

Walter became concerned, "No, that won't be necessary."

"Sir, you're in need of medical attention and we have to file a police report."

"No!" Walter said, "I'll go home. Someone's there who could take care of me."

"Sir, are you sure you have no idea who did this to you? Do you have any enemies?"

"No, none. Thank you, officer, I'll go home now."

"Sorry, we can't let you drive in your condition. You're a bit drunk."

"But—"

The officers put both Walter and Henry in the back seat and proceeded to drive them home. Walter and Henry were grumbling all the way. They took Walter home first. When he entered his home, as quietly as he could, he walked toward the stairs. At the top stood his mother who screamed at the sight of her bloody son. Walter, Sr. soon came running. In no time, Mrs. Hadley had made a crude diagnosis and called an ambulance. The parents followed the ambulance to the hospital, where Walter was treated and released against the wishes of the ER doctor. He had a broken nose, blackened eyes and several teeth were missing and multiple abrasions where his face had hit the concrete. He wasn't pretty!

It was now Walter's wedding day!

Chapter Thirteen

"We'll have to postpone the wedding, Son." Mrs. Hadley said, looking at Walter's bruised, swollen and bandaged face. "You can't get married looking like that."

"No, Mother, I will not postpone the wedding. A little ice will bring down the swelling."

"But, what will we tell people?"

"Well, we'll just tell them the truth; I was maliciously attacked by some persons unknown."

"Are you certain you don't know who these six attackers are?"

"Yes, Mother, I'm sure I don't know who they are, and there were seven attackers!" Walter answered impatiently.

"I'm sorry, dear, I just want to have them arrested and brought to justice."

"Well, it was dark, they were all wearing black clothes, I was drunk and I couldn't see their faces. They spoke a foreign language. Besides the officers who came got all the information I could give and that was that. They committed their deed and are off scot-free. They didn't rob me and I was glad of that. They didn't get the ring my fiancée gave me." He looked at his finger and there was the ring. "Please, Mother," he looked at his mother with pleading in his eyes and knew it would work, "let's forget all about it. I'll heal and the wedding pictures can be doctored up. I'm not going to change my plans."

Mrs. Hadley muttered under her breath. Mr. Hadley, Sr. simply looked on and listened. He patted his wife's hand and she barely looked at him; he was worthless to her.

They all trotted off to their beds to try to get a little sleep.

That afternoon at the wedding ceremony, everyone commiserated with Mr. and Mrs. Hadley and when most of the people saw Walter's beaten face, they were aghast. Many people urged them to call the police but Mr. and Mrs. Hadley assured them that they had already been called and all the records were at the precinct.

The bride was being escorted down the aisle by her step father, who was richer than her father. When her veil was lifted from her face and she saw Walter clearly, she gave a low cry.

"Wa…Walter, what happened to you? My mother told me you had an accident, but she—she didn't tell me you—you were so seriously hurt."

Walter took her hand, "Sh, don't talk now, dear. Let's get married."

Then they both looked at the minister, who was shocked at Walter's appearance but said nothing about it. He commenced the ceremony with dignity.

Walter tried to smile but the stitches to his lips constricted it to a smirk. He tried to reassure her he was fine. All she could do was stare at him throughout the ceremony. She thought, what a way to start a marriage! Luckily, Walter only had to repeat the words "I will," and the ceremony went off beautifully and they were pronounced man and wife. He kissed his bride gingerly because of his swollen, broken, stitched lips. She understood, but showed annoyance.

He thought of Lorraine.

At the reception, they drank to the good health of the bride and groom. Even during the dinner, Walter wondered who those seven guys were. They were stupid guys because Walter had a load of money in his pockets and none of it was touched.

Lorraine's beautiful face came in front of his eyes.

When the bride and groom retired to their hotel

room, Walter gave her to know that he wanted nothing to do with her. She was puzzled but not upset; he didn't look too attractive. In fact, he looked absolutely repulsive.

***

The following day, Sunday, at the Martini household, Carlo and Lena sat at the kitchen table drinking their espresso. They'd finished their breakfast and while they drank their coffee, Carlo read Il Progresso, the Italian language newspaper he bought every day.

Suddenly Carlo put his cup down. "Lena, get up. We go to get Lorraine. I cannot stand to be without my daughter another minute." He was breathing hard, his face was flushed. Lena knew he meant business.

Lena looked at Carlo, her eyes big with surprise. "But, Carlo, honey, we can't bring her home until—"

"NO," he shouted. "I don't care about what people say. To appease all the gossips and fools, we all must suffer? Nobody knows or cares how I suffer without my daughter, my innocent daughter. She's my daughter and she should be with me and you. Come on. We go to get her now!" He was breathing heavily and his fists opened and closed, his face showed determination. Lena knew it was time to move. She called her sons.

"Vinnie. Joe. Come here. Dad and I want to talk to you." Even before she had finished speaking, by the unusual tone in her voice, they were in the kitchen, waiting to hear.

"Boys, Dad wants to go get Lorraine. Right now."

Vinnie said, "Well, it's about time."

Joe said, "I was wondering how long it would take you to make up your mind, Dad."

"It's made up. We go now! *Andiamo.*" A happy look of anticipation filled his face.

"Wait," said Lena, "I'll call her and let her know. She can pack her things. Oh, I'm so happy; I'll see my daughter in my own home, where she belongs. Let's go!" But first she called Lorraine, who was surprised and happy about the announcement. She quickly got herself ready.

They left in one car, knowing they had to bring Lorraine's car home. They were sure there were things that Lorraine had accumulated and needed to be transported and one brother would drive it home.

They arrived in Garden Square in forty-five minutes instead of the usual sixty minutes. They descended on the Dolce household like the cavalry. In fact, Joe was singing "Ta ta ta ra ta ta ta," the cavalry song they used to see in the old cowboy and Indians movies. This caused some lightness in the family, though they really didn't need it. They were going to get Lorraine!

Gooma Nancy answered the door, glad to see all of them, she invited them in. They all entered respectfully because Gooma Nancy had been an angel in the storm and they loved her. Lorraine was up in her room, still packing and happy as a lark that her family had come to bring her home; they rescued her.

Lena stuttered, "Gooma—Gooma Nancy, we—we—well, we came—"

Carlo spoke like a gentleman and a father. "Gooma Nancy, we appreciate all you and your family have done for us and our beloved daughter. And we do not intend to offend you or insult you in any way. But, we have made a decision; I have made a decision. Our daughter should be home with us." He stood tall. "She is my daughter. She belongs with me and her mother and her brothers."

Gooma Nancy understood and smiled. "Yes, she does."

It was at that moment Lorraine had come down and heard what her father said. "Oh, Dad. Ma." She ran to her father and embraced him, keeping her eyes closed in order to stem the flow of tears. It didn't help. She knew he loved her and had forgiven her, though she was innocent of blame, she still felt guilty. Now she felt loved and forgiven.

"Lorraine, *figlia mia, figlia mia.* My daughter, my daughter." Carlo held his daughter gently but firmly as he was acutely aware of her growing belly. *Carissima figlia, torni da noi.* Return to us. We love you. I cannot stay another day without you. Come home!" He closed his eyes and pressed his face to hers.

"Dad, Dad, I missed you so much. I missed you, too, Ma. I—I'm so happy to see you. Vinnie, Joe, my wonderful brothers." She hugged and kissed them all, delirious with joy to see them and more so because they wanted her to come home. She turned to Gooma Nancy and said, "Gooma Nancy, you'll never know how much you've helped me." She went into Gooma Nancy's open arms and stayed there, held with such deep affection.

Gooma Nancy said, "Lorraine, you are a wonderful girl. You are fortunate that you have a loving family. If I had an available son, I would gladly urge him to marry you. I mean that."

Lorraine chuckled, "Gooma Nancy, you're wonderful and wise. I want to keep our relationship always. I have a great love and respect for you. I really do."

Gabe and Ida had witnessed all. Gabe smiled in understanding and Ida shed some tears. "Gee, I got so used to seeing that beautiful freckled face; I don't know what I'm gonna do now. She's great company for all of us."

Gabe and Gooma Nancy agreed. Then Vinnie and Joe decided they would retrieve all of Lorraine's belongings and pack them into the two cars.

There was a noisy farewell, hugs, kisses, thank yous, and remembrances of the past few months. Carlo, getting impatient, said, "*Beh, andiamo. Grazie, Gabriele, Ida e Gooma Nancy per tutto la vostra gentilezza.* Well, let us go. Thank you Gabe, Ida and Gooma Nancy for your kindness. You are all magnificent. Ciao and thank you again. If there is anything I can do for you, you just ask and it is yours. Goodbye." Again, hugs and handshakes.

Carlo couldn't wait for all of them to get into the cars and go. He insisted Lorraine sit in the rear of the car with him. He held her hand all the way home. He had his little girl back again. Carlo was one happy man.

Once back home, Vinnie and Joe brought all of Lorraine's things to her room. Lena prepared dinner. The chatter never stopped. The hugs and kisses to Lorraine went on and on. There was no doubt the family was happy about her return.

Lena asked, "Lorraine, I—I—want to ask and maybe I shouldn't but—but did any of them ever mistreat you?"

Lorraine looked at her mother with surprise in her eyes. "Gee, Ma, never. They are the best people; very kind, very gentle, very sincere. If they hadn't been, I would have been so miserable, I think I would have left there. But, no, they treated me like family. Gooma Nancy was like a grandmother to me. I thought of both my grandmothers, long dead and gone, and I said, if they had been alive, this is how they would be. So, I said a few prayers for the repose of theirs souls. Gooma Nancy took me to Mass with her every Sunday. Actually, they all went because the church is too far to walk and there are no buses, so Gabe had to drive us. Out of respect, I called them Uncle and Aunt. I think that pleased them."

Lena hugged her daughter, "Oh, Lorraine, it makes me so happy to hear that. You don't know how we missed you and how miserable we all were. Dad wanted to kill Walter. Every time, and this was every night, he spoke of it, cursing and threatening to kill Walter. Your brothers were able to control your father, I couldn't. Every night we prayed in front of the statue of *La Madonna* and the crucifix. One night your father said he saw tears in the eyes of the Lord. I didn't see them. But, I believe he did."

"Oh, Ma. I know how you feel. I want to kill Walter, too, but what would that accomplish? More trouble. Don't you think we have enough?"

Dinner was ready and they all sat to eat. It was like old times, except that Carlo wanted Lorraine to sit at his left. They took a long time to dine because they were all asking Lorraine questions.

After dinner, they were all in the living room, some watching TV and some reading the Sunday newspapers.

Vinnie spoke, "Hey, here's an article we'll all find interesting. It says here that one Walter Hadley was attacked by seven unknown thugs who left him unconscious with serious injuries as follows; a broken nose, two black eyes, broken lips and teeth missing. Gee, who would think something like that could happen?"

"What!" Lorraine said. "You're kidding. Let me see that." She attempted to rise from the soft sofa and had a bit of trouble.

"Wait," said Vinnie, "I'll bring the newspaper there. Stay where you are, okay?"

"Gee, who would do such a ghastly thing like that? That's so low class! Did they steal anything?" asked Joe, who smiled because the word "ghastly" was too…too uppity for him to use and he knew it wasn't lost on his brother.

"Nothing was stolen. It says so right here."

Lorraine looked around, puzzled. "My, who could have done this?"

Nobody answered her.

Both brothers looked at each other, suppressing smiles and covering their bruised hands.

Carlo looked at them, finding it very interesting. "That is what is really says?"

Vinnie looked at his father, now smiling broadly, "Yes, Dad, that's what it says. Who could have done such a fine thing for humanity?!"

Quietly, and very seriously, Joe said, "We'll never know."

Carlo looked at his sons with pride, "Somebody did our job for us."

Vinnie said, in all innocence, "Well, I hope these seven thugs did a good job."

Lorraine didn't make a further comment; she just wondered how Walter felt about getting his lumps.

Lorraine went into the den to call Lucy. "Hi, Lucy. It's me, Lorraine. How are you?"

"LORRAINE!! How happy I am to hear your voice! How are you?"

"I'm fine. I'm home. My family came to get me. They want me home. Isn't that wonderful?"

"Oh, yeah, that's great. So, now we can see each other."

"Yes, we can. I went to the Community College there. I'm sure my family told you all about my brothers bringing me a car so I could attend."

"Yes, Vinnie told me." Lucy became shy and smiled, "I don't know if you remember or not, but Vinnie and I are—are an item. We're going steady. We're in love." And she chuckled.

"Yes, I know and I'm very happy about it. Oh, Lucy, you should have seen the faces on them all when my father was telling them that I should be home with the family. I felt so happy."

"Of course. But—but what will you do now?"

"Well, I'll transfer to the college here and earn my certificate in Real Estate and Insurance. So, I'll see what I'll do. I'm due in about six weeks. I'm starting to feel nervous…well, not nervous, just something. I hope everything goes well. I'm going to change doctors. I need a local doctor and my obstetrician gave me the address of a few. All I have to do is choose. Lucy, I missed you and our good times."

"I missed you, too, Lorraine. I'm glad you're home. Vinnie is supposed to come here later and I'll ask him to take me to see you."

"Oh, that would be great. I have to go to go tinkle; hobby of the pregnant ladies, ya know. Bye."

"Oh, yeah, I remember my cousin, Annette, saying that all the time. Bye."

After her bathroom visit, Lorraine went into the living room again to watch TV. Carlo called to her to take a seat next to him. "Lorraine, I miss you a lot. Did you miss us?"

"Yes, Dad, I missed you all very much. Um, Dad, do you—um—forgive me?"

"But, *figlia mia,* my daughter, there is nothing to forgive. Yes, you disobeyed me when you went with Walter, I hate him, but he was not a gentleman and I cannot blame you. He made you drink and got you in a condition you are not used to. He's an unworthy character. I do not care how rich he is, he is a *merda,* a shit."

"Yes, Dad, I thought of that many times. And I felt guilty for the whole event. I never thought Walter would disgrace me. Now I see that he's as you say, an unworthy character. He's base and useless. I feel badly that the baby will have no father." Lorraine turned her face away in an effort to hide her concern. This is not how she envisioned her future.

Carlo took Lorraine's hand, and said gently, "Lorraine, *cara mia*, my dear, you must not feel badly the baby has no father. The father is a bad man. We will never speak of him to the baby. We, your brothers and I, will be fathers to your baby. I know it is not the same thing, but it is the best we can do. We have not stopped talking about it." Then he looked toward his sons, and said, "Vinnie, Joe, what were those packages you brought home the other day?"

"Oh, yeah, I forgot all about them." Vinnie said and smiled broadly.

Joe said, "Hey, yeah, I'll be right back."

And both brothers disappeared upstairs and in a few minutes came downstairs holding several packages each. They put them at Lorraine's feet. She knew the gifts were not for her, but for the little one she carried under her heart. She looked at her father and brothers, all smiles. She began opening the packages; one was a baseball glove, one was a baseball, one was a basketball, one was a package of marbles, and one was a New York Rangers hockey jersey.

Lorraine smiled and laughed, "But, what if it's a girl?"

Both brothers burst out, "No, it's gotta be a boy, we need a short stop."

The telephone rang and Vinnie answered it. "Hi, baby. Sure. Sure. I'll be right there. Bye." He turned to the family and smiled, "Well, I gotta go and pick up Lucy. She's dying to come here. Hey, what if I buy a cake and some ice cream? We gotta have a celebration."

Everyone agreed and out the door Vinnie went. "I'll be right back with my sweetie. Well, we might take a little longer; we gotta stop for kisses."

"Get out!" said Lena, in mock anger, "Stop for kisses! Whoever heard of such a thing?"

"Vinnie," said Joe, "can't you keep a secret? We don't want to hear such things. Don't forget, there's a baby present. You may think he can't hear but he can. Beat it!"

Very soon, Vinnie and Lucy returned, laden with a cake bought at the local bakery and ice cream. When the girls saw each other, they embraced, as gracefully as possible. "Oh, Lorraine, you look—look wonderful. How's the pregnancy going?"

"Oh, fine. I'm pretty good and so's the baby."

Lena rose from her chair and said, "Vinnie, come on, give me the cake and ice cream. I'll make coffee so we can have it with cake and ice cream we won't have to drink." She was in the kitchen in a flash.

Lorraine and Lucy walked arm in arm to the couch and sat down.

Lucy said, "Lorraine, did you see in the papers that Walter was attacked by seven thugs? He got what he deserved. That bastard!"

"Yes, Vinnie was reading it to us before. Yes, I agree, he got what deserved. Well, almost. He should have gotten more. I wonder who did this."

"Well, the newspapers didn't give names. That dope doesn't even know who did this. He must have a bunch of enemies if seven guys attacked him."

"Yeah," said Lorraine. "I only wish I could have given him a few kicks. He caused so much grief for me and my family. I thought I would have to stay on Long Island with Gooma Nancy and her family until after I gave birth. They were all so good to me but—but, it's not like being home with your family." She looked down because she was acutely aware that "family" didn't include a husband for her or a father for her baby.

Lucy felt for her friend and didn't know what to say, she held Lorraine's hand and said a quiet, "Don't worry. Things will turn out okay."

Lorraine looked into Lucy's beautiful brown eyes and saw the love and serenity that emanated and felt reassured, though she knew what her problem was and how long it would endure.

The telephone rang and Joe answered. He said, "Hold on a second." He turned to the family, covered the mouthpiece and said quietly, "It's Paul. What do I say?"

Lorraine looked pointedly at her brother and said firmly, "Tell him to come over."

Joe looked at her for a moment, and then returned to the phone. "Paul, why don't you come over? We're about to have cake and ice cream. Make if fast before the ice cream melts. Okay, great."

After hanging up, Joe said, "Lorraine, are you sure you—"

"Yes," Lorraine said, firmly. "Paul is my friend and he has to know sooner or later and I prefer that he knows from me. So," she sighed because the baby sometimes made breathing a little labored, "either he'll run like hell or he'll stay and be a glutton like the rest of us and remain my friend."

Joe looked at her, "Lorraine, Paul is a good friend to all of us. He's a good guy and I'm proud to know him."

A little while later, they were in the kitchen making a lot of noise setting the table. The ladies would not let Lorraine do anything since her feet were swollen. Then the doorbell rang. They all looked at Lorraine as though awaiting orders. She gave one.

"I'll answer the door."

Vinnie and Joe stood up, not to stop her but to offer their services. "You guys sit down. It'll be okay. Please stay where you are, all of you. Thanks."

She went to the front door and opened it, not too fast, not too slow. It was Paul. At first, his face was full of surprised delight. Then he saw her large, full belly. She was dressed in a dark maternity outfit. His face fell. It was as though he received a punch in the face.

"A gift from Walter." Lorraine said quietly and looked away.

Paul took a breath in. His puzzled look changed to understanding. Now he understood why Vinnie and Joe declined to take him to see Lorraine on Long Island; why they didn't speak of her. Then he took her in his arms and held her, not saying a word, just breathing, breaths that caught in his throat. She felt his hands, around her back, trembling. This made her cry.

When Paul was able to speak, he said, "Don't cry, darling. Lorraine, I'm so happy to see you. You look—you look wonderful. Don't cry, please honey, don't cry."

They remained in their sweet embrace for a few minutes. They were quiet. Paul gave Lorraine his handkerchief and while she wiped her tears, he bent and took the other side of the hanky and wiped his face, each aware that they were sharing. Then they laughed.

In the kitchen, waiting, they all were sitting or standing around, apprehensively. Since they didn't hear loud voices or anything else that would make them worry, they began to move chairs, just to make noise to let Lorraine and Paul know that they were still there.

Lorraine placed the hanky in her pocket and took Paul's hand and said, "Come on, let's go into the kitchen before those gorillas eat all our cake and ice cream." They smiled at each other and entered the kitchen.

"Hello, everybody. How are you?" Paul said, and he shook hands with all the males and kissed Lena and Lucy. His eyes were filled with pleasure. It was then that Lena and Carlo knew that Paul loved their daughter. It was obvious that he had loved her for a long time. Would he still love her?

There was noisy bantering and laughs and everyone ate the delicious cake and ice cream. Although they finished their coffee, cake and ice cream everyone remained at the table. They remained there for a more than an hour, talking and laughing. It made Lorraine feel good. This is how a family should be; not like the Hadley family, afraid to talk or move. Oofa!!

Vinnie and Lucy decided to take a walk and left. Paul, happy that he had been invited to share in their celebration; and asked Lorraine if she would like to go for a short walk. Lorraine declined, claiming swollen feet. Paul said, "Okay, let's take a ride. It's a beautiful evening. We could go to Astoria Park and park near the river. We could even yell, 'ahoy' to the tugs floating by. Remember we used to do that when we were kids? What about it? We don't even have to get out of the car."

"Gee, that really sounds nice. Dad, Ma, Paul and I are going out to the park."

Carlo looked at his daughter with love and understanding. "Sure, you both go out and enjoy the park."

They all bid each other good evening and Paul promised to bring Lorraine home early.

Once in the car, Paul wanted to speak but kept his mouth closed. He didn't want to make Lorraine uncomfortable but there were certain things on his mind.

"Paul, I know you're wondering about me."

"Lorraine, you—you don't have to tell me anything. It's your business to tell anybody what you want and don't want them to know. I know you and trust you." He had a sincere look on his face, which Lorraine noted immediately and was grateful for.

"Paul, you're my friend and I know you know me and trust me, but as my good friend, I want you to know what happened. Because, you see, when people see me in my condition, they'll naturally think I'm—I'm a slut." She breathed deeply and became emotional. "And I'm not a slut! I'm—I'm a good girl; a good person. I have a strong character." She couldn't help making a noise with her mouth, which she covered quickly.

"Lorraine, honey, I know you're a good girl. Nobody could tell me otherwise." He took her left hand in his hands, gently and caressed it. "Lorraine, you're the best."

She looked down at her belly; her right hand went to her belly to caress the baby she knew and loved.

Paul found a place to park, almost under the Hellgate Bridge. He was quiet. Then he looked all around, waiting; waiting for what, he didn't know.

He turned and looked at her, taking her hand in his. "Lorraine, I think you know how I feel about you. I think the whole world knows and has known for a long time. I love you."

Lorraine looked quickly into Paul's brown eyes. What does she say; what does she do? "Paul, you've always been a good friend."

"I want to be more than a good friend."

"I'm not gonna ask you what you mean by that. I think I know. But I want you to know how I got this way. I didn't lure anyone or entice anyone. I was a stupid, innocent idiot and I hate myself for it but I have another one to think about." She looked down at her belly, took a deep breath.

"Last December, after not hearing from Walter for a few weeks and—and thinking we were finished, he called me and invited me to a New Year's Eve party. I was happy, thinking that he loved me as I loved him and we—we would really get married. You know, his parents didn't approve of me; I—I'm not from his class. Well, anyway, he took me to a friend's house; there were only young people, drunk and crazy. He gave me a—a drink and I told him I don't drink, but he said it was okay because it was a weak drink. I—I trusted him. I drank and drank. We danced and ate and drank. I—I—didn't realize how much I had drunk. I was giddy. I laughed. He took me upstairs to a bedroom and I passed out and while I was out, he—he—he raped me." She stopped to gain control of herself. Paul sat quietly listening intently, feeling the pain Lorraine was feeling now, telling him and remembering and reliving the event. He waited. He held her hand.

"I really had no remembrance of anything that transpired. I instinctively felt something was wrong. When I woke up, I was frightened. I asked him to take me home and he wanted me to stay longer. I told him my father would kill us both. He laughed; he doesn't have an Italian father so has no fear or understanding. He has no morals. I was afraid. I—I was afraid because I knew something had happened and I didn't know what. I never—never thought it could be such an awful thing. I never thought he would dishonor me. After that, I didn't hear from him at all. I found out I—I was pregnant. Then I read in the newspapers of his impending marriage to a rich girl; a very rich girl.

"I haven't gotten in touch with him to tell him about the baby. I don't want him to know; I absolutely do not want him to know about the baby. I'm firm on that. I don't want to ever see him again or have anything to do with my baby. It's MY baby! Not HIS!" She was passionate and had to stop talking for a moment. "I can only think of my baby now. I'm gonna open a Real Estate and Insurance office after I give birth. I don't know when, but that's my plan. I have a certificate from the community college. I have to be free and independent and support myself and my baby."

After Lorraine finished her narrative, she looked apprehensively at Paul.

Paul held her hand all the while and was very attentive. Her words had pierced his heart. He hurt for her. He began, softly and with much emotion, "Lorraine, that was a terrible experience for you to live through. But—but please remember, that doesn't diminish my love for you. Not in any way. Not at all. I wish I could do something to alleviate your hurt. I can only tell you that I hurt, too. I would kill Walter for you. I would do anything I could to help you."

"Paul, thank you for your kind words. But, some guys, it seems a mob of guys have taken care of Walter already. I hope they don't get in trouble. And thank you for wanting to take care of him, but he's not worth the trouble."

"Lorraine, marry me. I love you and I promise to take care of you and the baby. I'll treat the baby as if he were my own. I promise you that." His eyes penetrated her soul. She knew he was sincere.

Lorraine looked at Paul; she was speechless and turned away and put her hand to her mouth.

He waited for her to compose herself before she spoke.

She cleared her throat. "Paul, you've made me feel so wonderful. I haven't the words to tell you how I feel. I can only tell you I appreciate your offer of marriage and the love for my baby; but I can't do that to you. You don't deserve it. You deserve a virginal bride."

"No, Lorraine! Please consider it. I do love you. I want to be with you."

"Paul, can you imagine what your family would say when you tell them you're gonna marry a big-bellied girl? No Italian mother wants that for her son. I know that and so do you. Please, my good friend, don't say any more about it."

"Lorraine, I don't care what my family thinks. I only know that I love you. I've loved you forever." He took her in his arms and kissed her. She didn't struggle; she felt comfortable but had the nagging, gnawing feeling in the back of her head, about Italian mothers who want a virgin bride for their sons. She knew she wasn't marriageable anymore. Who would marry used goods?

She began to cry even while he kissed her. Then she said, "Paul, thank you but please be my friend. That's what I need more than anything else. Oh!"

Paul became anxious. "What is it Lorraine? Do you feel sick?"

"No, it's nothing. Probably a bit of gas. Would you please take me home?"

"Right away." He started the car and in a few minutes, Lorraine was home and after making sure she was all right, he drove away.

Lorraine kept thinking of his words. There was no one in the world like Paul. Why didn't she love him? Why couldn't she love him?

Chapter Fourteen

It was late August and Lorraine was huge. She thought surely she would have a fifty pound baby. She wasn't due for about three weeks. Suddenly, she noticed that the baby had shifted and she was carrying low. It was a Friday evening; the family had just finished dinner.

Lorraine didn't say anything to anyone. She wanted to be sure she wasn't having false labor. Contractions started. She still didn't say a word. It was close to eleven p.m. Contractions had started to get stronger and closer together. She was watching TV with her parents; her brothers were not at home. She began to time the contractions.

"Dad."

"Yes, sweetheart. You want something to eat?"

"No, Dad. It's time to go to the hospital. I've been timing the contractions and they're five minutes apart."

Carlo and Lena, who had been dozing, became fully awake. Carlo, nervous at first, took command of the situation because Lena was losing it. She rose from her chair and said, "We gotta call the doctor and see what he says. Maybe we should not go now. We have to be sure the contractions are not false. *Madonna santissima.*" She began to make the sign of the cross and pray.

Carlo looked at his daughter as she had just gotten herself out of the chair and had one hand on her huge belly, and saw that she was unusually calm and in control of the situation. It gave him courage. Carlo, as he had been instructed by Lorraine, went to her room and got her little bag, which she had kept packed and ready, said, "Everybody in the car, NOW!"

The ladies obeyed him, especially Lorraine, who was helped by Carlo, since she didn't want her "water" to break in the house, but she knew that action was not under her control. They were in the car and at the hospital in five minutes. He was listening to Lorraine moan at each contraction and he knew what the closeness of the contractions meant. His heart pinched. He parked near the Emergency Entrance. Carlo ran to get a wheel chair, and as he attempted to put Lorraine in the chair, she groaned. He waited for the contraction to pass, and then he put her in the chair and ran with her to the ER.

Lena shouted, "Carlo, be careful, don't let her fall!"

Once inside, he shouted, "My daughter is going to have a baby. Is there a doctor here to help her?"

Lorraine looked at her father and chuckled as her face reddened with embarrassment. "Dad, please don't shout. A nurse will be here soon."

"But, Lorraine, you are in pain and the baby wants to be born now. I know it. I know my grandson."

"Oh, Dad—ow."

"Don't worry, Lorraine, everything will be okay." He looked around nervously for Lena who was already at the nurse's desk, giving information. She'd become calm.

Lorraine was taken into a slot where the nurse took her temperature. Carlo came in there and said, "She doesn't have a fever. She's going to have a baby. Can't you see that? I know, I had three babies myself. Please, take her to the operating room now."

The nurse, smiled and patiently said, "Sir, please don't worry. We know what to do. I'll get the doctor right now but you must wait outside in the waiting room. You're not allowed in here."

"But, I am her father," Carlo said, angrily, bunching his fingers and bringing them to his large chest.

"I know," said the nurse, "that's why you must wait outside."

Carlo opened his mouth to protest. Lorraine, in the middle of her largest contraction, said, "Dad, please get the hell out of here!!"

In that moment, the ER doctor arrived, put on gloves and prepared to examine Lorraine. As he did so, he asked, "Who is this gentleman?"

The smiling nurse, who was familiar with the doctor's ways, said, "He's the patient's dad. He's not a doctor."

The doctor gazed at Carlo and said, "Sir, if you insist on staying here, you'll have to be sanitized. Take all your clothes off and throw them in that container. That's for contaminated items. Nurse, get the number 4 needle and inject him in the ass. Wait, he's a big guy, I think you'll need a larger needle; make that a number 6."

Carlo didn't wait to see what size needle number 4 was. He made a hasty exit.

The doctor and nurse smiled. Lorraine knew what they had done and said, "Thanks, you two bastards!" And there was another large contraction and the water bag burst. "Oh," said Lorraine.

As the doctor examined her he said, "It's a good thing you came now. Oops! Here comes that baby. Nurse, pay attention; stop chewing gum!"

The doctor smiled, "Now, just push a little. This baby knows when to be born. Ah, here comes the head. A few more pushes."

Lorraine moaned and pushed.

They all heard the baby cry.

The smiling doctor said, "Nurse, did you ever see such a beautiful baby?"

"Only when mine were born," she said laughing.

The doctor held up a gorgeous, pink, screaming baby boy and showed the naked baby to the mother. "He's a very healthy boy!"

Lorraine looked at him and agreed that he was the most beautiful baby in the world. She wept, "Give me my baby."

The nurse smiled and said, "You'll get your baby when I have finished giving him eye drops and cleaning him. Oh, what a bruiser he is! He's adorable."

Any new mother would love to hear these words.

While the nurse administered drops to his eyes and cleaned him, weighed him, and wrapped him, she said, "This guy's a little gorilla. He's eight pounds."

The doctor looked on and said, "Ya know, we charge extra for gorillas!" He smiled at Lorraine while he gave Lorraine a shot to make her rest. The nurse gave the baby to Lorraine. She took the baby gently, looked at him and said, "Hello, little one. Hello, little Carlo. You are so adorable. I love you."

She looked up at the doctor and the nurse, "I'm sorry I called you bastards…"

"Please, don't worry about that," said the nurse. "We're used to that. Sometimes we hear worse than that. Sometimes we're threatened."

The doctor looked down at the new mother's perspired face, at her red curls plastered to her forehead and said, "Hey, your old man was great. I've been punched by other guys. This was the easiest birth I've ever assisted. We just have to conclude this segment. Then we can call your parents and tell them they have a grandson." He put the finishing touches on the delivery. Lorraine was sleeping, from the effects of the shot received after delivering little Carlo.

A sleeping Lorraine and baby, who had been put in a bassinette were both wheeled to Lorraine's room.

When Carlo and Lena were informed they had an eight pound, twenty inch, healthy baby boy, they almost fainted. When they went in to see Lorraine, they couldn't even talk; all they could do was stutter. She was awake after a short nap.

Lorraine looked beautiful and happy. Her brow was wet with perspiration and she had red ringlets on her forehead. She smiled when she saw her parents. The baby was in a clear plastic sided bassinette close by and Lorraine gazed lovingly at her gorgeous son, who had red curls like his mother.

"Dad, Ma, it's a boy." She turned to her baby and said, "My little Carlo."

Big Carlo burst into tears. Lena, who had not stopped weeping, wept anew. They had never discussed Lorraine's desire for the baby's name. And Lorraine, herself, really had never even thought about it. When she heard it was a boy, the only name that came to her was her father's name. He would be known as Little Carlo in the family.

The nurses told Carlo and Lena they must leave as mother and son must sleep. She advised them to come at visiting hours during the day.

Carlo said, "But, we just got here. We want to see the baby again. And my daughter, too."

The nurse smiled, "No, sir, you have to leave. Come back this afternoon. Goodnight."

Carlo, his chest bursting through his shirt, took Lena by the hand and said, "*Beh, andiamo, nonna.* Well, let us go, Grandmother."

Lena could only smile with great pleasure and they couldn't wait until they got home to tell their sons they were uncles to a fine healthy baby boy named Carlo.

Vinnie was the first one home and was surprised to see his parents awake at such a late hour. In a few minutes, Joe arrived home. Both boys asked what was wrong and where was Lorraine.

"Well," Carlo said, trying to be very calm and dignified, "your sister is in the hospital."

The boys became disturbed, "What's wrong?"

asked Joe. The brothers knew it was too early for the birth.

Vinnie said, "Let's go to the hospital now."

"No," said Carlo, "we cannot go until this afternoon at visiting hours."

Vinnie lost patience, "Dad! Tell us. What's going on?"

"Well, we have a little boy, no, a big boy and his name is Carlo."

The boys whooped and hollered. "How's the baby?" asked Vinnie.

"How's Lorraine?" asked Joe.

Lena said, "Mother and son are fine. Oh, boys, you should see that baby! He's so beautiful. A big hunk! He knows us; he smiled at us."

"Well," said Vinnie, "we got our shortstop!"

"*Ma che* shortstop!" growled Carlo, "he's going to be a concert violinist."

His sons fell all over each other laughing until they looked at their stern father's face.

"*Si, papa`, come dici tu,* yes, Dad, as you say." Then they all laughed, walked into the kitchen talking all at once.

Carlo said, "We just made it to the hospital and the baby was born. What a kid! Shoulder this wide." And he parted his hands at least three feet from each other.

Joe said, "Well, he's also a gorilla!"

"Ah," Lena said, "but what a beautiful gorilla. He has red hair like his mother. Oh, and me, too." And she strutted around the kitchen until her sons grabbed her and kissed her all over her freckled face.

Carlo, not to be left out, "He may have red hair like you and Lorraine, but he looks like me. He is built like me; like a Mack truck. My little violinist!"

His sons howled.

Just after dawn, it seemed, Vinnie and Joe went to

the florist and each bought the largest arrangement of flowers available and had them delivered. Then they went to the Sweet Shoppe and bought Lorraine chocolates, which they intended to help her eat.

That afternoon, they all went to visit Lorraine, with the chocolates; kisses from everybody to everybody. Then they went to the nursery to view the baby. On the bassinet, they saw a sign, "Baby boy, Martini." How proud they all were. The pediatric nurse saw them all looking at the baby and she went to pick him up and bring him to the glass partition. She held the baby up and loosened the blankets for the family to see the big bruiser.

"Man, look at those legs!" Vinnie said, admiration in his eyes.

Joe said, "Ya know, they look just like my legs!"

"Get outta there. Those are my legs." Vinnie said, as he gave his brother an elbow.

"You are both wrong," said Carlo. "Who's the soccer champ in this family?"

"Right, Dad," from both boys.

The baby began to cry and the nurse made a motion that he had to be changed. They left and went back to Lorraine's room. When they entered, she saw their big smiles. "A puny kid, no?"

"Are you kiddin'? He's the biggest baby there," Joe said.

"Yeah, he can take all those other little shrimps!" Vinnie said. A moment later he said, "Hey, I didn't even tell Lucy. I guess I better call her. I'll be right back." And he left to find a public phone to spread the good news.

While Carlo and Lena were whispering to each other, Joe talked in a low tone to his sister. "Lorraine, what if Paul calls? Should we tell him? I don't know if you want us to tell him or not."

"Yes, please tell him and give him my regards."

"Okay. Is there—like—what should I say; anything special?"

"No, Joe. Just tell him like it's a normal conversation. If he calls here, I'll tell him whatever. And thanks, you're a doll."

"I know." He took his sister's hand in his, smiled at her, and then looked away trying to stop his emotional tears.

More to change the subject, Lorraine said, "Ma, Dad, Joe, you should have seen little Carlo drink his milk this morning. All four ounces almost in one gulp. What a little piggy. Ma, you would be proud of him. And those burps; he really is a gorilla!" They all laughed. Lorraine laughed but there was a little sadness in her eyes, which her brother noticed. He squeezed her hand. She squeezed back, and then she said, "I'm a little sleepy. Do you mind if I doze off. But, please stay."

"Yeah, yeah, try to sleep," said Joe. "We'll be quiet." He kissed his sister's forehead.

But she slept heavily and they decided to come back in the evening.

Lorraine awakened for her dinner. Then they brought the baby in for her to feed. She held his little fingers to her lips and sang to him as he fed. He looked all around then burped and passed gas. Lorraine laughed and cried. "Oh, my little Carlo, we'll have so much fun that you and I won't miss your father, who is a total bastard and you will never meet."

Later the nurse came to take little Carlo back to the nursery and Lorraine rested, leaning back looking out the window, up at the ceiling, at the walls and at nothing. She heard soft footsteps in the hall and looked toward the door. It was Paul. He had a bouquet of flowers.

"Lorraine, are you awake?"

"Yes, Paul, I'm awake. How nice of you to come

visit me."

Paul kissed her on both cheeks. "Joe called me to let me know. Congratulations, Lorraine. I'm very happy for you. Did everything go well? Did you suffer? How's the baby?"

"Yes, everything went well. I didn't suffer and the baby is wonderful. Did you pass by the nursery and see him?"

"No, I came straight here. I—I wanted to see you—how you are. I'll go to see the baby now."

"Wait for me. I'll go with you."

"Are you allowed to get out of bed?"

"Sure, they want to you be on your feet as soon as possible. I've been lying in bed for more than twenty four hours. It's about time I get up. Could you please hand me my robe?"

Paul handed her the robe and then looked the other way, a lovely consideration which was not lost on Lorraine. He helped her out of bed.

"Ah, thank you. Let's go. My brothers are calling little Carlo a gorilla." And she laughed.

"You named him Carlo? That's wonderful, Lorraine. I'll bet your father is proud."

"Yes, he is. He didn't expect it. Neither did I. I just called the baby little Carlo so easily…I never even thought about it."

They were at the glass partition and the nurse saw them looking at little Carlo. She went to him and picked him up and brought him to the glass partition. She mouthed, "Is he the daddy?"

Both Lorraine and Paul looked embarrassed and uncomfortable. They just smiled and shook their heads gently. The nurse returned little Carlo to his bassinet and Lorraine and Paul walked slowly back to her room in a bit of an awkward silence.

Paul said, "Gee, Lorraine, he has your red hair. That's great. He's very cute. I—I—wish I could hold him."

Lorraine looked up at him as they walked. "Well, you will. When I get home, everyone will hold him so why not you?" She smiled at him and knew Paul was looking forward to holding little Carlo. Little Carlo; the more she said it the more natural it was for her to do so.

In four days, Lorraine and little Carlo were released from the hospital. In the old days, they used to keep mother and child in the hospital for two weeks. Now, everything was different; get the ladies ambulatory the next day, and get them out of the hospital in four days.

When Lorraine arrived home, she found her family had made some changes for her comfort. The little bedroom next to the master bedroom, which Lena used as a sewing/TV room, was converted to bedroom/nursery. Needless to say, Lorraine was pleased. During the two a.m. feedings, she would not have to go downstairs from her old room, heat the bottle and re-climb the stairs to get to the howling baby. Everything was neat and efficient and pleased Lorraine immensely. Having a new baby in the house hardly changed the routine of the normal household. Except, of course, the baby's presence drew the family into the room quite frequently. Lorraine was happy that her family loved the baby; who wouldn't be.

Lorraine fell into the new Mommy routine easily. She regained her normal, slim figure, she took little Carlo outdoors in his carriage. Some neighbors looked at her askance; some with surprise; some with genuine affection and congratulations. Some neighbors brought gifts and stayed to have coffee and cake, which Lorraine baked, having learned to bake from Gooma Nancy. The sweet yenta, Gooma Nancy, when she heard the news, was thrilled. She had called every day and even mailed some hand crocheted items for the baby.

Lorraine began to think of christening little Carlo, but was a bit worried because she knew that the Church would ask several pertinent questions. But on a sunny day, she took a walk to St Joseph's Church and knocked on the rectory door. It was opened by an ancient woman, who asked her what she wanted.

Lorraine, holding little Carlo, said she wanted to speak to Father Smith about christening her baby. The woman looked at little Carlo, saw the red hair and said, "Come in, I'll call him."

Lorraine watched the ancient woman walk away, with difficulty, after she showed them into the office and thought, "This woman was born to do this job. I'll bet she never had another position. I'll bet she knows all Ten Commandments by heart. I'll be she knows all the mortal sins and all the venial sins and all the ember days. I'll bet she still eats fish on Fridays. I'll bet—" Her thoughts were interrupted by the entrance of Father Smith. She was surprised to see him because he was young, tall and very handsome. She'd never seen him at mass.

Father Smith smiled at Lorraine and looked at the baby admiringly. He did not extend his hand for her to shake. "I'm Father Smith. What can I do for you?" he asked kindly.

"Father Smith, my name is Lorraine Martini. Father, I want to christen my baby. He's six weeks old and I thought it was about time."

"Yes, yes, good thinking. This is fine. I've come to this parish only a few weeks ago and this is my first real job. That makes me happy. Now, we'll fill out some forms." She could tell he was very nervous. He opened the desk drawer and pulled out some papers. "Now, then, the baby's name."

Lorraine stiffened. "His name is little…I mean, his name is Carlo Martini." She watched as the priest printed the baby's name.

"Now, the mother's name."

"Lorraine Martini. Oh, we need your maiden name." Lorraine told him that was her maiden name. She watched as he wrote that down. She could see that he was a bit unsettled.

"And the baby's father's name is?"

"No name. I don't want a name put on that line. Just write 'unknown'."

Father Smith looked horrified at Lorraine. "But—but, we must put down a father's name. Every child has a father."

"Not this child."

Father Smith almost fell out of his chair. "But, Mrs. Martini, you must have a name for the father, it's—re—"

"No, there's no father's name."

The priest was silent for a moment, his nervousness very apparent. He didn't know how to handle this situation. It was unusual and he was beginning to think—

"It's MISS Martini. I'm not married."

"Not married. But, that's—that's highly irregular."

"I know. I thought so, too." Now Lorraine was in facetious mode. She knew the priest was going to give her a hard time. She would not divulge the baby's father's name to anyone on this earth and that was that!

"But, Mrs.—Miss Martini, we need a father's name or there can be no christening."

"Look Father, this baby, whom I love more than life, will not be scarred by anyone. He's the result of a rape. This is my baby and no one else's. Now, if you can't or won't christen him, I will go to another church."

Father Smith knew she was verbally pushing him against the wall and he had been warned about some women who would try to "tempt" him. He smiled and said, "Well, if you want your son to be a heathen and go to hell when he dies, do that."

Lorraine stared at him a moment and when she knew he thought he had won, she said, "You should be ashamed of yourself, trying to scare me. Jesus would never say that to me. He would welcome me and my baby in His church. But, you sit there and think you're holier than thou. I'll find a priest in a Catholic church who will gladly welcome a new little Catholic. Goodbye."

She stared at him while she rose from her chair and left the rectory. Father Smith followed her, calling her name but she kept on going. She wanted nothing more to do with him.

She was outside, putting the baby in the carriage, when a penitent Father Smith walked swiftly up to her. "Please, Miss Martini, listen to me. I would gladly christen your son but we have rules."

"The hell with the rules. I'll go to another church to have my baby christened!"

Father Smith looked at her with a helpless, victim look. "You must understand; we have rules and regulations. It's not up to me—I—"

Lorraine faced the priest as a brave mother would. "I don't give a sh—a crap about your rules and regulations. I have an innocent baby. And I'm innocent, too. I was a victim. I don't intend to pay for being a victim my whole life. I don't intend to have my baby scarred for the rotten act of a thoughtless man. He doesn't belong in our lives."

Father Smith didn't know what to say. How could he argue with such logic and passion? She was right! But he knew his pastor would never consider performing the ceremony and would certainly prohibit any other priest from performing same. An illegitimate baby; it connoted ill for the church; a baby like *that*!

"Yes, I understand. It's one of those rules I don't agree with." He looked helplessly at her, at her determined eyes and her chin uplifted. He was at a loss for words. Then he took a deep breath and said, "Miss Martini, I'll be happy to christen your baby. Please come inside and we'll continue to fill out the papers and select a Sunday."

"Are you sure there will be no objections from the pastor? I don't want to make arrangements and have him call me and say that all has changed."

A very nervous Father Smith said, "Oh, not to worry. I'll speak with the pastor and tell him the entire story. What is the story?"

Lorraine almost laughed at his simplicity. She gave a rudimentary account, which Father Smith found appalling. "But, you should have reported this assault to the police."

"But, don't you understand, Father Smith? I don't want him to know about the baby. I don't want him in our lives."

"But, he has a right to know."

"A rapist has no rights!"

"Hmm." Father Smith obviously agreed with Lorraine but his collar forced him to keep tradition with the Church. "Please, come inside and we'll continue to fill out the forms and I'll write whatever you say."

She selected her brother Vinnie and Lucy to be Godparents, which at this moment they didn't know. They wouldn't refuse.

Lorraine was hesitant, but she was tough. If she had to lock horns with the pastor, she would do it!

She went inside the rectory, taking little Carlo with her and completed the necessary forms, choosing two Sundays from now for the baptism.

She and Father Smith concluded the routine, but she could see that he was still nervous. She also saw something very unpriestly in his eyes when he looked at her; it was a look she was accustomed to.

Chapter Fifteen

Two weeks later, Lorraine received a call from the pastor. He was gruff; cleared his throat many times and said, "MISS Martini, it's come to my attention that you have a baby, a fatherless baby, which you want to baptize in our church."

Lorraine had been expecting this call. She was aware of the pastor's stronghold on the Church and the parishioners. Many times, from the altar, he had bullied them into contributing money for an unimportant project. The parishioners always fell into his trap.

"Yes, Father Randall, I have a wonderful baby and I want to baptize him in our church. My family and I have been attending St. Joseph's for many years. Is there a problem?"

"Ahem, ahem, well, you see it's come to my attention that this baby has no father. We—"

"Yes, it's unfortunate that my baby, Carlo, has no father, but that shouldn't stop Father Smith from baptizing him. After all, if my entire family are good parishioners, it stands to reason that little Carlo will also be one. Why, I've taken him to Mass many times since he was born and you should see how attentive he is. I make the Sign of the Cross on him and he giggles. People see that and they smile. Why, my baby may grow up to be just like you and even make Pope. Oh, you were saying there was a problem. What is it?"

"Why—why, nothing. I seem to have made a mistake. Well, I'll see you at the christening. Goodbye."

"Goodbye, Father, Randall and thanks for calling." You son of a bitch, she said under her breath. She saw that her baby, lying comfortably in his bassinette looked at her. "You didn't hear that, sweetie. And if you did, you'd probably agree with me. Don't say those words until you're at least seventeen. Oh, okay, fifteen. I want you to be tough." She smiled at him, picked him up and kissed him. Then she replaced him and went on with her list of guests for the christening and the food that would be catered and prepared by Lena and Lorraine.

Gooma Nancy and her family, who were treated with great deference, were invited to the christening on a Sunday when little Carlo was seven weeks old. There were other relatives and friends who were invited; and Paul was one of them.

The Sunday of the baptism was a beautiful, cool, sunny day. People started arriving at the church and the ceremony went on so beautifully. Little Carlo smiled at everyone as though he knew the importance of today.

Lucy, as best friend, Godmother and future sister-in-law was present and she kept asking if she could hold the baby. "Of course, Gooma, you can hold the baby. Please be sure to put your hand under his head and neck when you pick him up." Lucy did as instructed; she was so thrilled.

The guests brought lovely gifts for the baby and Gooma Nancy had baked special Italian pastries for the Martini family. After the church ceremony, they all went to the Martini home, where the dinner was catered. Gooma Nancy had tears in her eyes when she first saw little Carlo because she had grown so close to Lorraine and had come to love her as Lorraine had come to love Gooma Nancy.

Gooma Nancy asked Lorraine, "Honey, could I hold the baby?"

"Of course, Gooma Nancy, of course. You should hold the baby; you're like a grandmother to me and a great grandmother to my little Carlo. Sit down and I'll get him."

When she placed little Carlo in Gooma Nancy's arms, the sweet old lady looked down at little Carlo and said, "Little Carlo, your mother is a wonderful woman.

May God always bless you, her and all the family with good health and good fortune. *Gesu vi benedica.*" She made the Sign of the Cross with her thumb on the baby's forehead and he looked very solemnly at her hands while she did this. She continued to gaze at the baby and rocked him ever so gently and hummed an old Italian lullaby then sang softly in her lovely soprano voice. Little Carlo closed his eyes and slept. Everyone was amazed because he usually smiled, kicked and squealed at this hour of the day. Lorraine sat next to Gooma Nancy; she was watching her son sleep very peacefully and the expression on Gooma Nancy's face, so happy, almost like an old Madonna. Lorraine thought, "What a wonderful, sweet woman. I'll always love her."

Paul took pictures of all three. Lorraine was conscious and shy while Paul smiled at all of them.

Gooma Nancy whispered, "Lorraine, take the baby and put him in his bassinet; he'll sleep well now. All my grandchildren used to do the same after I sang to them."

Lorraine did as she was told; she took her son very gently from Gooma Nancy's arms and brought him to their room and placed him in the bassinet. She kissed him before she let him go and covered him with a light blanket. As she turned away from her son, she saw Paul standing there, his eyes showing…something. Lorraine knew it was love for her baby. Paul came closer and looked down at the baby. "Lorraine, he's magnificent; just like you." He took her hand; he was choked up. There were so many things he wanted to say, but couldn't put his words in order. All he knew was that he loved Lorraine beyond words and now that she had this utterly fantastic son, his heart was bursting.

It was an awkward moment for Lorraine because she knew how Paul felt and knew he would propose again. She would have to repeat herself and it was something that hurt her but she thought by accepting Paul's proposal she was using and abusing him. He was too good for that.

He attempted to take her in his arms but she resisted him. "Paul, please don't do that."

And like a naughty little boy, he turned away. It was she who felt worse than he did.

They joined the other folks, who were eating, drinking, dancing and laughing. Paul walked to the other side of the room. He had changed his mind about asking her to dance. He became very quiet until Joe wandered to his side and they began talking sports. Joe was aware of the feelings that passed between his sister and Paul. He wished with all his heart that his sister would marry Paul. She couldn't do better than Paul, who loved Lorraine to distraction. Lorraine needed time to get over that bastard, whose name no one in the family wanted to mention or were permitted to mention.

Paul was quiet. "Joe, I think I'd better go."

Joe looked at Paul in surprise; Paul was never one to give up. "Look, Paul, stay a little bit more. I know how you feel about my sister. She's not a mean person."

"I know that," Paul said quickly.

"So then stay a bit longer. Lorraine needs a little more time and she needs a guy with patience."

"Yeah, but how long does this 'patient guy' wait. Maybe I'm really wasting my time. I think I'd better go. I'll say goodnight, Joe. Thanks for your support." And he went to say goodnight to all and when he came to Lorraine, he said, very quietly, "I'm going to leave now, Lorraine. Thanks for inviting me. If—if—you, well, goodnight." He turned quickly and left.

Lorraine was speechless, realizing that something strange just happened and she was powerless to rectify it. She felt as though a part of her heart just left. There was a hurt look on Paul's face that was evident to her and one other.

Gooma Nancy sidled up to Lorraine and said, "Lorraine, can you come in the den with me. I need some help."

Lorraine, looked away from the front door, as though she could still see Paul's aura, and then to Gooma Nancy and said, "Sure, sure. Let's go." When they entered the den, Gooma Nancy closed the door and looked at Lorraine with a motherly look.

"Lorraine, let's sit down. Ever since you came to our home, with your obvious problem, I thought I could help you by finding you a husband. Now, wait a minute, don't get mad. I haven't done anything and not because I haven't thought about it. You know, a single mother is not going to be easy to match with a nice Italian boy. Italian mothers may not love their daughters-in-law, but none of them want their sons to marry an unwed mother. That's a tough deal. But, I know you are a good girl and I was determined to find a husband for you. But, and that's a big but, I don't have to do that. Tonight, I saw your future husband."

At those words, Lorraine felt chills up and down her spine. "Oh, no, Gooma Nancy, really, I don't want you to do that. You don't have to worry about me. I know I'm a hard sell and I'm not looking for a husband and I'm not thinking about the baby's father, either. He's completely out of my life and my baby's life. Right now, I want to concentrate on my baby and my future career. Don't forget, you gave me good advice regarding that."

"I know, I know. And I'm proud of you; you showed you have intelligence and guts. You'll be successful; nobody can beat that. But, tonight, I saw a young man who's deeply in love with you. Okay, okay, you don't have to do anything now. You must heal and I mean that. Heal yourself, concentrate on your beautiful baby, but don't let this young man go out of your life. Don't waste too many years foolishly. You will regret it. That's all I'm going to say; if I talk too much, you may resent me and I won't have that. I want you and your family in my life and I want to be part of your lives. Come here and give the old Fairy Godmother a kiss."

Lorraine smiled. "You're wonderful and I feel the same about you. I'll always be grateful for all you and your family have done for me. Whatever I can do for you, let me know. Please don't forget that." And she rose from her chair and kissed Gooma Nancy on each cheek. Then they went to rejoin the party. But, in Lorraine's heart, she felt something missing. Then she went to check on the baby, who was stirring and beginning to fuss. She changed him and cleaned him until he was sweet smelling and took him with her to the kitchen where she gave him a small bottle of water. As Lorraine fed him, she thought about her life and how tangled it was.

Carlo came to his daughter, kissed her cheek and began to talk to little Carlo who smiled at his grandfather. Lena came close, too. "Look, Carlo, how he knows you. He loves you."

"And he loves you, too, *Nonna.* And so do I." He pinched her cheek, and then kissed her cheek. *La Nonna* smiled.

Joe had been watching his sister and felt in his heart, that she was feeling a little sad. But he knew his sister; he knew she couldn't be pushed to do something she didn't want to do. He knew she needed time; time to heal and time to make intelligent decisions. He hoped that she would not see the light when it was too late.

A few weeks after the christening, Lorraine got a part time job in an Insurance and Real Estate office. It was a store front office but it was quite busy. Lorraine fit in nicely; her hours were from noon to three p.m. She immediately threw herself into the office routine and worked well with the owners and other clerks and customers. She hadn't given up her car so she was able to take prospective buyers to see houses. When she made her first sale and proudly received her first commission money, she was ecstatic. She went home and threw the check on the table for her mother to see. "Well, what's for dinner? Money? Sure we can eat that. But it won't taste as good as chicken cacciatore." Then she chuckled as she picked her son, who was now seven months old, from his high chair and danced around the kitchen telling him she would buy him a present. Little Carlo didn't understand but he knew his mother and he laughed.

Lena threw her hands in the air. She and Carlo had not taken any money from Lorraine and this money would go into Lorraine's bank account, but the sight sent Lena into a *tarantella*! "Hooray! Oh, my darling daughter, how wonderful. How wonderful." And she kissed her daughter and put her hand on little Carlo's back and kissed him, too, and told him about his rich mother.

Lorraine hugged her mother with one arm as the other held her precious son, "Thanks, Ma. I couldn't do this without your help. You're great. Everybody's great." And she danced around the kitchen, hugging and kissing her son. She knew the sacrifice her parents made for their grandson and she appreciated it very much. Then the telephone rang and Lorraine answered it.

"Hello."

"Hello, Lorraine?"

"Yes. Is it—?"

"It's Paul. I—I haven't called you in a while. I hope you don't think I'm mad at you or anything like that."

"No, Paul, I never thought you were mad at me. I just thought you were busy. I understand that. I have a part time job and between that and taking care of little Carlo, I find I have little time to spare."

"I know. Well, how have you been?"

"Oh, pretty well, thank you. And you?"

"Yeah, I've been busy, too. I've been promoted."

"Oh, that's great, Paul. Congratulations." And she looked at Lena as her mother took the baby and put him back in his high chair and she went back to cooking, trying not to listen to the conversation.

"Well, it's a promotion that I really didn't chase after, but it was presented to me and I thought, well, why not."

"Wonderful." And an awkward silence followed. Then Lorraine said, "Well, I have sort of good news, too. I sold a house and today I received my commission. It's not a lot of money, but it's nice to have it handed to you."

"Oh, yeah. I know. Um, Lorraine, can you—I mean, would you—well, you might be busy."

"Paul, what is it?"

"Well, I don't want to be a pest. Maybe—I was thinking—maybe you'd like to go to the movies tonight. There's an Italian movie at the Cinema with Sofia Loren and I understand it's a comedy. But, if you're busy, maybe we can make it—"

"Paul, I'd love to go with you. What time will you be here? And since I'm flush, I'll pay." She chuckled.

Lorraine could almost feel Paul's happy sigh of relief. "Hey, I'll pay. I don't care how rich you are. I'll be there at seven thirty. Is that too early or late?"

"Well, I put little Carlo in his crib at seven thirty. But you can come here anytime you want. You haven't seen the baby in a while and you'll be surprised to see how big he's grown. Please come early. Okay?"

Paul was happy and said, "Gee, Lorraine, I'd love to see the baby. I—I really missed you and him. I'll be there before you put him to bed. Bye"

"Bye, Paul."

Lorraine had a smile on her face.

Lena noted it and started setting the table. "Gee, I wonder who called."

Lorraine laughed and helped to set the table. Soon the men started coming home and it's a funny thing, the first person they greeted was little Carlo. One by one, the men picked him up and kissed him. They walked around the rooms with him, talking to him and singing to him. The baby laughed.

Joe said, "This kid's getting to be a gorilla like his handsome uncles, Lorraine. What the hell do you feed him?"

Vinnie said, "I can't get over the resemblance to me; the handsomest uncle."

"What are you boys talking about?" Their father had walked into the room when the discussion began. "Look at his beautiful head. He looks like me. Look at his nose; it's like mine. That's why he's handsome. Get away from my grandson, *mascalzoni,* rascals.

Lorraine watched in happiness as they all fought over her son; who laughed and laughed. Then one of them produced a little rattle, which was quickly taken by little Carlo, who put the just unwrapped toy in his mouth.

Then they all sat down to dinner; Lorraine looking at the clock frequently.

Promptly at seven the doorbell rang. "I'll get it." Lorraine said, a bit too quickly, which made the men look at her and then at each other.

Lorraine opened the door and saw Paul with a bouquet of flowers and another little gift. She smiled because she knew the little gift was for little Carlo.

Paul smiled at her, bent to kiss her cheek. She looked up at him and said, "Paul, thank you and come in. You're just in time for coffee and maybe if the animals have left some cake, you can have some. It's the pound cake Gooma Nancy taught me to make and I make it often because I have steady customers here. Come on in."

They walked into the kitchen and there were a lot of noisy greetings passing around.

Paul looked at the baby. "Lorraine, wow, he's grown so much. He looks as though he's two years old."

Lorraine laughed, "Oh, get outta here, Paul, he's only seven months old and just sitting up, never mind walking like a two year old." Paul gazed at him. "Well, aren't you going to pick him up?"

Paul looked at Lorraine as though she were giving permission to do the impossible. "Gee, can I?"

"If you don't, little Carlo will be mystified. Everybody picks him up. Nobody asks me for permission, why should you?"

Paul carefully put his hands under the baby's arms and lifted him gently and held him closely. Paul and little Carlo smiled at each other. Paul was very pleased and he kissed the baby and tickled him saying, "Hey, Carlo, how's it goin'?"

Lorraine put the flowers in a beautiful base. Then she brought the gift to little Carlo and said, "Look, sweetheart, look at the gift Uncle Paul brought you. I'll open it for you." And she proceeded to unwrap it. It was a teething ring, which little Carlo quickly put in his mouth.

"Hey, look at that. He likes my gift," Paul said.

"Smart kid," said Lorraine.

Lena began to put the cups and saucers out for the cake. Lorraine put her pound cake on the table and all the men groaned in anticipation. Vinnie went to the freezer to get the ice cream. They all continued the conversation except for Paul, who still held the adorable little one.

Lorraine came to Paul, "Paul, would you please carry the baby to his crib?"

"Sure, sure."

Once inside the bedroom, Lorraine asked Paul to put the baby on the bathinette, and wrap the tie around him. The baby kicked and talked gibberish. Lorraine got clean pajamas and then prepared to change the diaper. She cleaned the baby until he was sweet smelling, gave him to Paul to hold and washed her hands. When she returned, she smiled at Paul and said, shyly, "You have to leave now. I have to feed him."

At first he didn't understand, and then he realized that Lorraine was still breast feeding her baby and she needed privacy.

"Oh, sure. I'm sorry. I—I—I'll be in the other room." He was obviously embarrassed and he smiled sheepishly and awkwardly made a hasty exit. He realized that Lorraine was by now, an expert mommy. He was filled with admiration. After the baby was full, she called Paul to come into the room. Soon, after burping him, she put the baby in the crib. Both Lorraine and Paul watched him until he fell asleep, which didn't take long. Lorraine whispered to Paul, "I always watch him fall asleep. He's so adorable, I can't help it."

Paul smiled at her and whispered back, "I don't blame you."

They walked to the table, sat down and joined the rest of the family having coffee and cake. Paul was amazed that the family talked so loud and the baby didn't wake up.

"He's used to our loudness," said Vinnie. "I taught him that."

"You did not!" Joe said, "I'm the one who teaches him all the good things. You teach him dopey things."

"Will you boys stop this crazy talk? I am the one who teaches him everything. I even teach him to speak Italian. Yes, when you think he is talking baby talk, he is speaking Italian and I am the only one who understands him," said Carlo, the grandfather. His chest was puffed up with pride.

They all laughed and then Lorraine rose and said, "I hope you'll all excuse us, Paul and I are going out for a bit. Ma, will you be babysitter for me please?"

"Oh, you have to ask! It's my pleasure to babysit. He's so good; he sleeps when his belly is full. Go. Go out and enjoy your free time."

Lorraine and Paul both left the house and got into his car and drove to the Cinema, a small theatre that catered to European films.

They talked very little but Lorraine was conscious of the lopsided smile on Paul's face. When they sat in their seats, they were aware of the audience's ethnic persuasion. However, they could see that there were a few intellectuals and some students of the Italian language who were present.

Paul turned to Lorraine, "How are you doin'?"

"Fine," she said. They both smiled at each other.

"I'm glad to hear that. I thought about you a lot and I've wanted to call but—but then I got busy and I knew you were busy. You seem to be so competent. I'm amazed."

"Oh, motherhood comes easily to females. I don't know what it is. Maybe it's maternal instinct or maybe it's love for babies that helps us. I don't know."

"Well, I'm very impressed. You're wonderful."

Lorraine smiled at Paul. Then the movie began and everyone, including them, became silent.

He took her hand and held it. He wanted very urgently to kiss her but didn't think this was the place to do it. After the movie was over, the audience applauded. Lorraine looked at Paul questions above her head. He smiled and said, "Many times people will do that when there's a foreign movie shown. Usually, they're shown in a small theater such as this one. I guess it gives the management the message that they would like to see more of the same."

"Oh, that makes sense. Did you enjoy the movie?"

"Yeah, a lot. I love Sofia Loren and when she plays a real Neapolitan girl, she's great, very sexy and beautiful, too. Of course, she comes from a small town near Naples."

They were outside in the lovely evening walking toward the car when Paul said, "Lorraine, I know you've never been to Italy. I went in my last year in college. It was a great experience."

"Oh, you sound like you met a lot of lovely Italian girls."

He laughed, "Yes, I did. But I also did a lot of sightseeing and Italy is a beautiful country and the people are friendly and when they heard that I was Italian American and spoke a little Italian, they didn't know what to do for me to make me feel welcome. I think every Italian American should visit Italy; they would be filled with a great deal of pride. Maybe someday, you'll make a trip there."

"Yes, maybe I will. I think I can make a lot of money in the business I'm in. You know, you've given me an idea. I'd love to go there when little Carlo is about ten or eleven. He'd get a great kick out of it. At least, I hope so."

"Sure, he will. Just keep your eye on your goal."

They had reached the car and were sitting, waiting for a clear moment when Paul could pull out of the parking space and onto the street. They were stopped for a red light. Paul took her in his arms and kissed her deeply. Lorraine didn't resist or push him away. She enjoyed the kiss. Paul kissed her again.

"Lorraine, I love you. I really do. I stayed away from you because—" the light had turned green and there were motorists behind them blowing their horns. Paul quickly put the car in gear and moved on.

He was frustrated. He pulled over and parked. "Lorraine, I had to see you tonight. I stayed away from you because I thought you never wanted to see me again. That thought bothered me. And I didn't want to be a pest. I don't want to pressure you into—you know, something you don't want to hear. But, I can't stop saying it. I love you. I want to marry you. I want us to be together. Please—please, think about it. And don't tell me the bullshit about Italian mothers and their precious sons marrying virgins. I know a lot of guys who married virgins and regret it. I—"

"But, Paul, I'm not thinking about Italian mothers, although it's a big deal and can't be discounted. I just don't feel it's right to use you to make me and my baby respectable. We are respectable, ya know. I wasn't and still am not a slut. I was raped. I told you that and you must know that I told you the truth."

"I know you did. I never doubted you, Lorraine." Paul said softly, "I know what kind of girl you are. I know how you were raised. You come from a family with strict morals and you have strict morals. Don't think because I kiss you—because you let me kiss you, I think you have low morals. It's exactly the opposite. I've loved you for a long time; ever since we were kids."

"Oh, Paul, I didn't know that. You make me feel so—so—honored. I don't know what to say." She looked at him as though she had just learned his secret. She had not been aware that he loved her for such a long time.

"It's simple; say you'll marry me. I know you don't love me but I'll make you and the baby very, very happy. I'll adopt him and give him my name, if you like, and treat him as though he was my own. I love him. And he needs siblings, ya know." He looked hopefully at her, his lopsided smile charming her.

Lorraine looked down at her hands in her lap. This was something she didn't expect and didn't know how to handle. Paul meant it when he said he didn't care about Italian mothers wanting their sons to marry virgins; she knew that and it touched her heart.

Lorraine knew Paul's mother very slightly. When she used to see her in the neighborhood, she always greeted her respectfully and that's where it ended. Could she just appear before this woman and present herself as Paul's future wife? And most importantly, was Walter out of her heart. How many times had she dreamt of him? In all her dreams he laughed at her and was illusive. After each of these dreams, she told herself that she hated Walter. And she believed it; as long as she was angry, she believed it. But when she was alone, she was lonely for him. But, now she realized she wasn't lonely for him. She was just lonely for someone and she didn't know who and maybe she would never know who. Maybe she was just being faithful but to whom and for what? Certainly Walter was not worth her time or energy. But, here was the wonderful, dependable, handsome, warm Paul asking her to marry him. Why couldn't she say "yes"?

"Paul, I don't know what to say. You've given me such honor tonight."

"Tonight? Did you not think I was ever serious about you?"

"I—I guess I didn't give it much thought. I mean, I thought about it but I thought the less I said, the better. I guess I was just overwhelmed with what had occurred that I couldn't think of anything else. I heard people say of other single girls who were pregnant that nobody will marry them and they might as well be whores; we're damaged goods. I never wanted that for me." She knew she couldn't express herself clearly and was embarrassed about it. She was talking to Paul, who was so sweet and tender. She was disappointed that she couldn't make her thoughts clear. But, he seemed to understand.

"I know. And I don't want that for you either. Lorraine, I hold you in high esteem. You should know that. Please, Lorraine, think about it. You don't have to give me an answer now or even soon. Just, please think about it. Okay? Will you promise me that? At least I'll know that I'm not making a fool of myself."

"Paul, I never could think of you as a fool. I have the utmost respect for you and for the way you treat me. And tonight, when I saw you with my baby, I was just—just—overwhelmed." She lowered her head and couldn't speak anymore. Paul put his hand under her chin and squeezed gently.

He smiled at her and said, "That kid loves me. I know it. I could feel it tonight. And I love him, too. Honey, I don't want to bug you about this. You may just get mad and tell me to take a hike. So, could we—I mean, is it—like if we see each other—ya know, not to go steady, just to be unhinged sweethearts, ya know, dopes. Would that be okay? And I won't mention marriage until you say it. Is that okay?"

Lorraine smiled at Paul. He had given her a clear road. It was okay. "Yes, Paul, that's okay. I think I could live with that. It's a clear understanding between us. Yeah, that's okay." She nodded her head and had a small smile on her face.

Paul had a big smile on his face and he hugged Lorraine. "Yeah, that's okay."

Chapter Sixteen

Little Carlo's other big holiday was Carnival, the last day before Lent, which is the last day meat can be eaten without fasting. All the family had gone to church on Ash Wednesday, even little Carlo received his ashes as Lorraine held him in her arms. The priests always made a big deal to include the babies. It gave the mothers and grandparents much pleasure; they thought their baby was the most beautiful, appealing and special. And aren't they right?

Then the family went home to eat a large fish dinner because after receiving Ashes, Lenten rules came into effect. Lorraine invited Paul to dinner. Paul was a frequent visitor and always made a big deal of playing with little Carlo, who was getting used to seeing him. Paul, true to his word, didn't mention marriage anymore, but his eyes spoke volumes when he looked at Lorraine.

Vinnie invited Lucy. It was pretty serious with them. They were talking wedding plans, for Heaven's sake. Vinnie had not thought of getting married, not for years and years into the future. But, then he realized that Lucy was a girl he wanted to be with for the rest of his life and Lucy felt the same. So, what's to stop them from getting married? Nothing!

Lena had cooked pounds and a variety of fish and all ate with gusto. There were platters of spaghetti alla marinara. Lena made sure there was plenty of grated Romano cheese on the table. She knew her family loved it on their spaghetti and she was sure they would urge the guests to eat as they did. They did.

After dinner, Joe went to visit a "friend." No one knew for certain if this "friend" was a male or female; but they suspected female. Vinnie and Lucy decided to go to the movies and invited Lorraine and Paul to go with them.

Paul said it was a grand idea, then he said, "Vinnie, I know you're inviting us because you think I'm gonna pay for you and Lucy. Wrongo! You cheapo, you pay for me and your sister or we don't go with you!"

With that, Vinnie said, "Forget the invitation. We don't wanna go with you two. I only asked you to be polite. And, yes, I'm a little short today."

"And short tomorrow, too." Paul retorted. They all laughed and got ready to leave.

After Lorraine put little Carlo to sleep, the four went to the movies. There was a lot of chatter and laughs and teasing. Then the talk turned serious with Lucy saying, "Lorraine, Vinnie and I are really talking seriously about getting married. So, right now, before we go any further with our plans, I want you to be my Maid of Honor. Please say yes. Please."

"Lucy, what an honor for me! Of course I'll be your Maid of Honor. Of course." They kissed and hugged, like the old Italian ladies did. "I'm gonna ask my two cousins, Tina and Adriana to be my bridesmaids. I'm sure they'll accept, since they're always after me to choose them."

Vinnie said, "Well, now that's settled. I've already asked my brother, Joe, to be my best man. Paul, I would like very much if you would be an usher. I'm gonna ask my cousin, Ciro, to be the other usher."

Paul didn't expect this but was very happy to be included in the wedding party. "Hey, Vinnie, thanks, it will be my pleasure to be an usher. Wow, I never thought about this. Thank you, thank you."

Lorraine smiled, "Well, that's all settled as far as we all are concerned. Too bad little Carlo is still too small to be a ring bearer." And they all laughed.

After the movie, they went for a snack at a diner located near the movie. They talked about the wedding, the date, the church, the reception hall and the wedding list of invitations. Vinnie and Lucy had to look for an apartment and buy furniture. They wanted an apartment located close to their parents.

Lorraine listened with contentment, but still her heart was tugged. She could never get married. She was considered "soiled." She felt rage beginning to rise. Paul, who had been observing her, took her hand and massaged it gently. She looked at Paul and met his compassionate eyes and felt her rage subside. She gave a lopsided smile to Paul and was surprised that Paul detected her feelings, which she had tried to hide. At the end of their snack, the couples separated as Vinnie and Lucy walked toward her home.

Paul took Lorraine's hand and said, "Would you like to walk a bit or go straight home?"

Without looking at him, she said, "Let's walk a bit." And they walked a bit in silence. Soon they were in front of Lorraine's home and they walked up to the front door. Lorraine had her key out; Paul took it from her and unlocked the door and handed it back to her. He stood silently; waiting.

Lorraine hesitated, she didn't know what to say, then looked up into his eyes and said, "Good night, Paul. Safe home." She entered the house and closed the door softly. Her parents mumbled, "Is that you, Lorraine?"

"Yes, I'm home. Was the baby any trouble?"

"No," Lena answered sleepily. "*Grazie, Gesu.* Thank you, Jesus."

As Lorraine started to walk toward her room, her heart was heavy and she cursed her luck.

***

Lorraine applied herself to her work and advanced. Soon she had enough money to open her own business. Her parents had helped her with the finances as much as they could and as much as Lorraine would permit them. She worked long hours and sometimes she worked seven days a week.

No matter how tired she was when she came home, she always devoted time to little Carlo. Lorraine would come home tired, but, was renewed at the thought of seeing her little boy who was growing like a weed. She would wrestle with him and tickle him and he would giggle until he couldn't laugh anymore. Then when she put him to bed, she sang to him in her sweet soft, soprano voice. His little brown eyes would look at every inch of her face and with his little finger, would trace her freckles and smile until he fell asleep.

***

Three years had passed and in those three years, Vinnie and Lucy had married and had two little boys. Joe had become engaged to a lovely Irish girl, Eileen. Lorraine remembers the first time Joe mentioned a girl he was seeing and her name was Eileen, Lena's eyes opened and her eyebrows went up.

"What's her name?"

Joe, a little subdued, said, "Her name is Eileen, Ma, and you'll love her. She's really nice."

"I don't know any Italian girl named Eileen. Is she Italian?"

"No, Ma, she's not. But she looks Italian."

"So, you don't have to tell me she looks Italian. It's okay if she's not Italian. Everyone should be proud of their national background. I'm sure she is. "

"She's a nice girl; a nice Irish girl. I want to bring her home for all of you to meet."

Lena stopped washing the table and looked at her son. "Joe, this sounds serious. You want to bring her home to meet us! Have you met her family?"

"Yes, I have. We're dating and I have to go to her home to pick her up; it's the only way she'll come out with me. I had to meet her parents. Her father is very strict with her. They've welcomed me with all sincerity and kindness. I like them a lot."

"But, you love her?"

"Yes, Ma." He said it so tenderly and softly that Lena could not doubt his sincerity.

"Okay, you bring her here for Sunday dinner. We will welcome her as her parents have welcomed you. Are you sure they like you? Ya know, sometimes in a case like this, people are not sincere."

"Ma, don't worry, they are. In fact, I worked on her father's car and he was so impressed with me and Vinnie, he invited me to meet his daughter. I thought she was gonna be a dog, but I couldn't refuse him and I was very surprised at what I met. She's a very sweet girl, very respectful of her parents and me, too. You'll see." And he came to his mother, whose eyes were getting big and beginning to fill with tears. He put his arm around his mother, kissed her and said, "Don't worry, Ma, no one can take me away from you. You're the best mother."

Lena lost it! She wept on her son's shoulder. Carlo could only look on and think how his little children had grown and become responsible adults. Where was he was this happened!?

Lorraine was not "settled" as people said. She remained a problem with her parents who knew Paul was waiting patiently. It was Lorraine who built a wall around herself; who thought she was unworthy, who withheld herself from going on with "that" part of her life. Little Carlo comforted her but she needed adult companionship for soon little Carlo would be big Carlo and coming home with a selection of his own.

Lorraine was not a complainer and as she worked in her store front office, her secretary, Joan, whom she'd hired right out of high school, studied her and learned to be prepared for any requests Lorraine might ask. Joan always had her pad and pencil ready. One day, she noticed a man looking in the store window; his gaze on Lorraine was very intense. Joan noticed his nose was crooked. She wondered why he didn't enter the office. Then he walked away slowly. She never mentioned it to Lorraine, thinking it wasn't important. So many men would look in the store front window and then walk away.

One day, Lorraine called home; Lena answered. She said, "Ma, I'll be home late tonight. Can you take care of little Carlo for me, please?"

"Of course, I can. How late will you work?"

"Well, I'm not sure. I have a client for insurance coming in and I have a few sales contracts to finish up and present. Maybe I'll be home by ten thirty. Is that okay; can you take care of my little rascal?"

"Yes, yes. Don't worry. I'll take good care of him. Maybe I'll make chocolate chip cookies for him and let him steal some of the chips to pop into his mouth. He loves that."

"Yeah, Ma, thanks for not spoiling him!" They both laughed because Lorraine never said anything like that to her mother. It was others who said Lena was spoiling little Carlo and Lorraine dismissed all they said as nonsense.

Lorraine was alone in the office and she poured over some contracts. She had a nagging urge to get up and lock the door. Her client, whenever he arrived would knock on the door; she could easily see through the glass door. As she worked, suddenly she stopped. Paul's image came into her head and she looked up at nothing, thinking about Paul. He was a great guy. So why--?

The telephone rang; it was her client who had to cancel their appointment. He apologized profusely and made another appointment, which he swore he would keep. Lorraine was glad of the cancellation. It was almost ten p.m.; she was tired, and as she quickly put her papers in order, ready for the following morning, someone came in the door. Fangool, she'd forgotten to lock it.

She came forward and noticed it was a man who dressed shabbily and wearing a stained, misshapen hat. She became frightened but somehow was reassured that nothing untoward would happen.

"Good evening. May I help you?"

"Hello, Lorraine." He held out his hand.

Lorraine was mystified; she didn't recognize him but he knew her name. Maybe he noticed it on the store window.

She looked at his extended hand and noticed it wasn't very clean but she didn't want to show ill manners, she took his hand.

"You're still beautiful." His faintly familiar voice was plaintive.

She gasped. She didn't recognize him until she looked at his steel blue eyes.

"Walter," she whispered.

"Yes, it's me, Walter. You look wonderful."

Lorraine couldn't speak at first, and then she said, "How—how have you been?" She was really taken aback by his appearance; like he had neglected himself or he was sick or something.

"Oh, I've been—been okay. I passed by your place and noticed your name and then when I looked inside, I saw your beautiful face."

"Oh, I've gotten a little older. I'm not beautiful anymore."

"How wrong you are. Can I take you for coffee next door?"

"Well, I—I really have to get home." She almost told him about little Carlo as it was her habit to talk about him to anyone, but thought better of it. Little Carlo was hers and hers alone. He was the biological father but he was no father and he would never know his son; *her son*. "But, okay, I can use a bit of coffee. Wait just a few minutes while I close up." She swiftly put things away and came toward the door so she could lock up. She didn't feel as safe as before, yet she knew she was worrying for nothing. For a strange reason, she suddenly thought of Paul and how nice it would be to go home to him; to somebody nice. She would tell Paul how she felt and her heart was warmed at the thought.

They went into the diner next door, where she was well known, and where Lorraine was greeted warmly. She and Walter sat at a booth and ordered coffee.

Walter removed his crumbling hat and put it in the space next to him. He gazed at Lorraine, and said, "So, how have you been? Are you married?"

Lorraine glanced quickly at her left hand that didn't show a wedding band, and said, "No, I'm not married. I just never got around to it. I started my business and it really keeps me busy."

Their coffee arrived and Walter put three teaspoons of sugar in it. Lorraine noted that, but said nothing. It's not her place to make a comment.

"Well, that's good. I got married, ya know."

"No, I didn't know." She lied and didn't care about it.

"Well, yeah, it was a big wedding. Her stepfather had lots of money. Still has. We—we're not together anymore."

Lorraine looked at him with compassion. "Oh, I'm sorry to hear that."

"Yeah, me too. It just wasn't to be." He looked around the diner and she knew he wanted to say more so she remained quiet.

"We were so in love but after a few years, we were incompatible. We couldn't stand the sight of each other."

He coughed and smiled weakly. "We have two kids, they're very young. She wanted a divorce and lots of alimony. You'd never have done that to me, Lorraine. Since I worked for her stepfather and he fired me, I have no money. I can't keep up with my obligations."

"Walter, what about your parents? Can they help you?" She said this and then regretted it; she didn't really want to prolong this conversation or even to remain with him a moment longer. She had more important things to do.

"No, my Dad lost everything; poor management. My mother was so ashamed, they moved out of state. They even lost their home. I would be a burden to them." He smiled sadly and stirred his coffee, which he didn't drink.

Lorraine looked at him, a stab in her heart. To think his parents, especially his mother, didn't want him to marry her because she was unworthy and low class and he's reduced to walking the streets. Was he hinting that he wanted to put the touch on Lorraine, she wondered. If that is the case, he is barking up the wrong tree. Not that Lorraine was vindictive, she just couldn't see herself falling into his trap, and she was convinced that was exactly what it was. She wanted distance between them. She wanted no further contact with him. And she began to think that now he knows where she works, he may become a constant visitor. *Oh, no. Fangool! I don't want him to know or be near my little Carlo!*

Walter looked at Lorraine with his eyes almost pleading. "Lorraine, I've always loved you. Do—do—you think we could get back together? I swear, I would make it up to you. I'll get a job, any kind—"

"Walter! Please don't even think about it," she spoke kindly but firmly, "I've gotten on with my life. I've been going forward. I would never think of going backward. I'm sorry but it's out of the question."

He got mad at her. "My mother was right, Lorraine.

You're nothing but an Italian bitch. You never loved me!" As he spoke, his voice rose and reached across the table and grabbed Lorraine's throat. She struggled.

Charlie, the counter man came running with the biggest knife he had and he called to the others to call the police. He grabbed Walter roughly, "Listen, you son of a bitch, you can't come in here and threaten Lorraine. We've called the police, you bastard."

Walter's eyes grew large with fear. He broke away from Charlie and ran to the front door and made a clean get away. When the police arrived, Lorraine gave them the minimum information; she didn't give them Walter's name. She felt sorry for him; he seemed demented.

Lorraine thanked Charlie, the others, the police and she went home.

When she arrived home, Lena, who was holding little Carlo, who was in his pajamas, by the hand, knew by the expression on Lorraine's face something bad had happened. Quickly, she put the little boy in bed, who obediently went to sleep.

"Lorraine! What happened? Tell me. Sit down." And she gave Lorraine a glass of water.

"Ma, Walter came to my office."

"What! Did he hurt you? Oh, *Maddona Santissima*, Holy Mother, what happened?"

"Well, he told me all his troubles. He's divorced and has no money. He wanted to get back together with me—"

"NO! I hope you told him to go to hell!"

"Well, not in so many words. And then he got violent."

"Oh, I'll kill him! I'll hunt him down; I'll find him and kill him!"

"Ma! Ma! Calm down. Stop yelling or you'll wake up the two Carlos. The police were called but Walter had broken away from Charlie and got away. I doubt that I'll ever see him again. And good riddance." And she sent a silent prayer to God that it should be so.

Lena was breathing hard from her parted lips. She had never liked Walter and when she thought of how he had abandoned Lorraine after he did what he did, she really, really despised him. "I'm so glad you never tried to get in touch with him and never told him about little Carlo. That was a very smart move, Lorraine. He doesn't deserve to have that wonderful little miracle for a son. Only you do."

"I know, Ma, I know. Little Carlo is mine. I'll never tell him about his father. Someday, he'll ask me, I have that feeling. I don't want to lie to him and I'll tell him the truth but not the whole truth. I definitely will not tell him his father's name. He doesn't have to know all that filth and unhappiness. He could never be proud of his father as though he were a hero. He was thoroughly rotten."

"Good," Lena said. After a few moments, she said, "Paul called."

Lorraine looked up, "Oh? What did he say?"

"He said what he usually says; 'please tell Lorraine I called.'"

"I'll call him later. I want to calm down a bit and I'm not going to tell him of tonight's episode. He's having a problem at work and he doesn't need to hear my problems."

"Lorraine, he—"

"I know, Ma. Please, let's not discuss it tonight. Please. I'm disturbed enough. I want to go see my little boy."

Lena watched her disturbed daughter go toward the little bedroom she still shared with her son. She prayed that her daughter would be totally free from Walter and that she and her son would have a wonderful, healthy life with Paul.

***

A few weeks later, not having heard from Walter at all, Lorraine had calmed down and didn't keep that episode in her mind; she thought less and less about it. She and Paul had gone out to dinner a couple of times and she was looking at Paul with a different expression. Still she had not spoken the words Paul wanted to hear. For some reason, it had to be a silly reason, she thought, she couldn't bring the words out of her mouth. She wondered why.

***

Lorraine was busy at her desk and it was close to closing time. Joan said, "Boss, it's past five pm. I know you don't want me to work overtime, so I'm giving you notice. I'm leaving now. Oh, I'll be back tomorrow. I'm not leaving this great office, because you're a slave driver and I'm a glutton for punishment and—"

"GO HOME! And report tomorrow at the same ungodly hour; five a.m."

"I'm going, I'm going, your sweetness."

"Joan, honey, can you drop these letters in the mail box?"

"Anything for you, Boss." They both smiled as Joan left the office.

An hour later the telephone rang. "Martini Real Estate and Insurance. Lorraine speaking, can I help you?"

A strange man's voice said, "Yes, Lorraine. I want to sell my house. I would like to give you the listing because you come highly recommended."

Lorraine was pleased to hear this because that's the way to increase your business. "Well, thank you. May I have your name and address please. I'll just take some pertinent information and come to see the house tomorrow."

"Oh, can you please come this evening? I'd like it listed as soon as possible because there's been a death in the family and I have to go to Europe and I'll be leaving tomorrow."

"Certainly. What is your name?"

"It's Hugh Johnson and my address is 45 Elm Lane."

"Where is that located?"

"It's located in The Valley and I'll give you the directions. It won't take you long since rush hour is over. I appreciate it very much, Lorraine. You are Lorraine Martini, the red head, aren't you?"

"Yes, I am."

"Oh, good. I'll be waiting in the house and I'll leave the lights on and the front door ajar. Goodbye, Lorraine."

"Goodbye, Mr. Johnson. See you soon."

Lorraine thought this whole thing is strange and goofy, but then when clients call, you answer. She called her mother.

"Hello, Ma?"

"Yes, Lorraine. What is it? You sound—well, sort of funny. Will you be home soon?"

"That's what I'm calling about. I just received a call from a new client and he wants me to come see his house tonight and put it on the market. He's leaving for Europe tomorrow and this has to be done now. I don't know how long this will take me because the house is located in The Valley and that's just over the Queens Nassau line. I think, anyway. So, if I get this job, the commission is sure to be big. Yippee. How's little Carlo?"

"Well, he's okay. I think he picked up a bug. And it may be bothering him. He's been a little cranky today and, ya know, that's unusual for him."

"Yeah, that is. Well, I'll try to come home fast. Does he have a fever?"

"No, no fever, which is good. I made some chicken soup for him, for all of us, and he ate some of that. There's some for you, too. He's watching TV now; my little doll."

"Yes, he is a doll. If he gets hungry, give him some of that pudding I made last night."

"Well, that was gone a long time ago. I made some fresh. Okay, be careful, sweetie. Bye."

"Bye, Ma, and thanks. You're a doll, too."

She quickly turned off the lights, left the security lights on, locked up and entered her car. She reviewed the directions and thought they were easy to follow. What she was concerned about was that it was getting dark and many local roads on Long Island were winding roads and had no street lights. If you had been born there, it was easy to know where you were going.

She was finally in Nassau County and trying to find the local street, which was difficult to find due to overhanging pine trees that obscured street signs. After travelling a while, she had to stop at a gas station and ask the attendant directions to the house. He told her he knew it well and she had passed the road and she would have to go back seven miles. He smiled, satisfied that he had knowledge and she didn't; she was a city slicker. Lorraine thought he was a country bumpkin who couldn't find his way to Times Square if the whole New York City police department was holding his hand and pulling him there.

She drove back and slowed down so she wouldn't miss the road which was easy to do because of the overgrowth.

"Gee, don't you guys trim the trees?" she said aloud to no one. But she shook her head. Then she found it and made a right turn. The driveway was long and went straight to the house, where it curved into a circle that had several parking spaces, and led back to the driveway that made its way back to the road. Luckily, it was a moonlit night and the house was large and white. It stood out in all its beauty. Tall cypress trees, gently swaying in the evening breeze, stood at each corner of the house. The landscaping, incorporating the shrubbery and trees nature had put there, was beautifully arranged; just what you'd expect for a mansion. The large lamps on either side of the white door were unlit. Strange, Lorraine thought, but she was getting excited because she knew if she could sell this house, which she thought surely would be an easy sell, she would earn a huge commission, part of which she would put toward their trip to Italy and part in little Carlo's college fund. She smiled as she pulled up and stopped the car. She picked up her clipboard and got out of the car. The darkness made a note in her brain, but she didn't dwell on it. She was eager to do business.

She saw the door ajar but inside there was darkness and Mr. Johnson had promised to leave the lights on. How strange. Then she saw a light go on in a second story window. "Gee, he could have left some lights on downstairs," she thought. But, she had permission to go on the premises and she went up to the door. She approached the slightly open door and called, "Mr. Johnson? Mr. Johnson? Hello." Receiving no answer she gently pushed the door open and gingerly stepped inside. She looked around but in the dark, there was very little to distinguish. She looked around for a light switch and found one near the door; she turned it on. There was a huge chandelier in the center of the large vestibule, but there was only one little electric bulb shaped like a candle that lighted. "Oh, fangool," she thought. "I can't see a Goddamn thing; how am I supposed to make any notes." She was able to make out a large, curved staircase to her left and started for it, calling, "Mr. Johnson? It's Lorraine Martini, Mr. Johnson, can you hear me?" She was beginning to get an eerie feeling. She didn't like it.

No answer. She heard shuffling coming from the lighted room upstairs. She thought, he must be an old man who's hard of hearing. "Mr. Johnson, it's Lorraine Martini, the Real Estate agent. I'm coming upstairs." And she proceeded cautiously up the stairs. She heard more noise. At the top of the stairs, she turned and went toward the lighted room. "Mr. Johnson, it's Lorraine Martini, I'm here." She entered the room. "Mr. Johnson. Mr. Johnson, are you all right? Can you hear me? I've come to list—" She didn't finish her sentence. She heard a noise in the hallway. Now, she was getting nervous and mad because she had seen no one in the room. Had she been lured here by some eccentric fool? She thought of her little son, not feeling well, she should be with him, and she's here being in a dumb game with some rich nut. Rich people! Rich dopes! She strode into the hall and looked around. She saw no one. She walked toward the top of the stairs, looking all around for the one who lured her.

At the bottom of the stairs she heard a voice, was it a familiar voice? "Hello, Lorraine. I knew you would come here. I know how ambitious you are."

She couldn't see the upturned face distinctly because of the dim light. She assumed it was Mr. Johnson. But why was he talking like this? They didn't know each other. Or did they?!

He looked up at her.

"WALTER!!"

He smiled. "Yes."

Lorraine felt chills going up and down her back and the base of her skull. Trouble.

"Walter, what are you doing here? Do you own this house?"

"No, my darling. I don't own this house. It belongs to my ex-wife, who detests me. She has all the money." He was ascending the stairs slowly and talking to her with a strange voice and a frightening smile on his face. Those silver blue eyes shown in the darkness like two swords pointed at her heart.

Lorraine looked at the room, still lit, and then at Walter, wondering how he had gotten downstairs without her seeing him.

He read her thoughts and smiled and said, "I used the elevator my lazy ex-wife had installed. She was never one to exert herself."

"Why did you tell me to come here? Why did you give me a false name?"

"Well, would you have come if I told you my real name? No, of course not. I needed to see you alone. I wanted to tell you that I've passed your office several times, watching you working, and you never looked up at me. I wanted to tell you that I've always loved you, Lorraine." All the while he was speaking; he was ascending slowly, menacingly, smiling his scary smile. Lorraine didn't like it and decided to get the hell out of there right now.

Edgy as she was, she realized that she would have pass him on the staircase; which would be a problem. He was almost at the top of the stairs.

Knowing she had to rely on herself alone, she breathed deeply and began to descend the stairs. A step above him, she stopped and said very firmly, "Let me by, Walter."

"No. Never. I'll never let you go again. You belong to me."

"It's a little too late for that bullshit, now get out of my way, rich boy!" Now, she was fighting mad.

"Lorraine, I always loved your spirit and I always loved you. It was my mother who said I shouldn't marry you. She said I would be disowned and disinherited. I married the other girl because her family had connections. I never knew my family would lose everything and desert me."

"You're making me cry. Now get the hell out of my way!" She was angry and he loved the way she looked; so adorable and beautiful. She was as he remembered her.

"Lorraine, you still love me. I know it."

"Get the hell away from me. You and your family killed my love for you. My life is wonderful without you and them. Now get the hell out of the way!"

He made a grab for her. She struggled.

"Let me go, Walter!"

"Never. I love you. You belong to me."

"You're crazy. You smell of alcohol. You're drunk. Let go."

He had her by the sleeve of her jacket. He was unsteady on his feet. She was pulling her arm away from him and attempting to hold him away from her. Suddenly, her sleeve ripped and both, losing their balances, went tumbling down the stairs. The sound of their bodies bumping against every step frightened Lorraine. It was a long stair case and she thought she would die in this darkened house, while her baby was ill. "Oh, *Gesu, aiuto.* Jesus help," she prayed aloud. She wanted desperately to see her baby again. She passed out before she hit bottom.

There was silence once both of them reached the bottom. The whole house was silent. There wasn't even a wood cracking sound. And it was dark!

After a few minutes, Lorraine regained her senses and looked around. She saw Walter, his head at an abnormal angle and knew instantly that he was dead! "Oh, no. Walter. Walter." No sound. She tried to get up but her leg gave way and she fell. She looked at it, even in the dim light; she could see that it was broken.

She looked around at her plight. She had to get out of here. Little Carlo was sick. She should be with him; he's her little boy. Then she thought of her family. She was near hysteria. "Well, my life hasn't flashed before me, so I know

I'm not gonna die. But, my little Carlo, I should be with you." She began to cry, not for the pain in her leg, but for the pain of a mother who should be with a sick child. She knew she had to get out of the house and get help. She struggled on her elbows as she had seen soldiers do in the movies. After a long struggle, she made it outdoors. She looked at the driveway, long, dark, tree lined, silent and lonely. "Couldn't that stupid gas station bumpkin make a trip here?" she thought. She heard animal noises. The wind picked up and it was getting cold. The pain in her broken leg was overwhelming.

She thought of little Carlo, his smiling face, his red curls, his lisping, his cute brown eyes and how wonderful it was to hear him say, "Mommy, I love you." Her eyes filled with tears. "Help, Help," she called but no one answered. "Oh, Dad and Ma, if I had listened to you then, I wouldn't be here now. How good you both are to me. Maybe I didn't show my appreciation and love for you enough. Oh, God, Jesus, please help me. Have mercy on me. I only did this because I believed he was a legitimate client. Please help me. Oh, my little Carlo, my baby. I love you so much. You've brought so much happiness to my life. You made my life worthwhile. I thank God for you. If I die here, you'll never remember me. Oh, God, please don't let me die here alone and with a dead man close by."

She thought of Paul, the good, faithful, patient Paul. She realized she had come to love Paul some time ago, but was too stubborn to admit it. "Oh, Paul, please forgive me. I've been so stubborn. I don't deserve you. I'll die here, I know. You'll never know that I love you. I hope you find someone worthy." She'd been crying.

"Help, help."

Silence.

She put her head down on her arms. She thought of her son, her parents, her brothers and Paul. Paul. How good he was. How patient he was. How sincere he was. How cold she felt. Her exhaustion put her to sleep.

***

The clock in the kitchen at the Martini home said nine fourteen. Lena, whose nerves were making her nuts, said, "Carlo, I'm worried about Lorraine. She should have been home by now. You know she wouldn't come home after little Carlo has gone to bed. Call the police."

Carlo knew his wife was right and was going toward the phone.

Having heard their mother's agitated voice, Vinnie, who had come to visit Joe on business, and Joe came downstairs with concerned looks on their faces.

The doorbell rang. "Oh, it's Lorraine," screamed Lena. "Lorraine." And she ran hopefully to the door, ready to embrace her beloved daughter.

Both boys said Lorraine would have her key. Joe went to the door before Lena could get there. It was Paul, who saw the worried looks on their faces and asked what was what.

When they told him, he said, "Well, maybe she's at her office."

Lena said, "I've been calling and there's no answer." She twisted her hands and said a quick silent prayer.

Paul said, "Why don't we go to her office. Maybe something—some—" he couldn't finish.

Joe said, "Hey, that's a good idea. Lorraine keeps a duplicate key in her room. Let's go. Dad, Ma you both stay here with little Carlo. We'll go there and call you from her office."

"Yes, yes, go," said an eager and worried Lena.

Carlo said, "As soon as you get to her office, call us."

They promised and all went into Paul's car and

drove to Lorraine's office.

Chapter Seventeen

The three worried young men arrived very quickly and entered Lorraine's office. They turned on the lights and looked around. Paul went to her desk and found a pad and pencil in the middle of an otherwise orderly desk. He picked it up and examined it carefully. "Hey, guys. Look here." He said.

The brothers quickly came to Paul. "Look, the imprint of some of Lorraine's writing." He picked up the pencil and lay the side of the sharp point against the imprint and slowly and carefully, shaded the area. "I saw this done in the movies once. I wonder if it works in real life." Soon they saw the address emerging. They all smiled, got in the car and left.

Paul drove as fast as he could, exceeding the speed limit and hoping that a police officer would stop him because they needed help from law enforcement. But, as usual, where's a cop when you need one. They crossed over into Nassau County. Now they had a bit of trouble finding the road marked Elm Lane. It was dark and street signs were difficult or impossible to see. They stopped at a gas station to ask directions.

The lanky young man said, "Hey, you guys are the second people to ask about that address tonight."

"Yeah? Who asked you before?" demanded Vinnie.

"Oh, it was a pretty red headed girl. I told her she passed it and should go back about seven miles and then turn right. They sure don't make the street signs clear and they been promisin' that but they don't get around to doin' it. Hey!"

They left him standing there. They had no time to listen to his stories. Since they left the house, they'd been travelling for over an hour and that time frame worried them. They didn't speed back because they didn't want to miss Elm Lane; therefore, they travelled a little slower. They found Elm Lane and made a right turn; it was the only turn since it situated on a T. Soon after they saw a large mail box with the number 45 emblazoned on it. They turned in and drove carefully to the house, they saw Lorraine's car. Paul stopped the car and all three dashed toward the house.

They saw an unconscious Lorraine lying on her stomach near the open door. Paul reached her first, turned her over gently and called her name. Soon she opened her eyes, and remembering what had happened, became frightened. She screamed, "Let me go, Walter. Let me go."

Paul tried to calm her, "Lorraine, Lorraine, it's Paul." He held her closely, "You're safe now. We've found you. Look, here are your brothers. Don't be scared. It's okay, Honey, it's okay. Shh."

Lorraine's eyes were wide with fear and confusion. "Paul." Recognizing him, "Oh, Paul. I called you and you heard me. Paul." She put her arm around his neck and pulled him to her so that his cheek was against hers. "Paul. You heard me; you heard me. I needed you. I really did."

Paul was touched and heartened by Lorraine's action. Her brothers had stayed a few feet away, recognizing the situation.

"Lorraine, are you hurt? Can you get up?" Paul asked.

"I don't know, I think I hurt my leg. I had to crawl out here." Paul looked at her legs and saw that the left one was definitely broken. He was glad the moonlight was very bright so that they could see well.

She looked at all the men, "Walter—Walter is in there. He's—he's dead. Oh, I can't believe it."

At the mention of Walter, all three men talked at once, asking why she was there and why she was meeting

Walter. Paul immediately felt a slight betrayal, especially after she had called his name so lovingly just a few moments ago.

"Wait, wait. I didn't come here to meet Walter. I'd never do that. Oh, my leg." She winced with pain.

Vinnie said, "We gotta get her to the hospital."

Paul whispered, "Lorraine, I'm gonna pick you up and put you in the car. I'll try not to hurt you. Then we'll go look at Walter. We have to call the police so they'll know there's a dead body here and it was an accident. I'll try not to hurt you. One of you guys open the door, please."

Paul placed Lorraine carefully in the front seat, while she grimaced a bit. Out of the glove compartment, he got a flash light and all three guys went back into the house to see about Walter. They saw his body at the foot of the stairs, his head at a weird angle. The brothers didn't go up too close but Paul walked up to the body. "Yeah, he's dead. Look at his head. Come on, fuck him, he's dead and not going anywhere, we gotta get Lorraine to the hospital and then call the police. Let's go."

They all piled into the car and Paul drove down the long driveway and turned left toward what he hoped was the main drag. After travelling for five minutes, they saw a police car coming in the opposite lane. Paul flashed his lights on and off and the two cars stopped in the middle of the deserted road.

Through the open windows, policeman and Paul conversed, Paul telling him as much as he knew. The officer said, "That house is unoccupied at the moment. I'll have to call in. Who's injured?"

"This young lady. It appears she has a broken leg. Can you take us to the nearest hospital?"

The policeman got out of the car, came to the passenger side of Paul's car to ascertain Lorraine's condition. "Yep, she's got a broken leg. I'll call in for assistance and you can follow me to the hospital. Stay where you are and I'll make a U turn. And be sure and follow me." Paul did as he said and in a few minutes, sirens could be heard on the road. The policeman could be seen talking into his radio and he kept an eye on his rear view mirror.

In a few minutes another patrol car appeared in the rear, following Paul. Paul saw this and muttered, "Boy, they sure don't trust anybody, do they?"

"No," said Joe, "and you can't blame them. We could be a bunch of hoods! Vinnie looks like a hood!"

"Yeah," said Vinnie, "and you look like the Mayor of New York City!"

Even though Lorraine was in pain, she smiled and said, "I can always count on you two for laughs. Ow!"

Paul looked at Lorraine and said, "Does your leg hurt, honey?"

"Only when I laugh. Oh, I can't believe I said that, but I've waited many years to be able to say it." They all laughed and Vinnie said, "Lorraine, you're hot shit! Even in pain, you make jokes."

Lorraine moaned, "Yeah, I'm a regular comedian. Ow!"

"Lorraine," said Joe, "tell us what happened."

"Well, when I was alone in the office and about to close up, the telephone rang and it was a man calling to tell me he wanted me to list his house and could I come there tonight. I said okay and took the address. Then I called Ma and she told me that little Carlo didn't feel well and I wanted to cancel but I thought I'd better go because I thought the commission would be high and he said the house had to be listed tonight because he was leaving for Europe tomorrow.

"When I finally got there, it was already dark outdoors and there were no lights on in the house. Then I saw a light go on, oh, my leg, in a room on the second floor." She was trying not to moan. "I went up to the door, which was ajar, and I called Mr. Johnson, that's the name Walter gave me. No answer. I went upstairs, but the room was empty. Then I heard noise in the hall and I thought whoever it was was going to get a black eye since I'm here playing games with some fool and my baby is not feeling well. I should be with him. Anyway, I was at the top of the stairs and Walter was at the bottom of the stairs, coming up slowly and telling me it was all his mother's fault that we didn't get married. I knew I was gonna have trouble. I told him to let me by. He grabbed my sleeve, we struggled, my sleeve ripped and we tumbled down the stairs. I was unconscious for I don't know how long and when I saw Walter in the dim light, I knew he was—was dead. But, I knew I hurt my leg and got myself outside. I kept yelling for help but no one came until you guys showed up. Oh, here we are at the hospital."

The police wouldn't let Paul remove Lorraine from the car. The Emergency Room staff came out with a gurney, lifted Lorraine so that she felt very little pain and placed her on the gurney and in they went.

Paul said he would park the car and meet them inside.

Joe said, "We gotta find a public phone to call Dad and Ma."

"Oh, yeah," Vinnie said, "they must be out of their minds with worry. Oh, boy, wait until they hear the story. Can you imagine what they're gonna say?"

Joe asked the nurse at the desk if there was a public phone and she said he could use the phone on the wall."

Joe smiled at her; she was pretty, thanked her, and went to the phone. He dialed and Lena answered before the first ring ended. She was very worried, almost in tears. Joe assured her that Lorraine would be fine.

"What happened to her? How did she break her leg?"

"Ma, it's a long story but I'll tell you some facts." And he gave her a condensed version of what Lorraine had told them.

"Oh, that son of a bitch! I'm glad he's dead. I wish I could have killed him myself with my bare hands!"

"Ma, Ma, you're so tough. Try to relax. I don't know what time we'll be home so you and Dad had better get some rest. It's close to eleven thirty. We'll see you later. Oh, call Lucy, so she'll know Vinnie will be home late. Bye. Oh, how's little Carlo?"

"He's feeling better, thank God. Tell Lorraine. Bye, Sweetheart. Thanks for calling. I'll call Lucy now."

Joe hung up the phone and heaved a heavy sigh. He went to Vinnie and Paul and told them how worried Lena and Carlo were and little Carlo was feeling better. "Vinnie, I told ma to call Lucy. Is that okay?"

"Sure, sure. Thanks. I'll give her a call now." When he returned, they sat quietly and then they saw Lorraine, with her leg in a cast, being wheeled to the nurse's station opposite them. All three young men questioned the doctor and Lorraine simultaneously, not realizing it.

The doctor said, "Lorraine is doing fine. She doesn't need to stay overnight. I gave her a pill for pain and I've given her some pills for pain for tomorrow or whenever she needs them. It's a simple fracture that will heal nicely. No dancing! She told me you live in Queens. Can you transport her comfortably in your car?"

"Yes, she can sit in the back and the three of us will sit in the front," Joe said.

"Excellent. I've given her the number of an orthopedist she can go to in Queens. I went to school with him and he's excellent. Okay, any questions, you can call me. Good luck. Goodbye and goodbye Lorraine. You're a great patient."

A nurse brought Lorraine crutches to use when she got home.

They all said goodbye and wheeled Lorraine outside. Paul went to get his car and they all helped put her in the back of the car with her leg propped on the entire back seat. All the boys sat in front. They didn't talk much. Lorraine fell asleep.

In front of the Martini house, Lorraine was awakened and Paul carried her inside. Lena and Carlo were awake and got out of bed, Lena in tears and Carlo a frown on his face. Paul, who had carried Lorraine inside, put her gently on the couch. The brothers knew that Paul wanted to do that and didn't insist they carry their sister.

She turned to her brothers and Paul and thanked them. Then Vinnie went home to Lucy. She motioned to Paul to come to her and bend down, kissed him and said, "Paul, thank you so much. I really, really appreciate all you did for me tonight. Can you come see me tomorrow night?"

Paul smiled, "With pleasure. I'll be here early."

"Yes, come for dinner. Goodnight, Paul." She kissed him again and Paul smiled and sailed out the door. He was very aware that the kiss wasn't a brotherly kiss.

She would have to go to the bathroom and brush her teeth, but first she wanted to see her son. Joe helped with her crutches. She went to little Carlo's crib and looked down at the sleeping little redhead. She felt his forehead; no fever. She sniffled. She wanted to kiss him but knew she wasn't able to do so while on crutches. She would have to practice using them.

She made her way to the bathroom, did what she had to do and Lena helped her into her pajamas and got her to bed.

When Lorraine was comfortably in bed, she looked up at her mother, "Ma, thank you so much for all you do for me. I'll tell you the whole story tomorrow, okay?"

"Yes, yes, my love, go to sleep. You need your rest. Goodnight."

Carlo had come into the room. He wanted to reassure himself that his daughter was well. He bent down to kiss the forehead of his already sleeping daughter. He cleared his throat several times and blinked his eyes. He murmured a little prayer of thanks.

When he and Lena were in their room, he said, "Well, it's a terrible thing to say, but I'm glad that Walter is dead. But, I wanted the pleasure of killing him myself."

Lena looked adoringly at her husband, "Oh, Carlo, you know you don't mean that. I wanted to kill him." They both laughed. They snuggled and before they fell asleep, Lena, knowing how lucky she was to have a husband, thought of Paul and remembered the invitation issued tonight by Lorraine to him. She smiled. Maybe Lorraine would soon be "settled."

***

It seemed like a few minutes and it was morning. Lorraine heard some noise and looked toward the crib that little Carlo still occupied. He was making noises and calling "Mommy, Mommy."

Lorraine had a smile on her face, "Good morning, my little man. How are you today?"

"I fine, Mommy. Come get me, Mommy."

"Sure, my love, just a minute."

Nonna heard and was in the room in a second. "Good morning, my loves. How are you both? How are you feeling, Lorraine?"

"Very well, Ma. How are you and Dad?" She was struggling to get out of bed.

Lena said, "Wait, wait, I'll help you." She held the crutches until Lorraine could get herself out of bed and on her one good foot.

"Oh, that Goddamn Walter!" She said a curse but knew he was already dead and could harm her no more. She came close to her son. She smiled at him and he smiled back at her. "Hey, Big boy, can you climb out of the crib? I know you can do it."

Little Carlo showed her how agile he was for an almost four year old. His eyes were wide and he giggled at his mother and Nonna. "I'm so proud of you Carlo. I'll be needing your help for a while. Do you think you could help Mommy, sweetheart?" Lorraine said.

"Sure Mommy. I a big boy now."

"I know. Can you please get my slipper? No, not that one, the other one."

He placed the slipper on her foot. "Oh, you're wonderful! Thank you very much."

"You welcome, Mommy," Little Carlo was pleased. He kissed his mother, and they all went into the kitchen, where Lena had already started the coffee.

"Well, my sweeties, what would you both like for breakfast?"

"Hmm, I don't know, Nonna. Carlo, what would you like?"

"Pancakes!"

"Pancakes coming up!" Lena said proudly and she quickly got all the ingredients out of the cabinet and started mixing with gusto. Soon, they were all eating delicious pancakes and soon, Carlo and Joe came downstairs. And Lena got busy and made more.

Vinnie arrived, greeting everyone and saying Lucy sends regards and will call Lorraine later. He sat down and had some pancakes.

The kitchen was a noisy place, joking, talking, laughing and teasing of little Carlo. The two uncles fought over Carlo, who was thrilled and laughed and laughed as each tugged at him.

The telephone rang and Lena quickly answered. "Lorraine, it's Paul. Can you come to the phone?"

Lorraine looked at her mother with concern. "I'll get it in my room, Ma, thanks."

She struggled on her crutches but she was able to make it to her room and she answered the phone, heard Lena click off and said, "Good Morning, Paul. How are you?"

"I'm fine, honey. That was my question to you. How do you feel?"

"Oh, I feel fine; I feel wonderful. We're all having pancakes and there's so much noise in the kitchen that we hardly heard the phone." Then she lowered her voice, "But, I'm glad we did. Paul, I want to thank you so much for helping me last night. You were wonderful; a prince in shining armor. You're my hero."

Paul laughed, "Well, I wouldn't go so far as to say that."

"Well, this morning my brother, Joe, told me of your detective work. I think that's wonderful. I don't know what would have happened to me if you hadn't done that."

Paul said, modestly and quietly, "Well, Lorraine, we'd have found you a little bit later. But, I'm glad we found you sooner than later. It was a moonlit night; it was so bright that we saw you almost immediately. I knew it would be scary if you had been there a bit longer." He stopped talking for a moment. "Lorraine?"

"Yes, Paul."

"You—you said something last night and held me close. I—I hope you remember it."

"Yes, I do, Paul."

"Did you mean it?"

"Yes, I did, Paul."

Paul's heart skipped a beat. "Lorraine, I want to say so many things to you but not on the phone."

"Well, what's stopping you from coming here tonight? Do you have a date?"

"A date? Me? No, how could I? Well, I mean. No, I don't have a date! Do you?" A flustered Paul said.

"Well, that depends on you."

"What? Gee. I—I"

"Yes, Paul?"

"I—I lo—well, I'll tell you when I see you. Bye."

"Okay. I'll tell you, too. Bye." Lorraine smiled as she spoke to him.

She returned to the kitchen, the smile still on her face. Everyone stopped talking and looked at her.

"Well, what are you all looking at?" She smiled as she talked. "I have a date tonight with Paul. That's all. So, go about your business. God, I never saw such nosey people!"

Vinnie as the first who was able to speak, "Well, if that doesn't beat all. Lorraine, you're hot stuff!"

"I know," she said.

Vinnie continued, "The whole Goddamn world knows that Paul's in love with you. You probably knew it yourself and you wait until you break a leg to tell him."

"Well, Vinnie, I've had too many things to think about. Don't forget, many people would say I'm 'damaged goods' and not fit to marry anyone let alone a fine person like Paul."

At the sound of "damaged goods," the whole excitable, Italian family began to argue and shout.

Lena said, "You're not damaged goods. And never think of it again."

Carlo said, "*Nah,* my daughter is the best girl in the world and anyone who marries her is very lucky and fangool to all the busybodies who keep talking and talking. *Maledizione!* These lazy women should wash under the sink!!"

Vinnie said, "Lorraine, I don't want to hear you say that ever again. You're the best. And Paul will be very happy to marry you."

Joe said, "Lorraine, some of the guys we know, who've seen you, always ask about you and some of them wanted to meet you, but we know how crazy you get when we mention it, so we kept quiet. So, stop thinking you're unwanted or unattractive because you're not!" And he took in a deep breath, not able to hide his emotion.

Loraine looked at everybody. Little Carlo, who had been quiet through this whole explosion, looked at each person, then his eyes falling on his mother, seeing how serious she looked, took it to mean she was some sort of culprit, began to cry. At once everyone gathered around him, someone picked him up, hugged and kissed him and prattled on, and he was passed around to all the clucking adults, who had begun to scold each other loudly, which only made little Carlo cry louder. Lorraine, who sat down, motioned for someone to hand him to her. Once he was in her arms, she tightened them and began to snuggle and sing to him. He smiled at her. Her eyes were glistening and he said, "Don't cry, Mommy, I take care of you." She kissed him and held him tightly.

Everyone sniffled. "What a smart kid," Vinnie choked.

Lena began to clear the table and then everyone decided to help her. Lorraine cuddled and played with her son. She realized how lucky she was to have such an adorable and healthy and smart little boy. She thought of Paul, who already loved little Carlo. And, a new thought entered her mind. Everyone in the family loved Paul!

Lorraine decided she must dress particularly attractive that evening. She wanted to look spectacular. She couldn't wait for the sun to go down.

***

Lena had prepared a lovely dinner and all of them had almost calmed down. Lorraine was a bit nervous and she tried to calm herself but was unsuccessful. At dinner time, Paul rang the doorbell. Lena jumped up to answer the door, embarrassed that she'd not set a place for him.

"That's okay, Ma," said Paul, a bit emboldened. Lorraine smiled at him. He had brought her flowers and when he gave them to her, he bent to kiss her and said, "Hello, darling. These are for you, but since you have a good excuse for sitting there, I'll put them in water. Okay?" He pinched her cheek.

"Okay," she said and smiled at him and watched him as he walked away.

He went into the kitchen and Lena had already found a vase, took the flowers and put them in the vase and brought them to the table.

Little Carlo, sitting in his high chair, held up his arms to Paul, "Uncle Paul, come and kiss me." Without another word, Paul did what he was asked. By that time, Lena had set a place at the table for him.

Lorraine looked around and thought it was the most natural thing in the world for Paul to be sitting here at the table, next to her, holding her son; their son, who was soon returned to his high chair so that they all could enjoy their dinner.

He took her hand and held it under the table. And even as he spoke to other members of the family, he would squeeze her hand. She squeezed back.

After dinner, since it was difficult for Lorraine to sit in the front seat of the car, they decided to stay at home. They sat in the living room and put on the TV.

Lena put little Carlo to bed, then she and big Carlo went to their bedroom to watch TV and maybe do other things, which are nobody's business.

Joe left to visit Eileen.

Paul and Lorraine sat on the couch together.

"Lorraine, I have a lot to tell you."

"Me, too, Paul."

"Ladies first."

"Well, I wanted to talk to you about last night, when I went to Nassau County, to that house."

"Yes, I'm listening."

"Well, I didn't go there to meet Walter. I don't remember if I said so or not."

"You said so and I believed you."

"I knew the sale included a large commission and I was thinking about that when I agreed to go there. Remember you said once that I should go to Italy and I said I wanted to go with little Carlo when he reaches about ten or eleven years old. I was planning on saving all that commission."

Paul had one arm around her shoulder and one hand holding hers. "Yes," he said, "that's a good idea." He kissed her.

"Well, I didn't know it was—"

He kissed her. "I know. You said so. Tell me more. I'm waiting." He kissed her. She was losing breath and was thrilled with all his kisses.

"Please don't stop kissing me."

"I never will. Please tell me."

"I—I love you, Paul. I love you. I realized it when I was lying outside the house in pain, your image came to my mind and comforted me and I said to myself, 'what am I holding back for, Paul loves me and my baby and why don't I love him and then I realized that I really did love you and—"

He kissed her.

"I want to marry you. Is it okay?" Lorraine whispered half afraid.

He kissed her. She put her arms around his neck.

"Oh, baby, you don't know how okay it is! I've been waiting for this for a long time."

He kissed her. She kissed him back.